bared

HONOR BOUND: BOOK ELEVEN

ANGEL PAYNE

bared

HONOR BOUND: BOOK ELEVEN

ANGEL PAYNE

WATERHOUSE PRESS

For all the WILD girls who have believed
in this world since Garrett & Sage.

You've kept me going in so many ways, and I'm so grateful.

CHAPTER ONE

The truth.

It bared so much.

Joyous things. Beautiful things.

But sometimes—many times—too many things.

Dark corners. Buried secrets. Exposures that altered lives.

Princess Jayd Cimarron was trying to weigh which side of the truth had done just that to her world. As she stood on the veranda outside her big brother's royal receiving room, looking over the Mediterranean waves below, she might as well have been looking into a bottomless abyss—called the rest of her life. She did not jump there yet, but was preparing to. It was likely a given, based on the revelation that had blown her world apart in the last twenty-four hours.

But the dread was weirdly comforting. An affirmation of sorts, matching so many of the feelings that had lurked in her belly for as long as she could remember. The constant thunder clouds in her psyche despite the bright sunshine defining most days on the island of Arcadia, this one included.

The knowledge—the uncanny certainty—that this day would come.

That she would be standing on this very balcony, watching as a pair of men strolled in and faced Evrest with vindictive glee.

Trystan Carris was the polished protégé of Fortin

Santelle, down to his slicked hair, dark suit, and mafia-movie stance. Oh yes, despite the balmy temperature of this June day, both men looked ready for a scene in some violent spy thriller. But they matched only up to the neck. Where Fortin's face was set in pure business neutrality, Trystan wore a smirk empowered by the familiarity of knowing his king since their grade school days.

Times that were long gone.

Evrest was now His Majesty King Evrest of Arcadia, determined to guide his kingdom into a modernized era—and Trystan Carris was a member of the movement determined to stop him. Never mind that the Pura, their island's version of a radical fundamentalist sect, had suffered more setbacks than successes during their tumultuous history. Apparently, literally naming themselves the Latin word for *pure* was their self-written invitation to take the dirtiest advantages whenever luck and opportunity collided in their favor.

Collisions like this one.

Fate had definitely delivered all the luck on a giant platter. The aligning stars that resulted in the "reliably sourced information" the men presented to Evrest just twenty-four hours ago. Their upper hand was so significant that they had room for benevolence, granting their king the night for reviewing copies of their incriminating documents before delivering their demands for keeping quiet about them.

Thankfully, Evrest had not been prideful about seizing the offer. He closeted himself in that office, reading the documents well past midnight.

Jayd had not let the hours go wasted either. If today's meeting went down as she anticipated—as she feared—she would have to pull the proverbial trigger on her own response plan.

From the moment Carris stepped forward, her trigger finger began to itch.

A small comfort came as Requiemme emerged from a side door, joining her on the veranda, confirming she was not alone in the instinct. Despite the golden glory of the afternoon, her lady's maid shivered before muttering, "Why is it little surprise that the monsters are right on time?"

Jayd looped an elbow with her friend but did not reply. Emme's accusation was comforting but not necessarily true. Santelle and Carris were not monsters. They were just men. *Arcadian* men. Which meant they were also proud, stubborn, determined, and dogged—to the point of turning into fanatics.

Which also meant that they had not given up on digging deep for one specific truth. The fact she had always sensed. Perhaps had always known. And was now validated by the Pura's physical evidence.

She was not the true Princess of Arcadia Island.

And not even her brother, a monarch who'd been named after a mountain, could move this one.

She knew that already too. Worse, she sensed the same comprehension had sunk into Ev. She saw it in her brother's bloodshot eyes and furrowed forehead. She followed it in the tense finger he rubbed along his bottom lip. And yes, she felt it in every awful clench of her chest.

Her brother, who topped every internet search for sexiest royals, was currently a train wreck. He'd been ruling the island for almost four years now, but he was a brand-new husband and father. Those were extra loads in and of themselves without having to deal with this new challenge from the Pura bastards.

"Highness!" Requiemme's scandalized gasp confirmed how she had let the profanity slip out. But mustering a shred of remorse for it was impossible.

"What?" Jayd retorted. "You would prefer I state the truth? That they are filthy *kimfuks*? Is that better?"

"*Highness.*"

"Let me have the fun, Emme." She freed a long sigh. "It may be my last for a while."

"Bah." The woman flung her glare toward the glistening aqua waters just below the terrace. "These two will not have a leg to stand on after His Majesty is done with them and these silly allegations, especially right now. The world is in love with your brother, his queen, and their fine, beautiful new prince."

More aches up and down her throat, as a heavy swallow made its way down. "All the world's adoration cannot help my brother fight the truth."

"Bah," the woman spat again. "You cannot honestly believe that—"

Jayd cut her off with a raised hand. She lowered it into a tense fist at her middle while watching Santelle and Carris move in, taking up imposing stances before Evrest's regal oak desk. That was when she noticed the subtle differences in their style between yesterday and today. Their pristine suits and shiny boots were enhanced by small touches. Their ties were more costly. Their lapels were embellished with Arcadian flag pins. Their formidable features seemed . . . smoother. *Were they wearing makeup?*

"By the Creator," she rasped, concluding that they were— and why. They were expecting Evrest to be making some kind of public announcement. The recognition would have panicked her at once except that her brother looked more ready for a shower and a three-day nap. He wore black slacks and a wrinkled button-front shirt, with one shoulder dotted in baby drool. His shoulder-length waves were contained at his nape beneath a scrunchie printed with baby tigers.

"*Bon sonar*, gentlemen," Evrest greeted, taking command of the conversation at once. That was also Jayd's cue to return inside.

She stepped into the space just over her brother's left shoulder, with Requiemme taking position behind her. As Santelle and Carris dipped quick bows to Ev, she yearned to smack their smug faces. Her nerves were soothed somewhat by Emme's squeeze at her elbow. How the woman could convey calm and chastisement in the same move was truly a mystery to Jayd, though right now, it was bested by a more dominant dilemma.

How—and why—had the secret of her true lineage been kept such a tight secret for twenty-four years? Kept from all the Arcadian people? From her brothers? From *her*?

That question, along with a thousand others, had taken over the real estate in her mind since last night—though she had not dared utter any of them aloud. Truth be known, she did not have the courage. An admission that led swiftly to shame. She was Jayd Dawne Cimarron, damn it. She had always held her own against three daunting brothers with guts and grit and tenacity, but now she had to accept that it might have all been for nothing. That she was not actually "the sass of the Cimarrons." That she was the princess of nothing at all.

The sister of no one at all.

The realization that cut the deepest.

Emotional blood that Requiemme, thank the Creator, saw right away. Her fierce whisper in Jayd's ear proved as much. "Until His Majesty says otherwise, you are still our beloved princess."

In that moment, those words were more vital than air.

But oxygen fell off her priority list as the younger man moved out of his bow and took a confident stride forward. As he inclined his head toward Evrest again, the afternoon light mixed with the amber glow from the room's chandelier, snaking through the oils in his hair product. *There* was a moment Jayd would never get back. From that instance, the man would always be Belly-Crawler Carris in her mind—down to the unctuous undertone of his voice as he addressed her brother.

"Your Majesty Evrest. Thank you for welcoming us back to the palais."

"You gave him a *choice* about it?" Jayd's sneer earned her a cocked brow from the viper before he addressed Ev again.

"We trust you have reviewed the materials we presented yesterday?"

"I have." Evrest finished by nodding toward Jayd. "Which is, of course, why I asked my sister to join us for this follow-up."

Carris wasted no time before ticking an eyebrow again as well as shifting his slithery weight.

Jayd straightened too, stiffening as if her cotton shift dress was a regal evening gown. Two could play the let's-pretend-we're-in-the-throne-room act. But the thing was, she had logged more hours at it than the snake. They could strip her of her birthright but not her experience.

"As you know, Majesty, I am one of the princess's greatest admirers ..." Down came both the man's brows, as he flicked another discomfited glance Jayd's way. "But with all due respect, are you quite certain—I mean, at this particular point—to involve her so fully?"

"Wise?" Jayd's incensement overrode her decorum

before she could think. "To involve me? With *all due respect,* Mr. Carris, does this entire situation not *involve me?*"

Her quickest ally was also the most unexpected. Though a chuckle played at his lips, Fortin Santelle sauntered up and said, "My favor of agreement with Her Highness." He dipped a serene nod at Trystan's scowl. "This verdict directly affects Jayd, after all."

"Verdict?" And of course, she still could not seem to find the mute button on her affronted snips. Her nickname had been well-earned. She really was a sass, but only on her best days. On her worst—and this was going down as one of them—she was the shrew of the Cimarrons instead. "I was not aware this was a trial, gentlemen. If that is the case, what is the accusation? Do I get to mount a defense, or have you already erected the gallows?"

"*Pardondais,* Princess." Santelle dipped a stiff bow. "A regrettable but accidental choice in vocabulary."

"Bullshit. Of the highest order." Luckily, she kept it to a low grumble this time.

It did not stop Ev from driving a fast elbow into her thigh while rising to his feet.

"In any case, gentlemen, we have arrived at the nucleus of your point," he said. "The facts you have managed to kindly unearth and bring to my attention."

Kindly?

Jayd kept the riposte completely silent this time. Aloud, she filled in, "Yes. The facts. About my lineage, correct? Oh, come now, brother," she chided in response to Ev's surprised gawk. "Do you think I have not suspected until now? Not heard the scandalized whispers in the palais halls as I pass? Not noticed the slurs about our *maimanne,* uttered too loudly to be misspoken? So now you all do not have to be so coy, do you?"

"We mean no disrespect, Princess." Santelle's interjection was harder to pick apart this time around. His tone was earnest, but his gaze was shifty. "Our only goal here is the truth."

"So you can take it public to every man, woman, and child in Arcadia," Evrest supplied.

"Not necessarily," Carris cut in.

Jayd spurted out a laugh. "Well, of course not. Because the *necessary* thing here is...what, I ask? What serves the people...or the Pura?"

"And what would *you* have them know, then?" Santelle rebutted. "That the princess they have adored for twenty-four years is a sham? A pretender without a drop of actual Cimarron blood in her veins? That she is the product of an affair Queen Xaria was having while King Ardent was fighting with his men on the Mediterranean? That while he was helping to thwart a secret invasion from Muammar Gaddafi's forces, Xaria was consorting with a commoner? That we have collected physical evidence, including your *maimanne*'s recorded confession, to confirm all of it?"

"A recording the queen was not aware of," Evrest countered. "Secured by a woman she considered a trusted friend." As he snarled the last three words, he rose to his full height. Jayd could not remember her eldest brother ever looking so terrifying but terror-*filled* in the same moment. "She was confessing the contents of her deepest heart to that friend, who kept the recording because she knew it would fetch a high price one day—a bribe the Pura were apparently willing to pay. For what it is worth to any of you, that woman's betrayal has sent my mother to her sick bed."

"She will see no one," Jayd all but accused. *She will not even see me. The daughter who needs her the most right now. The girl who needs so many answers.*

"Perhaps she should have considered the consequences when spreading her legs for someone other than—"

Santelle's own croak was his interruption, as Evrest charged over his desk and into the man's personal space.

Jayd hissed in satisfaction as her brother wrapped his huge fist around the *bonsun*'s neatly knotted necktie.

"Shut. Up." Ev's order was low and lethal, making the air itself shudder. "I refuse to suffer the muck from your sewer of a mouth, Fortin Santelle."

For a second, Santelle looked like he'd be smart about heeding that order. But only for that second. Soon enough, he sputtered, "Every word I speak is—"

"The truth?" Evrest twisted his hold tighter. "You dare use *that* as your justification, when everyone in this palais knows you were one of the cockroaches who helped my father sneak into half of the brothels in the Eve District?" He loomed in closer, narrowing his glower. "Or is that why you have such solid knowledge of how a woman opens her thighs?"

Santelle's face became a cosmetic vegetable salad. Tomato red. Beetroot magenta. Eggplant purple. His seething mouth was a contrasting line of furious white. "How *dare* you, sir!"

"I am not your sir," Evrest seethed. "I am your *king*, and you will address me as such."

"Ev!" But Jayd did not move to stop her brother. In truth, a diced vegetable salad sounded delicious.

"Perhaps we should all take a deep breath and a step back." Despite the placation, Carris moved up and brushed the air with his palms. "We are not here to start a war, Your Majesty."

"Just a one-sided trial," Jayd countered.

"No." The man spiked a frown her way. "We are here in a spirit of... let us call it partnership. To work together on the challenge before us all."

"Said the viper to the hawk?" Evrest bit out.

"Say the loyal subjects to their king."

"Bullshit, the sequel." Again, Jayd submerged it well below her breath—which did not stop Ev from firmly squeezing her shoulder as he spun and stomped back to his chair.

Her cheeks flared from shame. She was not helping anything with her running commentary, even at the sneaky volume level.

Ev proved as much with his visible tension. His shoulders strained at the confines of his shirt. He lowered back into his chair with the jerking doom of a felled tree.

"This matter is simpler than you think, Majesty." Trystan Carris's tone was still disturbingly diplomatic. "You have but to render a few defined decisions."

"Which are?" Ev prompted.

The Pura bastard spreading his hands like a self-appointed messiah. "Well, now that all the facts are on the table..."

"You mean the bribery materials?" Jayd gritted.

"We *all* have a few choices," Carris went on as if she had merely sneezed. "After all, the information we have obtained would be vastly interesting for the Arcadian people..."

"Then why are you not just *doing* it?" Another effort to tamp her temper was wretchedly unsuccessful. "What are you waiting for? Does it feel that good to stand there with your balls in your hand, or are you going to actually put the things to use and follow through here?"

"Highness!" Emme gasped.

"What?" Jayd darted a desperate look from her maid to her brother. "Is that *not* what is going on here? *Majesty?*" At least her formality got Ev to jog his head up. "These two are leveraging the hearts and minds of our kingdom. The people who have been through more than enough in the last two years!"

"Ah. An outstanding assertion, Princess." Santelle was just as deferential as before, though the slick smirk he hooked on the end was already a red flag. But since Jayd knew not why, she had to let the man go on. "They *have* been through so much," he asserted. "Scandals that have changed cherished traditions and then respected laws. Rogue terrorist groups inside this very palais, and then blowing up the Grand Sancti Bridge—"

Evrest grunted. "Rogues you know nothing about, of course."

Santelle's glower was brief before he pushed on. "After all of that, a medicane storm destroyed valuable land, beaches, and homes, which were already eroded after being overrun by film crews and—"

"Stop." Jayd jerked away from Emme's calm hold on her shoulder. "Just *stop.*" She stomped forward, coming level with Evrest. "Are you *imbezaks* honestly blaming the medicane damage on the select outsiders Evrest has allowed onto the island?"

"*Select* outsiders?" Santelle charged. "In the form of hundred-member film crews and Americans now betrothed to all three of our monarchs?"

And there was the bullet that silenced Jayd's dispute.

And her tongue. That happened when one was too busy gulping down bile. *Our three monarchs.* The man had already written her out of the Cimarron family succession.

Thank the Creator for Evrest and his growl. "Regardless of all your factual lapses, gentlemen, shall we return to the *one* reasonably verifiable truth of your narrative—as well as what you want for keeping it silent?"

"No." Jayd rounded the desk and clutched a hand onto Evrest's bicep. "No, damn it. There is nothing for you to discuss with these curs, brother. Let them go ahead and break their stupid story to the world. They only think they're dealing with a doll here. I can take the backlash."

Carris nodded with entirely too much deference. "Nobody is doubting that you can, Princess. But there are other layers to consider here."

"Layers?" Jayd dropped her hand back to the area in front of her stomach. "What in saints' name are you—"

"Can your brother's credibility take that blow?" the sneaky *prispoul* insisted. "And not just His Majesty Evrest. What about Their Highnesses Samsyn and Shiraz? What will come of all the good work *they* are trying to do for your kingdom, especially right now? Samsyn is building and organizing our security personnel into an elite force. Shiraz is making smart alliances with contractors that will improve our infrastructure but not break our coffers. And this is all just the beginning—unless they are impeded by another kingdomwide crisis."

She swallowed again. No bile slid down this time. Only pain, brimming up from the depths of her heart. It worsened when she dared a look at Evrest. He was grinding a finger across his bottom lip again. His forehead was like buckled concrete.

Damn it.

Ohhh, damn it, damn it, damn it.

The snake was right. And Evrest already knew it.

Nevertheless, Carris smiled wider before twisting his dagger deeper. "Your Majesty has insisted on adhering to the facts—and there is an unchangeable one right here before us. The Arcadian people have had a great deal of their world changed within the last five years. But so many new things at once…makes people unsteady. They seek what they can trust. They want to feel that when looking to their monarchy, as well. Monarchs who, like them, were born in this land. Who have a shared history here. Who cherish its treasures as deeply as they do."

"And they do not believe we are that monarchy anymore?" Jayd did not try to hide the sorrow that seeped through her query.

If Carris was speaking but half the truth, it meant many Arcadians were *not* happy. That every development for which she and her brothers had worked—improved roads and harbors, national security teams, better plumbing and electricity, actual internet access—there were thousands of Arcadians who still craved an island with wooden wagons, primitive homes, and archaic laws.

"The Cimarrons are still adored," Carris asserted. "And even grateful…"

"But?" Evrest inserted the man's implied word.

"But everyone has been asked to readjust their lives—and their thinking—at supersonic speed. Many see that our new electronic wonders have come at a price to our landscape and resources. They view the American newcomers to the palais not as fresh young voices but as harlots who have bewitched their princes and usurped their daughters of rightfully deserved positions. Many even think Arcadia will become a US territory before long."

Evrest's nostrils flared. "*Harlots?*"

Jayd wanted to be mad too. Instead, she sputtered with half a laugh. "A US territory?" She tried to laugh again, but desperation was not a merciful master. "Do they think all three of my brothers to be dolts of that degree? That they would not have better judgment of their hearts? That they would not see through to a woman's true character?"

"That would depend, hmmm?" Suddenly, the Belly-Crawler was inching back to true form—and Jayd felt like the skinny mouse in his hungry sights. "Because if we release the actual recordings, and your *maimanne's* true character is made public..."

A pall of silence. Interrupted only by a slithering sound that Jayd swore was real. That she felt in every one of her vertebrae...

Until Evrest stomped back out from behind the desk.

He braced his stance wide. His shirt got tauter than before as he popped his shoulders back with noble pride. "My patience grows thin, damn it. State your compensation terms or get the hell out of my sight."

Another extended silence. Jayd drew a blank on reading Carris. *Not good.* Because when a snake slithered beneath the rocks...

Within seconds, she understood the reason for those rocks. And exactly why Carris had been sent on this mission with Santelle at all. The younger man was indeed the snake, while Santelle swooped in as the crafty mongoose with the bitterer bite. All too experienced about it too. The man had, after all, sold his own daughter's virginity to lift the family out of bankruptcy, a deficit caused by his bad business decisions and overreaching embezzlements. All those details clung to the forefront of Jayd's mind as the elder courtier firmed his stance and pulled in an extended breath.

"Compensation," he finally said, practically separating the syllables into words of their own. "Hmmph. Such a *murky* word, am I right?"

Evrest flared his nostrils. "You would favor bribe instead? That makes everything easier for me, Fortin."

Santelle stiffened. "What if we would not prefer monetary offers at all?"

"And why was I afraid of just that?" Ev rumbled. Though Jayd darted a look at her brother's profile, the precaution was unnecessary. She already knew his sardonicism was just a front. He was not joking about this—because clearly, neither was Santelle.

That was no help for her churning nerves.

Which raced faster, driven by a new—and awful—theory.

Which turned into the furious but desperate question on her lips. "So what *are* you after here, gentlemen?"

The demand she already flogged herself for vocalizing.

Because in so many ways, she knew it was the beginning of the end.

Hers.

Already, her eyes stung. She averted her gaze from Ev, refusing to let him see her stupid tears, but her stare swung to the worst place possible. The center of Trystan Carris's quietly preening face. She fought back by hiking her chin and hardening her fear into fury. The cobra would never swallow her for breakfast. Or lunch or dinner.

The thick but brief silence was broken by Santelle's calm but firm statement. "We have a few simple requests."

Evrest grunted, and Jayd swore the sound had not changed from their childhood, when Samsyn paid her to eat his vegetables. Still, he muttered, "Go on."

"Everyone knows that Orion Sheere has nearly both feet in the grave," Santelle returned. "When the man finally passes to the Creator, you shall ask me to fill the extra seat."

Ev spewed a dark laugh. "Despite the fact that you were ousted from the council in disgrace less than two years ago?"

"Folly for which I have publicly apologized," the man countered. "*Many* times."

"It completes Fortin's redemption arc," Carris offered with slick grace. "And if you present it as such, acknowledging that his wisdom and guidance have been missed on the council, you appear like the benevolent and forgiving monarch. Everyone wins."

Ev twisted his lips again. Clearly, that line meant no more than its empty predecessors. Still, he bit out, "All right. But only after Sheere is gone and properly mourned."

"Of course."

Santelle's posture eased.

Evrest's did not.

Jayd barely tethered her wince. She loathed watching her brother struggle like this. He had made a deal with the devil and looked ready to throw up because of it—and it was because of her. All right, not directly. But he would not be in this position, filled with palpable agony, if not for her. And though they were not fully tied by blood anymore, Ev was still her beautiful, beloved big brother. Nothing would ever take that truth from her.

"What else?" Evrest prompted. Because everyone knew a bargain with a Beelzebub never stopped at one demand.

"If the high council votes to abolish a tradition-bound law, there will be a trial period for the people to adjust to said abolishment," Santelle asserted. "After the year's trial, the Arcadian people will vote whether the law will be permanently changed or reverted to its original."

Evrest nodded. "Remarkably, that request makes sense. Done."

Though Santelle murmured his thanks and loosened a little more, Jayd careened toward the opposite. Her belly clenched, her hands coiled into balls, and her mouth went dry. They still had not reached the end. She had streamed enough reality competition shows to know. The judges always saved their most destructive comments for the end.

"Wise choices, Your Majesty."

Carris's drawl confirmed her suspicion. The man was still too serene, too ready. The snake was still waiting, just under a giant fern.

"And your praise is premature, Carris." Evrest eyed him with new intensity. "Because you are not finished yet, are you? Everyone wins, yes? Santelle is getting his council seat and his law reform. But what is the thing *you* want out of all this?"

By the time Ev finished the question, it was irrelevant.

Jayd already knew the answer. Every moment that went by, it stabbed deeper into her psyche. But not like the drive of a dagger.

Like the plunge of a snake bite.

And she knew.

The man did not want some*thing* out of this agreement. He wanted some*one*.

"Me."

It tumbled out with more certainty than her next breath. She was that positive of its truth—yet oddly, that settled with its surety. Her belly roiled with horror, but her mind was centered with truth. It was the comfort she clung to while pivoting to face Carris again. His comportment was expected. Arrogant but sanguine. Unmoving but all-knowing. Everything she needed for affirmation of her assertion, though she forced herself to voice it anyway.

"It is me," she repeated, raising her chin by another notch. "That is *your* ask, Mr. Carris. Yes?"

One edge of the snake's mouth quirked. "You are an astute woman, Highness."

"What. The. Hell?" Ev emphasized his snarls with a trio of brutal stomps, shaking every polished tile in the floor.

"Was the man not clear, brother?" Jayd swept around, hoping she did not appear as jittery as she felt. Thank all the stars in heaven she had been raised to hide every emotion behind a graceful shell. "But of course he was. You heard him. I am astute, Ev—likely because I can spot a snake even if he's hiding in satin. That *is* what you meant, Mr. Carris, yes? That I can discern when a reptile wants to slither his way into the highest echelons of the palais? And is especially eager about it when offered such a fat branch to do so? Truly, a snake would be foolish to settle for slogging in the swamp at that point, right?"

The man continued to work his jaw around words that wouldn't come. Under other circumstances, this would have been *her* chance for a savoring smirk—but these were not those times, nor that opportunity. As Carris kept indulging his wounded—and surprisingly sincere—scowl, Evrest's outrage became a battering ram on the air.

"Let me be clear about this, you *bonsuns*. We are here to discuss the safeguarding of my sister's honor, not the sacrifice of it. Especially not to a dickless Pura puppet!"

"Oh, dear Creator." Jayd barely prevented herself from dropping her face into her palm. The urge was just as strong to use it across Ev's face.

"Your brother is right, Highness." All too quickly, Carris was back to his slick statesmanship—not exactly a soother for her nerves. "Clarity is a fine idea right now. So might I remind His Majesty that should the truth about his sister's lineage be revealed, he shall be praying for *anyone*, dick or not, to accept her troth."

If Evrest's energy was beating at the atmosphere before, it decimated everything now. Everyone, Jayd included, stepped backward from its force as her brother swept toward the door and then yanked open the portal.

As the heavy wood slab pounded back against the wall, Evrest commanded, "Get out."

Santelle was brave—or foolish—enough to scoot forward, hands outstretched. "Majesty. Come, now. If we all simply take a breath and—"

"Get. *Out.*"

"King Evrest!"

"Stand. Down." Carris's dictate, coming halfway through the man's shout, unnerved Jayd three times as much. "I mean it, Santelle." With hands clasped behind his back, he stepped into the open doorway. "Clearly, His Majesty needs some time to contemplate the nuances of our offer."

"Nuances?" Evrest spat a bitter laugh.

"But of course. We *are* only asking for one council seat.

And the marriage contract will only have a twenty-year fidelity clause."

"For *both* sides? Wait. No." Ev raised a stiff hand. "Do not insult me with an answer."

Carris drew up his posture in a new bid for mobster charisma. "Your Majesty. It would be my utmost honor to—"

Evrest's new bark gashed the air. "Honor? Spare me, Carris. All of it. To evoke honor, you have to know what the stuff is."

Santelle leaned forward. "Your Majesty—"

"*Silence.* You are treading on ice as thin as your character, you traitorous, scum-sucking—"

"*Enough.*" She scared herself, uttering the order with authority that came close to Carris's. "Leave them be, Evrest." She clutched him by both elbows, needing it for her composure as much as his. "We will *all* take the night and think this over."

"Ah, yes." Santelle exhaled with fervor. "Take the night. Outstanding advice for everyone."

Jayd shot the man a derogatory glance. *Of course it is, you treasonous oaf. Because that is all I will need to fully resolve this issue.*

"Once again, Her Highness proves to be as wise as she is beautiful."

Jayd responded to Carris's insertion with more than a glance. The snake received the full force of her glower. "Flattery lends men time they cannot afford." She lifted her head, calmly meeting the *prispoul's* darkened glare. "*Bon sonar*, Mr. Carris. We shall summon you back tomorrow."

She forgave herself for the fib before the Pura scum were even gone from the palais. She had to. Not a second could be wasted now. The resolve seared the forefront of her mind as she rushed into her suite located nearly at the opposite end of the building from Ev's office and the other governmental operations suites.

Most days, Jayd bemoaned the distance, but it was an extra blessing right now. Providence dished out another favor in the form of a surprise squall over the sea. As the small storm rolled closer, the waves below her balcony became a kaleidoscope of colors. Another seamless coincidence, since her nervous system was a similar cacophony of feelings.

She had thought herself ready for this. Had spent the better part of last night in its preparation. Reviewing the details. Smoothing at every possible wrinkle. But now that it came time to really squeeze the trigger, could she?

You have no choice here, Jayd.

"There is no other way."

She repeated it a few times after that, hoping the desperate whispers would become a motivational mantra while hurrying into her closet and peeling off her sundress. But the words got no easier to say as reality barged in. Off came her bra, replaced by a chest cincher that held back her cleavage by at least a few inches. Over that, she donned a plain shirt and a basic suede vest along with rugged trousers that had likely never been washed.

"Oh, by all the sweet stars." The blurt was Requiemme's, issued as her maid entered and beheld her in the new ensemble. "Ohhh, Jayd Dawne," she moaned. "You are . . . well and truly serious about this scheme?"

"Schemes are for *bonsuns* like Carris and Santelle." She directly eyed the woman via one of the space's full-length mirrors. "This is a plan intended to blast their dirt into dust."

And then, if the Creator kept smiling upon her, into

nothingness on the wind.

Requiemme sighed heavily, though her stance was still resolved. "So ... I am to summon him, then?"

"If you would like." Jayd actually smiled while turning and rocked back against a wall full of her formal gowns. It was nearly a relief to think about not being squeezed into one of them again. "But if I know him, that will not be nec—"

A defined pound, followed by a bunch of thuds, interrupted her. They came from her suite's main room, into which she rushed behind Emme, to behold the prone form of the *him* they had just referenced.

But the next moment, Jagger Fox rolled to his feet with the same speed and grace as his animal namesake. He shook out his russet spikes and then slanted a grin their way. The expression was wholly wrong but right for the occasion, which came as no huge surprise. Unpredictability was Jagger's norm—and right now, that was another welcome comfort for Jayd.

"Oddly, I might miss sneaking in here through your laundry chute, Ripley."

The nickname, his unique privilege due to sharing her love for the character from the *Alien* movies, made her lips quirk up a little too. And then, as she helped yank the super-strength suction cups from his palms, even a bit higher. "Well, nothing is stopping you from making the climb just for fun."

"Except that you will not be here to do *that* at the end." Jagger tagged it with a blissful groan as Jayd dug her thumbs into the centers of his palms.

"*If* she is not here to do that."

Requiemme's rebuttal earned her Jagger's scowl. "Way to support your princess there, angsty Emme."

"Her, I support," the maid snapped. "But the rest of this insane plot..."

"*Plan*," Jayd injected.

"...which shall carry *many* more ramifications than simply sneaking out for a nectar binge at Asuman Cove, young lady!"

"Damn. I shall miss those too," Jagger muttered.

Jayd jabbed him with a swift side-eye. "Before *you* start with the 'young lady,' just remember that I know where your balls are."

Jagger obliged with a violent choke. "Yes, my princess. You certainly do."

But that was enough of that subject. At least for now. There were times for revisiting the not-so-distant past, when the two of them had decided to heed the million rumors about their blatant "sexual" chemistry and take things to that equally apparent climax. Except that it was not so apparent— or climactic. But conclusive. Definitely that. Though she and Jagger shared no bodily fluids, they had exchanged something more significant. Secrets. Intimacies they had sworn to take to their graves—or anywhere else the Creator would take them.

That night, they had chuckled about that last part of their vow. Laughter that had come through tears—since they agreed that neither of them would be free from Arcadia for more than a few weeks at a time. Diplomatic trips were the "vacations" of her future, and military training trips were the excursions of his.

That was all about to change.

The realization socked her in the gut as Jagger crossed to her writing desk and propped his backside against it. With deft precision, he unsnapped the long side pockets in his black cargo pants. From the compartments, he pulled out thick sheafs of paper. He stacked them atop each other and then held them out as Jayd walked over.

She picked up on their freshly copied scent, making her newly aware of the huge risk she had already asked of her friend. After Ev had refused to let her read the incriminating dossier, "protecting" her in his own ridiculous way, her friend sneaked into her brother's private office—yes, the room right next door to where they met with Santelle and Carris—and copied every single sheet for her.

Now, he was going to help her do more than read them.

So much more.

But she had to make sure he still knew that. Or if he wasn't, to give him permission to get out of here while he could. While he could still hope that her brothers would let him keep one of his testicles. After this point, if they ever learned about his part in her plans, the poor guy would probably be singing soprano during his lifetime of palais latrine duty.

She lifted her head and bored her gaze right into Jagger's caramel browns. "Are you very sure you want to do this, Lieutenant Fox?"

"Are *you*, Your Highness?"

Though he ended with his typical sarcastic lilt, his tone was mostly serious. She was grateful for both. More than that, she was glad that Jagger knew how much she needed both. "To be honest, I have no idea," she confessed. "But there are no more easy choices here. If Evrest does not cave to Trystan's ultimatum, the Pura will release all of this, no doubt adding a few sordid embellishments."

"But marrying the *kimfuk* is also out of the question."

"Regrettably, so is killing him," she lobbed back, perversely comforted by Jag's commiserating nod.

"And so we return to the hard part," he concluded.

"Says the one who does not have to read this whole thing." Jayd winced while simply thumbing through the pages in her grip.

"Says the one who skimmed enough of it while copying it for you," Jag countered. "And a good thing, at that. I believe I saw what we are looking for around the two-thirds mark of the stack."

She dug in a thumb to the approximate spot he suggested, while her friend circled around and sat himself at her desk. He lifted his shirt from the bottom, exposing chiseled abdominals for the three seconds it took to retrieve another item from a hidden pocket in the shirt's lining. The smart pad bloomed to life as he tapped knowing fingers across the small touch pad.

"Make sure you are looking in the written transcription of the taped conversation between your *maimanne* and her friend." His deliberate sneer on the last word was yet another secret solace for Jayd. Clearly, some people were more loose about their interpretation of the word *friend*. Jagger was not one of them, demonstrated by the risks he had taken just to get up here tonight.

She would say exactly that to him right now if she were not so stressed about getting him out of here before palais security started their late-afternoon sweeps. Which, if she knew Evrest, would be especially vigilant in this part of the complex. For her own safety, of course.

Her safety.

By the Creator. The expression was a joke at this point.

Would she ever feel safe, here or anywhere, ever again?

To get that answer, she would have to take the most

frightening chance of her life. Break out of every boundary that, until this night, *were* her life.

And there was Jagger Fox, grinning like he was simply helping her with an update patch for one of her *Alien* video games.

"Ermmm...Highness Jayd?" he finally prompted in a matching drawl.

"Uhhh...yes?" she blurted. "*What?*"

"You going to stand there in a trance about my abs all night long, or are we going to get this show on the road?"

He got a snicker out of Emme for his trouble with that one.

Jayd still struggled between giggling and scowling. Fortunately—or maybe not, depending on how a girl was supposed to perceive things when beholding the name of the man who was likely her father—she was neutral to both, allowing her to plunge down Jag's proverbial road. "Here comes the show. And its name is Louis LaBarre."

"On it," Jagger confirmed, his fingers flying across the keypad.

Requiemme was no longer laughing. "Louis La who?"

"LaBarre." Jayd was just as stoic about the repetition. She could not afford to be any other way. Not outwardly. Doing so would fan the flames on her inner chaos, and it was too damn soon for anything more than stinging nerves and a roiling stomach. Letting in the rest of the firestorm depended on what Jagger found. *If* he found anything.

By the Creator, she hoped he found something.

Otherwise, this mission of discovery would swiftly become, as Emme had labeled it already, a wild stab at insanity.

Maybe, in a few ways, it was.

But was staying here any less crazy? Hiding her head in the sand until the day she surrendered to Trystan Carris's lifelong ownership?

There was always option three. The one where she allowed Carris and the Pura to erode Evrest's credibility beyond repair.

Wrong. That was *not* an option.

So she commenced pacing laps around the suite as Jagger kept tapping, clicking, and staring at his pad.

More tapping.

Clicking.

Staring.

For minutes that felt like hours. Then longer.

Jayd kept pacing. Rubbing at her aching belly. Nibbling her thumbnails down to nubs. Contemplating which of her fingers to start on next.

Breathe, Jayd. Breathe.

And believe. Damn it, believe!

She had no other choice. She had no other path.

For a long moment, she paused her pacing. Was this what Louis LaBarre went through twenty-four years ago? Had he stood somewhere in this palais, looking at the whitecaps across the sea, wondering if he would ever see the beauty of Arcadia again? If he would ever see *her* again? Was that a wrenching decision for him?

Or . . . not?

Had he been relieved to keep his silence about all of it? About her? Had he even stayed until her birth? Had he given half a thought about her health, her happiness, what she looked like? Or had he been relieved about the cover-up? Perhaps even happy to step away from acknowledging her? From ever knowing her?

As the queries built up in her mind, the ache pushed harder at her heart—and a glaring certainty took over her soul.

No matter what those answers were, she had to seek them out. Had to find the one person on this planet who could fill in so many blank spaces for her. And—*oh dear Creator, please*—bring her new clarity along with them. A new direction. A solid purpose.

She needed to know, once and for all, who she really was. What she was really doing here. Or anywhere.

But not if Jagger found nothing.

A possibility she forced herself to consider with every new step she took, pacing again through the maddening minutes of her friend's continuing search. If Jag really did come up short on the hunt for LaBarre, she would have to fall back on a desperate Plan B—aka, the needle-in-a-haystack maneuver. Finding her father would not be impossible. Just harder.

But life never gave anyone a promise for easy. Not even fake princesses. Perhaps, especially *not* them.

After another collection of long minutes passed, Jayd decided she could give Jagger just another thirty seconds. Then twenty. Then ten.

"Got him."

Jag's proclamation had to be the most blessed pair of words in the history of words. After giving herself permission to breathe again, Jayd managed to croak, "Wh-Where?"

Jag hitched a shoulder back, implying his invitation for her to step over and join him. Once she did, her eyes widened at the digital pin in the map on his pad. "France? *Paris?*"

Jagger leaned back in the chair and folded his arms. "They call it the City of Light, yes? Maybe this is fate already giving you a sign."

Jayd let out more air, turning the whoosh into a sigh. The exhalation was threaded with an energy she had not allowed herself to feel all day.

Hope.

"From your lips to the Creator's ear, my friend," she uttered at last.

No. Not uttered.

Prayed.

CHAPTER TWO

They said Paris was the easiest city in the world to get lost in.

But it was here that Max Brickham always found a few things. Most notably, himself.

"And it's too damn early in the day for that mush, asshole," he muttered under his breath, happy when his booted footfalls covered for his hushed decibels. The polished wood floor of the Louvre Museum's Denon Wing also cooperated, turning his determined pace into resounding echoes that made their way up to the curved skylights.

But his senses were blended into sentimental smoothies from the moment he entered Gallery 77. The sensory slush worsened as he continued on, nearing the sole reason why he'd stayed an extra day in the city.

A smile prodded the corners of his mouth as memories tugged the edges of his psyche. Years ago, when he'd first stood before Delacroix's iconic painting, *Liberty Leading the People*, he'd been visiting the city with Zeke Hayes. By then, a lot of shared missions had forged his and Z's friendship into something deeper. They weren't a couple, but the term bromance was too fucking trite. What *was* it called when a guy had seen damn near every skeleton in your closet but stood by you anyway? So yeah. Whatever that was. Zeke was the guy who got it all. Who understood most of it and accepted what even Max didn't. Not back then.

Most importantly, he was also the only person Max knew

who'd gazed at this painting and didn't see just a gal with great tits tromping over a pile of dead bodies.

He'd seen exactly what Max had.

A barricade that had been demolished. A group of people who dared to think beyond their norms. Rebels who'd declared freedom from the rubble. Even the nobility in their pain.

After that, Zeke and he had left the Louvre and wandered the city for hours. Talking about why they'd thought the same symbolic stuff about the same piece of art. Talking about other symbols too. Insignias like the Dominance and submission triskelion. About black leather chokers with specific symbols, and the people who wore them. About the shield of ownership, and the people who wore those. A secret language they both knew but had been terrified to admit to. *Them.* A pair who'd been through some dank shitholes together, confessing things that only came out when death was closer than life, but still without learning those incredible details about each other.

That night, when they ended their walk at the Place de la Bastille, they shook hands and agreed on the next level of their friendship. They became business partners. The Bastille Seattle, providing a safe, sane, and luxurious environment for the city's kinksters, would soon become a reality.

Though he still cherished the memories from that night, he was itching to move on again. As in, getting all the way back home. But the Bastille Club, and the freedom it granted to his own dark side, was still half a world away. And the growing crowd in the gallery was getting too damn close. Closing in on him, several bodies at a time, until he practically shoved his way clear of the throng, moving away to suck in huge, hard breaths.

Too late.

More memories barged in on his senses. This time, not the pleasant kind. The darkness was no longer composed of tourists, school kids, and art nuts. It became floors of dirt, walls of rock, and blackness filled with helplessness.

And horror.

The terrible, inescapable horror inside his mind. Of what he'd watched there. What he'd done there.

No. No. No.

He was conscious of the litany spilling from his lips in a rasp as he pushed down the hall like an overeager newb in field training.

"Not now," he gritted at his raging pulse and dizzy vision. "*Not now.*"

But adrenaline and imagination hit his bloodstream like hydrogen and oxygen. Mixing. Combusting.

Spiraling into full panic.

He clamped his teeth, struggling to hide the surge.

His heart rate doubled. His balance faltered. Sweat broke out from every pore.

"Fuck," he choked out.

Fuck, fuck, fuck.

Without another crowd to elbow aside, he applied the same force to the rioting neurons in his mind. "You're okay," he muttered. "This is Paris, not Bamiyan. *Not* Bamiyan. You're okay, you big wuss."

Goddammit.

When would this bullshit end? It had been nearly four years since his first panic attack, three since he popped smoke from the big green military game and left black ops for good.

But *had* he?

Because wasn't he the one to jab up a hand when old

field buddies needed special help with off-the-grid missions? Wasn't he doing it before the payout was even discussed? Wasn't the rush of the risk better than a month's worth of anxiety pills, calming him in ways he couldn't explain? And wasn't the shitty aftermath worth it?

Probably best to defer on answering that one.

Because this assignment had come with one hell of an Aftermath. Capital fucking *A*.

Logically, he could trace the reason why. Hadn't been the money—a sweeter than sweet deal, thanks to the contract being for renowned billionaire Reece Richards—or even the team setup. He couldn't have asked for a better squad than his buddies, former feds Sawyer Foley and Dan Colton, as well as badasses Mitch Mori and Kane Alighieri from Richards' private security team. But despite their thorough prep and expensive gear, the op had cost Mori his life—as Alighieri, his husband, had watched.

So yeah, a reason like *that*.

Aftermath.

The kind that clung ruthlessly to a guy.

And here was the evidence, on high-def display across his whole mind.

Yay fucking yay.

No fucking way.

He fought back again. Compelled himself back to the mumbled affirmations. "You're okay. You're not there. You're right here. Sunlight. Civilization. Sanity."

No more darkness or piss or fear.

Most especially, no more stone walls.

As he emerged from the main pyramid into the full sunshine, a deep inhalation helped to drive the thought home.

As he sucked in another, he willed the rays to sink in deeper, through his close-cropped skull and tense neck, to the places he needed them most. The drops of his bloodstream that were still a wild river ride. The atriums and ventricles of his heart, still a deafening rock concert.

"Breathe, damn it."

Finally, *finally*, it seemed to be working.

A little. Not enough.

He walked across the museum's main courtyard, heading for one of the wide reflecting pools. Water was his favorite natural relaxer of choice, as he'd learned during extensive therapy sessions with Doc Sally at Joint Base Lewis-McChord. She'd helped him determine that it likely stemmed from growing up in downtown Emerald City and escaping the ugliness of the south side by watching sunsets over the Puget Sound. Images of those waters were what his mind called forth the most during those black, life-changing hours deep beneath Bamiyan. That night, hundreds of hours long, in which he'd finally given up on ever seeing the sun again . . .

Just like that, the panic returned with a vengeance.

"Fuck." He battled the urge to just go and sprawl in the reflecting pool. The weather wasn't blistering, but these attacks always made him feel like he'd humped a hundred-pound ruck across the Registan.

Thanks, Afghanistan.

Enough fun and games. Sally had also taught him when to stop, pause, and admit he needed help. When to recognize a moment just like this one.

"Suck it up, buttercup," he mumbled, plodding over to one of the cart vendors on the plaza. "*Une bouteille d'eau,*" he requested, and quickly twisted the cap free from the water.

After chugging half the contents, he fished a small pill from his back pocket and swallowed that too.

Goddammit, how he hated taking the pharmaceutical escape hatch from this shit—but again, Sally's words echoed through his head. *Brick is your call sign, mister—not your credo.*

He wanted to laugh at her now just as much as he did then. And he would—just as soon as he finished up with shaking like a daisy in a rainstorm.

It'd be a few minutes before the chemicals took hold and brought that miracle, though. He endured the wait by slumping against one of the columns bearing witness to the museum's origins as a military fortress. The smooth stone was warm against his back. He focused on the heat, mentally mixing it with the rise of his dopamine while scanning the plaza with lazy eyes. Okay, whatever counted as lazy for him these days. After eight days away from the tranquility of his place on Whidbey Island, his middle name had likely been changed to Paranoia.

Still, he didn't flinch at a movement in the shadows beyond his right shoulder. When the man who'd materialized there took three steps in cowboy boots without a sound, Brick relaxed again. "You plan on coming out anytime soon, Wizard of Oz?" he murmured.

"Cackled the bad witch to the good witch?"

The comeback, in Ozias Demos's trademark drawl, already had Brick twitching with a smirk. "Hold up. I'm the one who looks better in pink sparkles, remember?"

"Crikey. Forgot about that detail. Just like I must've forgotten that you switched up our meeting spot. I mean, I don't *remember* getting a text, but that'd be what a *decent* guy would do..."

"And I'm no decent guy, so we're all good, yeah?" Yet he contradicted himself at once, pushing off the pillar and holding his arms out to keep the passage clear for a passing group of chattering middle-school Brits and their frazzled chaperone. "But you probably also forgot this is *your* meeting, yeah?"

"Uh...yeah."

The guy's hesitancy wasn't just in his timing. The very timbre of Oz's tone switched, causing Brick to do the same with his stance. He pivoted in time to get a visual copy on the rest of his friend's explanation.

"It's...not entirely mine this time, mate."

And wasn't this going to be his new entry for the irony diary? Because the second Brick comprehended that he and Oz weren't alone, his damn meds kicked in. Mellow battled mistrust for control of his reaction, making him vacillate—and their new friend took advantage of that moment to step forward.

If Brick didn't know that Oz had no brother, he'd have taken the guy to be that hazel-eyed, celebrity-grinned, semi-ginger of a sibling. The dude even swaggered like a modern-day Eastwood as he stepped forward, meeting Brick's stare while extending his hand.

"Good day, Mr. Brickham. It is a deep honor to meet you."

So much for the Eastwood thing.

"Because Oz has told you so many lovely things about me?" he quipped, mentally replacing the reference. Eastwood was now Hiddleston or Tatum, one of those pretty boys with a rugged edge who'd be a better prince than a cowboy.

"Well, now that you mention it..." The guy filled in his own inference with a courtly chuckle.

"Christ." And now Oz was laughing too, as if they were

getting ready to go have tea. Brick started hoping this would wind up with knocking back some Macallan at the Ritz's Bar. "Where are my manners?"

"*You* have manners?"

With smooth grace, Oz ignored his gibe. "Jagger Fox, I'm happy to officially introduce Maximillian Brickham—but call him Brick if you value your testicles. And my mate Brick, please allow yourself the treat of being cordial to my friend, Lieutenant Jagger Fox of Arcadia."

Against all his efforts to contain it, a chuckle sputtered from Brick. Goddammit, Oz knew how he respected a subtle verbal backhand. "My boosted serotonin and I say nice to meet you, Fox."

But hell, why not blame the meds when he could? Though he regretted the choice as soon as *both* men's regards turned openly wary. And they said a lot had changed about perspectives on mental health.

"Didn't know things had gotten that bad for you, mate," Oz said with entirely too much sap.

"Only when people make me stop and think about them," he growled.

"But you're fine with the crowded meeting place?" Oz pressed. "I had to pick somewhere we'd all blend in."

"Yeah," Brick returned. "Yeah, I'm fine. There's the sky. There's the exit. I'm good. *I'm good.*" He even stabbed a dorky thumb in the air. "Props to modern medicine for keeping vets relaxed across the world."

"And thousand-thread-count sheets, courtesy of the Hotel Ritz?"

He hadn't expected the observation from Fox—or the chance it gave him to lob an approving chuckle. "Someone's been doing his homework."

Fox shrugged. "Some investigations are easier than others."

"Meaning?"

"That once you made Oz's recommended short list for this, I backtracked through your lodging records in the city. You do have distinct preferences."

"You backtracked . . . distinct preferences . . ." He cut in on himself by laughing harder. "Guess I should be thankful we're on the same side, then." Another stop, in which he cocked a hard eyebrow at the Arcadian. "Wait. We *are* on the same side, right?"

Ozias swung in, holding up a hand. "Easy, meat eater. There are no sides this time."

"Oh, my sweet little wizard." Brick smacked his now-empty water against his palm. "There are always sides."

"Your friend is a wise man."

Fox's words were, shockingly, *not* a shock. Something about the guy resonated with Brick. A specific sternness he normally didn't connect to the people of Fox's country. But he also knew the Arcadians were as reluctant to leave their island as allow others to visit it. Jagger Fox must've ventured this far for a damn good reason.

"Christ on toast," Ozias muttered. "You two are peas in a pod."

Fox snorted again. "Not every pod."

"Dare I ask for an interpretation of that?" Brick charged.

Fox straightened, accentuating his tall frame. The guy reminded Brick of a sprinter, his lean but powerful muscles ready to activate at any second. "It means that we both like being the one in control," he said. "Only you have more success with certain females than I do."

"Which also means what?" Brick took a second to fortify his stance too. "Or should I now be asking . . . who?"

For the first time, Fox was outwardly discomfited. Though Oz sent the guy a reassuring nod, Brick began to wonder exactly what woman the guy had messed with. How deep of a hole was Jagger Fox in, that he was screening operatives in places like the Louvre's main plaza?

The museum's most famous resident, the *Mona Lisa*, had nothing on the mysterious glances department on this guy. It was even true in the moment he finally looked back to Brick, his irises like bronze daggers despite how he narrowed them from the impact of the sun.

"Ozias informs me that you are the proprietor of a notable kink society dungeon."

Brick swung his bugged stare at Oz. "Well, shit. Sharing really *is* caring with you, mate."

"Grab a chill, man." The Aussie motioned to Fox with a jab of his head. "He's good for the confidential. I'll vouch right now."

"He vouches," Fox chimed in. "And I really am good for it."

"Thanks. I feel *so* much better."

A fresh scowl from Oz. "And now it's really time you untwisted your knickers, flamin' galah." He pushed at the air, making it clear Brick would be next if he didn't listen. "You think I'd openly rabbit on about you and Bastille to just anyone? For just any reason?"

"That's rhetorical, right?" Brick riposted. "Or do you want to really know how your 'rabbit' can hop after you've had a few too many?"

"I probably deserve that," Oz muttered. "Though not *this* time."

"Because this time, he was under pressure," Fox inserted before Brick could conceive a decent comeback. "From me."

"He had to know you could be trusted with secrets," Oz added.

"Huge secrets," Fox embellished, before clenching his jaw taut enough to turn it into a right angle. "I found it hard to believe we might be able to get someone of your caliber on such short notice."

Brick didn't veer his gaze from Ozias. "You did give him the whole former black ops angle, right? About all *those* secrets?"

Oz nodded but shrugged. "Guess your discretion about all of Seattle's kinksters means more in the long run."

"I wish that didn't make so much sense." Brick wheeled his scrutiny back to Fox. "But I'm still in the bog about the rest of that. You're 'getting me'? For what? And on what kind of short notice?"

For a long moment, neither of the men spoke. They all stood there in the loose triangle, listening to the food vendor hum off-key to the song in his headphones. Nearby, teenagers laughed while posing for selfies, and a couple moaned while ramming their tongues down each other's throats.

None of it seemed to matter to Oz, who stuffed his hands back into his pockets and splattered an affable grin across his lips. At once, Brick recognized what he was doing. Feigning a chat-up between two old friends, so anyone watching on the museum's security cameras wouldn't know anything different.

Hiding in plain sight.

"Right, then," the guy finally murmured. "That ought to

do us right for the watch cams for a while." Without faltering his smile, at least across his lips, he nodded toward Jagger again. "You ready to do this, mate?" he asked.

"Ready to do what?" As Brick pushed out the demand through barely moving lips, Fox laughed as if he'd cracked a joke with a good zinger.

"Are you...familiar...with our royal family, Mr. Brickham?"

"Familiar?" He almost guffawed. Who in the civilized world didn't know at least a little about Arcadia and its colorful evolution over the last three years? "Familiar enough to know the Cimarrons have helped put your little island on the world stage. King Evrest has led the way toward bringing your kingdom out of the Dark Ages. Thanks to him and his two brothers, you all are seeing great improvements in your lifestyle and external trade opportunities." He forced himself to stop, noticing the proud uptilt of Fox's strong smile. "Buuut you already know this, don't you?"

"It is fun to hear others say it," Fox assured. "I am proud to be an Arcadian under their leadership. I am even more proud to be a security lieutenant, directly reporting to Samsyn Cimarron himself."

"A good man," Oz inserted, garnering a new look from Brick.

"You know him?" he queried, genuinely curious.

Oz dropped a nod. "Had the honor of serving with him on a few interesting missions." As he drew out the syllables on the last two words, more perplexity pressed Brick's mind. "And then to visit Arcadia itself, which is where Jag and I got to know each other better. I also met the rest of the Cimarrons, including His Majesty Evrest."

"Who's not a *king* king, right?" Brick queried.

"Correct," Oz supplied. "He's a constitutional monarch, meaning he has no direct power, despite his sway with a lot of the people."

The line seemed like Jagger Fox's cue to clench his right-angle jaw again. "Just not *all* the people," he murmured.

"Ah. Right," Brick replied. "I'd heard about all that."

Though that was the extent of what he could provide on the subject. Back on Whidbey Island, he never turned on the TV or used the internet beyond emails and digital book purchases. When going to the mainland a couple of times a week to check on the club and pick up groceries, he steered clear of any news except weather reports and local happenings.

Every once in a while, he'd stay overnight at Bastille for special parties and to catch up with the regular kinksters who'd become friends. But the gregarious front he showed to the rest of the world was just that. A convenient ruse for the mess of a human being he was on the inside.

Exactly the way he liked it to be.

Needed it to be.

Continuing to care about the world, even at the level of a tiny island kingdom with localized terror problems, wasn't the excuse any of his triggers needed.

He'd found that out the hard way.

And was happy to put *those* memories aside when Oz took a turn to speak.

"Evrest hasn't been the only Cimarron in the public eye," his friend relayed. While the king father and queen mother, Ardent and Xaria, have remained largely private—"

"Sure," Brick interjected. "The whole family's involved in different aspects of things." So he *did* know more than he thought he did. "There are two brothers. Samsyn oversees military and security. Shiraz is the money, logistics, and infrastructure guy."

"And then there's Jayd."

"Jayd." He ignored how Oz and Jagger smirked at his rasping repetition. To be honest, he didn't really care. Not when he had something much better to focus on. The youngest Cimarron royal. "Ah . . . yeah. The princess. Didn't remember her."

Remarkably, he succeeded at a show of wry indifference.

"The hell you didn't," Oz snarked.

Or . . . not.

"Goddammit," Brick groused.

"Nothing to be ashamed of," Fox soothed. "The woman has that effect on most people."

Brick didn't argue. How could he? What man—for that matter, what person with a pulse—wouldn't respond just like him to a simple thought of the woman? Those glossy black curls, tumbling against her regal, sleek cheeks. The eyes in that face, glowing like huge opals and framed by lush lashes. That was just everything above her shoulders. Brick remembered a lot about her lush, rocking curves too.

A lot about them.

He yanked himself out of the lust-weighted reverie by homing in on Fox's comment. "Most people," he noted. "But not you?"

The guy's expression remained smooth and neutral. "Once upon a time, yes," he replied. "Until I realized that princesses are not exactly my preference."

Brick chuckled. "More the stablegirl type, hmm?"

"More like stable*boy*."

Oz snorted. "Stable*man.*"

Fox hitched half a smirk. "Whatever you say, koala baby."

Brick let a small smile curl his own lips. Well, that explained a lot about Oz's historical hesitance about invitations to go kink clubbing to celebrate successful missions. Though by now, the guy had to have figured out that when a dude *owned* a full-service dungeon, anything was okay short of dragging in minors or donkeys.

In the time it took him to generate that thought, Ozias wrested the subject off the air with his return to an all-business demeanor. "This is all semantics, anyway," he asserted. "As of this moment, or any from the last three days, we're not talking about *anyone's* princess."

"Three days?" Brick jerked up his head and nailed his friend with a perplexed stare. "What the hell happened then?"

Despite Oz's brief flare of dominance over Fox, the Arcadian stepped forward to lead the conversation again. "She disappeared," he supplied. "Not literally, of course. Not into thin air."

"Then in what way?" Brick pressed. "Symbolically? Temporarily?"

Oz stuck in a grunt. "Brickham, how are you not truly aware of all this? Even the rock you live under in Seattle isn't that big. Never mind that we're *not* in Seattle…"

Their exchange was forced into some tense beats as a tourist group tromped by. As they thinned out, Fox said past his still-gritted teeth, "She departed Arcadia." His jaw clenched tighter. "No. She escaped. That is the clearer truth."

"Escaped?" This time, Brick didn't issue the echo for the sake of logic. Not when there was none of that shit to be had here. "All right, officially down the hole of confusion, kids.

Escaped how? And why? From what? And are you absolutely sure?"

"We've got video footage," Oz supplied. "She was in a good disguise, but thanks to enhancement software, we picked up enough details to know she boarded a fishing trawler off the western coast of the island."

"Which was *not* her original plan," Fox offered by way of a disgruntled mutter.

"Which part?" Brick countered. "The escape or the disguise?"

"The trawler," the Arcadian clarified. "She and Requiemme were going to get across the water on a helicopter."

"And you know that how?"

"I was going to be their pilot."

"That's solid." But Brick cocked his head with another question. "Who the hell is Requiemme?"

"Her lady's maid."

"Her lady's *what*?" He barely kept his laugh subdued. "I mean, you all actually still do that kind of stuff? Lady's maids?"

"The role has grown into more of a personal assistant now," Fox explained.

"Regardless," Oz inserted, "and whatever the title, we need to be mighty grateful about her commitment to Jayd. Without her there, we might not have snagged a positive ID."

Fox added a steady nod. "We were able to confirm the dockside security cam footage by recognizing Emme first. From there, it was a matter of interviewing the trawler's crew and double-checking some important tells about Jayd."

"Such as?" Brick prompted.

"Her very steps, to start," the guy replied. "She walks at the same pace that most people jog. When she manages to stand still, it is not for long. She fidgets, especially if her stress levels invade her stomach."

Brick acknowledged all that with a short grunt. "Sounds like all this qualified as stressful." Though the guy had yet to divulge *why*. But if this tale was even close to its end, Brick was a brain surgeon with nerves of steel. Alternate realities weren't that easy.

Sure enough, the Arcadian paused for only half a breath before continuing. "She enjoys pacing and usually taps a matching cadence on her thighs. If she sits, she will do the same to tabletops, counters, balcony rails ... Any surface that is readily available. And of course, no matter what she does, the woman cannot hide her distinct eyes."

"Nicely done homework," Brick complimented, though the guy had a handicap on the last point. The woman's eyes were practically her calling card. Even if she cloaked their unique shading with contacts, there was no way of concealing their huge expressiveness, enhanced even more by their lush lashes, sultry lids, and expressive brows.

Expressive was damn right.

To the point that just a few thoughts of those eyes led his brain to a matching number of fierce fantasies about them. Visions he could *not* afford right now, if he was sticking to the theory that they still danced on the tip of this proverbial iceberg.

"But as we all know," he went on, "homework isn't always full preparation. And your plans for recovering your royal asset have hit a few glitches." He swung a knowing look between the men. "How am I doing so far, kids?"

Ozias huffed and rocked back on his heels. "Hotter'n a fried crotch hair, as per usual," he drawled. "But now we're running out of tarmac on keeping the news contained from the global press. Ears are starting to prick at the screams of the Arcadian royals watchers. If Jayd's absence from the public eye is picked up and goes viral, and then the whole world starts hunting for her, we don't have an edge of anonymity. We'll have less of a chance to find her before..."

"What?" Brick demanded into the guy's sudden silence, prompted by a fast and terse look from Fox. "Finding her before *what*, Oz? Or whom? Maybe the people behind why she left—*escaped*—in the first place? And maybe *why* you're frantically trying to get her back, after you helped her leave in the first place?"

He paused to sliced his own hard stare into the mix. "Look, you guys can't trust me with just half the details here. Unless you really don't need me after all and just want to stroll inside for a look at the large-format paintings?"

When neither man told him to fuck off right away, he accepted the pause as a figurative opening of the secret clubhouse door. But stepping inside the clubhouse didn't mean access to the decoder rings. Years of experience, infiltrating the clubhouses of his country's darkest enemies, had taught him that truth.

In the years since then, his attentiveness for those kinds of details had served him well as a skilled floater for privately funded ops, helping him pocket enough side money to actually think about buying a second home. The talent also served him well for unraveling stubborn submissives, who eventually came around to thanking him for the fun in the end. But that was when they were actually headstrong instead of acting the feisty part just to get in his pants.

But nothing in his pants was important right now.

That much was proved out when Fox, encouraged by a new nod from Oz, dropped his arms and moved forward. The guy looked like he was stepping out of a cave and grimacing at the sunlight. Brick was tempted to tell him how thoroughly he related but decidedly bit back his words. Wasn't his turn for the talking stick right now.

"I grew up with the Cimarrons," he stated at last. "And there was a time when Jayd and I were so close, everyone predicted we might betroth." He swung his gaze to Ozias before finishing, making Max notice how tightly that twisted the Aussie. "But that was before I accompanied Samsyn on a spec ops trip to Syria. We were chasing down gun runners who'd grown fond of using our old port as a stopover to Syria."

The Arcadian finished that with a warm smile, prompting the same from Oz. "And I was in Latakia on a few days of R and R after my unit had sprung some embedded reporters out of Aleppo. And there, in a tiny bar, off a tiny street, in that little seaside city..."

"All right, all right," Brick filled in before Fox could. "I got the picture. Magic, fireworks, everyone's eyes turning into hearts." In short, everything that was awesome and aces for *other* people, not guys named Max Brickham. At least not in this lifetime. Not with this twisted mess he was still trying to call a brain. "And I'm happy for you two—and I mean that—but let's get back to basics. Like the subject of Princess Jayd Cimarron, and your tear to find her quickly and quietly."

"Yes," Fox emphasized. "As quickly and quietly as possible."

"Though we're not on a rogue tear here, mate," Oz assured. "So don't go there. We've come with Samsyn Cimarron's full stamp of approval."

Brick narrowed his gaze. "So you know that just leads to my next question, right?" The rhetoric invited his purposeful but fleeting pause. "If you're sanctioned by your own government, why haven't you just taken this to the Paris prefecture? Won't the police's resources be easier than scrambling your own team?"

"No." Fox ramped his tone to an impressive growl. "No police. No public records. No cameras or recordings. Nothing that can tip off those Pura *kimfuks* to what we are up to." He flung nervous glances over both shoulders. "It was even a risk to meet here, but the fountains and the crowds will drown anyone trying to tap us."

"Tap us?" Brick's perplexity rocked his whole head back. "For what?"

"To learn if we're laying deeper Arcadian state secrets on you," Oz said.

"Which we are," Fox added.

"And if we sought you out because of what we plan to do about them."

"Which we also are."

Now Brick looked over his shoulder. "Secrets like what?"

Oz took a thick beat before answering. "Like the fact that Jayd Cimarron isn't a full-blooded princess."

"The hell?" Brick countered.

"It's true," Oz rebutted. "Well, true enough that the Pura faction went diving after a half-baked lead but gathered enough evidence to prove it as truth—at least in the court of public opinion. They uncovered some paperwork, along with a recording, implicating that Xaria Cimarron had an affair—and that Jayd is the product of that liaison."

"Shit." Brick's astonishment helped him draw out the word.

"Naturally, they took all the evidence to Evrest—"

"To use for political leverage," Brick went ahead and filled in.

Ozias lifted his head and smiled, acting as if he was enjoying the sunny weather. His snarl wasn't so easily shrouded. "They had a whole list prepared," he said. "And it included a demand for Jayd's hand in marriage to one of their own guys."

"Fuck."

"Younger member of the party," Fox supplied. "A real... How do you say it? A piece of work... named Trystan Carris."

"Fuckstick-on-high works too," Oz muttered during the moment it took Fox to summon a photo of said fuckstick to his phone's screen. "But if you ask me, he's as good as a *Sopranos* extra."

"Solid confirm on that." Brick grimaced while beholding the image. "But it wouldn't make a difference if he looked like Reece fucking Richards," he added, referencing the famous good looks of his most recent employer. "This isn't the dark ages. Fundamentalism isn't a license to treat a human being like property."

"All right, all right. Easy, mate. I happen to agree with you, okay?"

Brick nodded tightly, indicating his return from the brink of his mental abyss. No way should it have been so easy to crawl to that edge, considering the pill he'd just popped. But an overcrowded gallery was one kind of trigger. Hearing that men were bartering a human like a horse was another.

Even Oz didn't have all the details on that part of his past, nor would the guy be getting them today. He'd never see Brick's scars, physical and mental, from the mission that had changed him forever. The fuckup he'd never forget. The woman he'd failed to save. The fate she'd faced because of his mistakes.

Asha. I'm so sorry.

"We are *all* in alignment on that thought, then," Fox asserted, his palms-up stance working with his vest and shirt for a modern peacemaker vibe. "Which is why we have come to you with such urgency, Mr. Brickham."

He scowled. "Just Brick, okay?"

"All right, Mr. Brick."

He tolerated Oz's soft chuckle while regathering his thoughts on the safe half of his brain. The side still properly plugging logic and conclusions into each other.

"All right, let me see if I understand this story so far," he finally said. "Once upon a time, you helped your princess slip off the island so she could escape an arranged marriage to a . . ."

"Fuckstick-on-high," Oz supplied.

"Right. Thanks." As Brick slowly paced, he scraped a hand across the top of his short-buzzed skull. "But now, you've hopped the rock, as well—understandable, since it seems Sir Fuckstick and his minions have also run down the princess's plot."

A wry grin played at the edges of Fox's mouth. "You can pen a wise narrative, Mr. Brick."

"Gratitude for the upvote, Mr. Fox. But I'm still missing a giant plot point here." He jabbed a new scrutiny at his companions. "Why here? Why Paris? You know the princess could've fled much farther by now. For that matter, she might've stopped sooner. Arcadia is over twenty-five hundred kilometers away. Just a wild guess, but there are probably a lot of great hidey-holes between here and there just perfect for a runaw—"

He stammered into silence the second Ozias jammed an

image in front of him.

A photograph, filling the guy's phone screen, that contained three undeniable elements.

First, and most unmistakably, it was an image of Jayd Cimarron. Though her face was framed by a bolder, shorter haircut and topped by a dark beret, all the gorgeous basics were there. Those proud cheekbones. That heart-shaped mouth. And holy God, those eyes. Somehow, her dark makeup made them more huge and luminous than ever.

Second, there was a security camera stamp on the picture. It indicated the day and time. It was recorded three nights ago at eight sixteen p.m.

Third, there was a sign over her head from the place she was exiting. A tavern on Rue Gabrielle.

In Montmartre.

Four kilometers away. Not twenty-five hundred.

"Well, damn," Brick muttered.

"We caught a lucky break with it," Ozias inserted. "But it was luck created by this nifty bugger." He elbowed Fox in the ribs, an innocuous but wholly flirtatious move in one. Under any other circumstances, Brick would've been tagging himself as the weird third wheel on this bizarre Louvre date, but there wasn't time for that luxury. There was deeper information to get to.

"Hit me with it, crafty Fox," he prompted. "Brag about your brilliance."

"No brilliance," the Arcadian protested. "If that was the case, that sneaky little *preesh* would not have cut me out of the second half of the plan, leaving me to hunt for her on security feed files instead of guiding her safely out of the palais. She also would have remembered that I was ready to face His

Majesty Evrest's wrath for it. Samsyn's and Shiraz's, as well. They cannot continue to keep shielding her like this. She is a grown woman, deserving of the truth—*her* truth—and overdue for their respect about what she wants to do with it."

Ozias gave his main guy another quick shoulder bump. "You're still a hero, babe. Sneaking into the king's office and copying those evidence files for her took some mighty clangers."

Fox snorted. "Clangers that'll be in a steel bowl, cut straight from my scrotum, if my king ever learns what I did."

A rumble rolled up Oz's throat. "No one's getting near your scrotum without my say-so."

"And *I* say that's more than enough scrot talk for the day," Brick ordered before focusing directly on Fox. "Files that contained *what*, exactly?" he pressed. "The intel had to have bled some good juice, or you wouldn't be standing here dreading the wrong end of a prostate exam."

Unbelievably, the Arcadian's stance tautened even more. "The name of her real father," he muttered.

Brick's nostrils pinched as he sucked in sharp air. "Well, there's some healthy platelets."

Ozias continued the explanation. "It was couched in an audio recording from years ago. Xaria Cimarron admitted the affair to a woman who was once a close friend." He huffed. "Obviously, the queen didn't know she was being spied on, and even led by some questions."

Brick's exhalation was heavy. "Revealing stuff?"

"Enough to be incriminating."

"Define *enough*."

"Her Highness talks about her husband's continuing indiscretions before revealing that she found someone special for herself. He was an artist, commissioned to work on a custom piece in the palais. There was a great deal of that going on since the king father Ardent had just added a new wing of the palais. And since Queen Xaria has taken to her bed and refuses to speak to anyone about the matter now, some deductive reasoning had to take place before identifying the lucky fellow."

Brick narrowed his stare. "She didn't just name him in the recorded exchange?"

"Now where would be the good time in that?" Oz tossed out, clearly enjoying the comment more than his others.

Fox was nowhere near that jovial bandwagon.

Brick was no sooner finished with his what-am-I-missing gawk than the Arcadian swiveled with a sour glare.

"Oz is amused that I had to read a transcript of the queen mother Xaria in full swoon about a man who could paint poetry all over her body."

"All right. That at least narrows it down a little, right?" Brick, feeling at once for the guy, opted for sticking strictly to business. "Now you know he might have been an artist."

"Yes," Fox concurred, still flinging a fierce glance toward Oz. "But of course, the Pura deduced that too."

"Which means what?"

Oz quelled his mirth as quickly as he'd enacted it. "Only that once they figured it out, they dived right in on the follow-up research and then included all those details in the report they submitted to Evrest." He gave in to a small smirk. "Flamin' galahs led us right to the mother lode of intel—including the fact that Jayd's real papa has likely resettled here in Paris."

"An artist in Paris," Brick gibed. "So original."

"His name is Louis LaBarre," Fox stated. "And right

now, that is only our educated guess, based on more of the transcripts from the queen mother's conversation with her friend."

"The one from over twenty years ago?" Somebody had to get it out there, so Brick took the initiative.

"That is correct," Fox said. "But we have reason to believe he remained here after departing Arcadia. The dossier also contained a string of aliases the man has used, though all are traceable back to the same apartment address in Oberkampf."

"Ah. An artist who wants to be near wild nightclubs." Brick almost rolled his eyes. "There's more originality."

"Those rave crowds might work in our favor soon," Oz asserted. "Because if the Pura beat us to finding LaBarre, and Jayd either shows up or is already there, the skirmish won't be pretty. But with civilians as part of the equation, less lead will fly."

"Good point," Brick conceded. "But why are you so sure the Pura are as close as you? If the palais press office is still keeping this a tight secret, then those bastards are probably still wanking off back on Arcadia."

Fox thinned his lips. "They have their ways of learning things."

"And millions in financial clout," Oz added. "They've had some hefty foreign funding over the years and love saving it for ideal occasions—as well as the right palais voices to bribe."

"Zealots with deep pockets." Brick shook his head. "The deadliest enemy to have."

"And this time, they will not stop in their endeavors," Fox declared.

"Agreed," Oz issued. "This is their Holy Grail. Finding Jayd Cimarron and getting her wedded and bedded by Carris translates to a huge chunk of political clout."

"No," Fox grumbled. "Clout is only the tip of this ice cream."

Oz pursed his lips. "Baby, I think the term is ice*berg*."

"And *I* think Brick already understands the scope of this issue."

Brick flashed a grin. "The Arcadian for the point, man. You know it too, Oz. Carris doesn't want to expose anything about Jayd Cimarron except her womb to his dick. The sooner that happens, the closer he is to the inside track at the palais."

Ozias took the point with scary ease—until Brick watched him lean against a pillar like a surfer relaxing on a palm tree. "So you *do* see it our way."

"Dude, I've *been* seeing it your way since the start of this tea party. That's not the issue here." He scraped a hand up the side of his neck and started rubbing at his nape. "Why the hell are you inviting *me* to your cake cart?"

Oz maintained his casual slump, though his gaze got incisive. "You didn't seem to have a problem with the Reece Richards cake course."

"That gig was protection only, not extraction." Most importantly, it was in a new hotel in one of Paris's most elegant areas, not a terrorist cave beneath a squalid sci-fi landscape. "And it sure as hell wasn't an investigation. Not to the tune of finding a very determined woman in a very big city."

Fox absorbed his gripe with a small roll of his shoulders. "Well, the Cimarrons have authorized me to contract you for more lucrative . . . cake."

"It's not about the money," Brick bit back. "Oz knows that already."

"I certainly do." Oz passed off the remark as a casual

comment, adding a charming grin as a group of flirty college girls strolled by. "But I also know that you enjoy a nice thick slice of sweet stuff from time to time. This sugar will guarantee you enough flow to afford that place you've been eyeing up in Whistler."

"Damn it." He shook his head in time to Oz's lazy chuckle. "I should have never told you about that."

"Bah," Oz blurted. "You were blotto that night. We both were."

"Which is why you remember what I said?"

"*Pffft.* It was interesting."

"Fuck you." He dragged his hand forward, angrily scratching at his skull again. "For the record, empty compliments won't soften me up."

He didn't say it to make Oz back down. But he didn't expect the guy to jog his head back like Brick had simply let out a ten-second belch. "Mate, I think you're already softened fine—and my words, empty or otherwise, had nothing to do with it. Only person who has yet to see that is the one in your skin."

Brick ignored the telling tickles along the back of his neck. "Thanks, Yoda," he groused. "I'm still not levitating the star speeder out of the bog for you."

Fox cut into the air with an audible clutch of breath. "Did you just compare Princess Jayd to a mud-covered spaceship?"

Oz held him back with an iron hand across the shoulder. "I think our friend is battling deeper demons," he stated before turning a similar regard on Brick. "Specters, I reckon, that could be banished with the right mission as a nudge?"

Goddammit.

Brick craved to spit it aloud at the Aussie, but his teeth

were going at each other like grinders on sheet metal. How did Oz *know*? It hadn't gotten spewed during a night of "blotto" ramblings, since Brick had stopped getting that drunk with anyone after Bamiyan. And all his sessions with Doc Sally were strictly confidential.

Maybe the bastard was gambling on a calculated guess. In which case, he'd struck a damn artery. Nothing Brick could do about it either. He was a blood spill of major tells even before the gnashed teeth. He'd sucked up too much air through his nose. Averted his gaze way above the quotient for normal. Oz didn't miss a single speck of it.

Because he was right?

Fuuuck.

Probably because he was right.

But Brick wasn't ready to admit that. Not to himself, and certainly not out loud. Not yet.

"I need a few hours," he finally said. "Can you give me that, at least?"

"Of course." But Oz dotted that by scooting his gaze out to Fox. "I mean, that's all right, yeah, babe?" After the Arcadian nodded, he told Brick, "It's all right, mate. Here's the twenty of the safe house we've secured."

Brick peered at his friend's phone screen, committing the Montmartre address to memory while faking a hey-look-at-that-fun-vacation-picture laugh. Didn't hurt to give the security cams a good lasting impression. "Got it," he affirmed.

Past an equally feigned grin, Oz said, "So if we don't see you by midnight, we'll assume you've pussied out."

"Or actually found some common sense?" he returned.

"Yeah, yeah. Fuck you too."

It was their version of a mushy goodbye hug, and that was

just fine by Brick. He was never one for mushy, even before Bamiyan. He'd always done better getting to work shit out for himself, which had been his biggest strength—and ultimately, downfall—in the black ops game.

Right now, he chose to look at it as the former.

But with every step he took around the city, wandering streets and alleys even as the afternoon grew into evening, he started feeling it as the latter.

Because he still didn't know what to do about this damn offer.

About everything Ozias had said when bringing it to him.

Fuck, fuck, fuck.

Oz.

If that meeting had been with anyone else, he'd have already told them to go pound sand. Ironically, no one would've understood that answer more than Oz. Well, usually. The Aussie, normally as laid-back as a tequila sunrise *and* sunset, had been uniquely aggressive out on that plaza, all but demanding Brick's answer on the spot. Relatable, considering his blatant adoration for Fox. And seeing the Arcadian's clear concern about finding his princess before the Pura dickwads . . .

His princess.

No. Not really a princess anymore.

So what *was* she?

Just Jayd now. Jayd Cimarron, a missing Arcadian beauty.

A woman who'd had the guts to sneak away from her home, her family, her comfort—all in the name of seeking her truth. Perhaps, for the first time in her existence, *living* her truth.

Which meant she was proud, determined, and brave.

Which also meant she was intractable, impetuous, and

not open to taking instruction. Possibly—probably—from the very team who'd come to rescue her.

So why hadn't he already turned this gig down? Why was he still out here as the streetlamps turned on, instead of back at the Ritz and ordering a steak dinner on Reece Richards's dime?

The questions pounded his brain as he stopped on a tree-shrouded corner in the heart of—*surprise, dumbshit*—Montmartre.

What the living fuck?

But no way was he adding that one to the mental quandary file. He wasn't ready to tick it off as answered either.

He needed some clarity. Which was exactly what he *thought* was happening for the last few hours, only to realize his wandering had treated his brain like a gardener's air blower. The clutter wasn't gone, just pushed to different places.

Another magic pill wouldn't help either. He was mired in confusion, not panic. Besides, one visit to the figurative pharmacy was enough for the day. For *any* day.

As he peered around, shops and landmarks started looking familiar. They, more than anything else, disclosed how close he was to the Très Particulier. The bar was aptly named considering their nearly secret location. He only knew about it because he'd been here just last week, with Colton and Foley, after the op that had gone horrifically sideways. They'd needed to drink themselves into oblivion, though not in the full public eye. Colton, with his semisuperstar connections, had suggested the Particulier.

Brick couldn't think of a better place to hide out. Hopefully, from his own chaotic mind. Thank God for friends who knew about bars as secret as Xanadu but as lush as Honolulu.

After ringing at the Hôtel Particulier's main gate and gaining entrance, he made his way directly to the bar. It was already fairly busy, though most places in Paris didn't start really bumping until nine or ten p.m. Still, he was able to order a decent brand of whisky and then claim a red velvet chair at a small table near the wall, where he could park his head against the large painting of an exotic forest. Hopefully, the tropical bird residents in the picture would fly away with some of his mind's heavy conflict.

Which continued to make no sense.

At all.

He didn't need to accept the damn job. Did he even want to? And if he didn't, why hadn't he written off Oz's offer already?

Oz, who'd understand more than anyone if he never showed up. Who already knew that Brick needed the sanity in his head more than the chalet in Whistler. Who, very obviously, comprehended the value of well-kept secrets ...

Just as Brick was about to break down that thought—more specifically, how Ozias had kept his relationship preferences so thoroughly cloaked from him—a woman walked by, at once zapping all his senses like an electromagnetic pulse.

"Christ," he croaked. "What the living f ..."

He stopped as soon as she did. She pivoted quickly, as if peering out across the terrace for someone, and the EMP hit him again. Dismantling his cognition. Erasing his equilibrium. Funneling his focus.

Her profile ...

It was nearly as jolting as her scent, which he hogged in his senses for a few seconds longer. It wasn't often that he smelled amber and honey and fire and forest in the middle of a Paris cocktail bar. In the middle of *anywhere*.

But as he finally pulled in a new breath, he accepted the rarity of the sight in front of him too. The crazy coincidence of it...

Or was it?

Wasn't this entire thing just like a classic Ozias stunt? Had that bastard yanked Fox along for the ride, sneaking behind Brick all afternoon just to set him up for this moment? This insane instant, realizing that the beauty *was* as familiar as she *seemed*.

That forehead, high and golden and smooth as a Mediterranean wave. Those long and decadent lashes. Her cheekbones, astonishing and bold. Her hair was different, which was what had thrown him off at first. The blunt pixie looked hand-chopped pixie, which actually made sense now. Her wardrobe didn't contain any trendy pieces, though she still made the black, lace-trimmed tee and matching leggings look like ritzy designer wear. The stiletto boots likely added to his impression, but he credited most of his conclusion on her sure-shot tells. The way she approached the bar as if getting ready to leap over it. The nervous tap of her fingertips against her knee, even as she sat down instead. And her constant, continuing vigil of a stare—from those eyes too huge and luminous to hide.

Brick went to hooded mode with his own gaze not a second too soon, avoiding more than a passing glance from her. But years of surveillance experience served him well. He was still watching her—even as he ordered his pulse to cut itself in half and his blood to stop overheating as if he were gawking at bare tits for the first time.

But this was way more than that.

The decision that had damn near marched itself right into his lap.

But because of that, it felt . . . ordained. Destined. Yet still, goddammit, the hardest choice of his life.

Because as he watched, three larger guys got up from their table across the aisle from him—and sauntered their way toward the bar. Directly toward her.

Eyeing Jayd Cimarron like the main course of their next predatory meal.

CHAPTER THREE

Anonymity was a bizarre feeling.

Not as freeing, or easy, as she had always imagined.

Instead, sitting here without a retinue of staff or a crowd of bowing subjects, Jayd felt naked. Vulnerable. Despite her basic cotton shirt and jeans, along with the recesses of her cushy chair, the discomfort was an incessant gnaw at her nerve endings.

"*Bonsoir.*"

The waiter's cordial greeting had her snapping around. She gave him a prim smile and braced for the flash of recognition across his face. It was taking a while. A long while.

She reached to calm her nerves by twirling her hair. That was when she remembered: no hair to twirl. Or any makeup on her face. Or latest-news clothes on her body. To the young man who stood there so patiently, she was just another random customer, stopping in for an early Sunday cocktail. One who was now holding him up from serving others.

So she rushed out, sounding too clumsy about it, "Ermmm . . . *bonsoir*, monsieur."

"What would you like to drink, mademoiselle?"

She smiled again, appreciating the man's consideration. Though the last few days in the city had ensured her French was improving, her years at Stanford had ensured she maintained a distinctly American accent. He had switched over to English for her benefit.

But his query presented a new dilemma.

Never in her life had she ordered a cocktail for herself.

That felt as awkward as it sounded. But never in her life had she been in a position like this. Her entire life, food and drinks were always just brought or presented to her. Yes, even during the Stanford years. On the few occasions she could slip from her security detail and get out to a party, she had always been a known entity. Entirely too known. Someone was always there to serve, to suck up, to "help." Nobody had ever seen her like this. As a simple girl in Paris, out on a simple Sunday evening, having a simple drink.

She wanted to embrace that. To love the freedom of it as much as she always imagined she would.

But she felt more naked than ever. More unsure.

"Well, there you are."

Requiemme had never arrived at her side with better timing. She refrained from hauling the woman into a full death squeeze, just dragging Emme down into the chair next to hers. "Yes," she finally said. "All of me. Right here."

"Are you all right?" Emme leaned over, studying her. "What has happened, Highn—ummm . . . Hiiighlll-degard. Yes. Uhhh . . . are you quite all right, Hildegard?"

For some reason, it was just the medicine she needed. "Why, yes," she returned past a small snicker. "Are *you*, Agathenia?"

"Agatheni*what*?"

The poor waiter cleared his throat with mounting impatience.

"Oh my," she muttered. "*Desonnum*, sir. I—uh—I mean, we are truly sorry. Please bring us some . . . red wine, I suppose? Whatever you recommend."

As soon as he nodded and departed, Emme scooted in closer. Her lips were pursed and her voice was taut. "Never ask what he recommends. It will always be the most expensive thing on the list."

Jayd winced against the twinge in her stomach but perked before answering, "Well, we have been watching our funds carefully, yes? And we are certainly not here to drink the night away."

"So we hope."

She was not fond of the fresh twist that brought to her belly. "I assume that means you did not see LaBarre in the lobby?" The Particulier offered a few hotel suites as well as this notable bar. While she had come straight in here after they arrived, Emme had circled through the little lobby for the hotel just in case.

"Not a soul to be seen," her maid relayed with a fresh frown. "So the man is now officially late."

"We are also in *France*, my friend—where he has been living for twenty-four years and likely being fashionably tardy through all of it."

"Hmph." Emme absently traced some swirls along the top of the table. "Late is late."

"And customs are customs. So please try to relax. Fidgeting like a raccoon on a ledge will not bring him here any sooner."

"If he has the decency to show."

"If you are so certain that he will not, perhaps we should just get up and go to his apartment now—"

"No!"

"Why?"

"You know why, Jayd Dawne," the woman scolded,

sounding for all the world like *Maimanne.*

Jayd hated it when that happened. She especially hated it now. One, because she currently needed a friend, not a mother. Two, because she ached from missing her real mother. Yes, truly. Despite all Xaria Cimarron's enigmas and sins, including the one that manifested into a twenty-four-year-long secret, there was a bond to the woman that she could explain to no other. Nothing and no one took the place of one's mother, no matter how odd that relationship seemed from an outside view.

But right now, there was no running to that special suite, high in the palais. No extra moment for indulging all her unanswered questions.

Why did you do it, Maimanne? *And why-why-why did you never tell me about it?*

But it was useless moping. Wasted time. Minutes she could not afford.

She refocused on the business at hand, snipping back at Requiemme, "Fine. We shall adhere to your plan, despite its architecture of paranoia."

"If paranoia saves your skin, then I wear the badge proudly."

"Do you want the golf claps now or later?"

"Whenever you like, as long as you consider this: if we were able to hunt down LaBarre's address so quickly, others can too."

"Others like who?" she countered. "Evrest is not disclosing my escape to the press, which means he has likely not leaked the news past Samsyn and Shiraz, either. The three of them know I am alive and all right. Our private mobile communication window is secure."

"I am aware of that, Hildegard." The woman was not teasing about the nickname this time. "And am also appreciative that you have switched out your mobile device several times since your chat with them..."

"But?" Jayd provided it with a gentle smile but was answered by the continuing nervousness of Emme's darting gaze.

"But Carris, Santelle, and their band of goons are wily. We know this. They might have spies in places we do not know about. Even if that is not the case, your brothers will not be able to make excuses for you forever. And then—"

"And *then* there will be no point to your argument." She settled back in her chair and widened her grin. Sometimes feigning confidence was the best way to summon it. "This part of it, at least."

"Meaning what?" Emme demanded. "What part?"

"The part about you fretting over something that should have happened a long time ago. A *long* time ago."

The grimace she finally allowed across her lips was Emme's. Finally, Emme softened. At least a little. "I am not trivializing your pain, Highness. Being kept from this enormous truth as you were..."

"But this is not entirely about that either." Jayd could say it and mean it. "The man has a right to know about what has happened. The secret that has been leaked. *His* secret."

Requiemme drummed a finger on the top of their table, eventually hard enough to make the flames dance inside the votive candles. "On that, we are agreed," she murmured. "I only wish the timing was—"

"What?" Jayd prompted. "Different? Would that make this any better? Easier?"

Emme was clearly heading into an answering fume but schooled her features when the waiter reappeared. Or so Jayd assumed—until sensing the second body mass in the air.

She looked up, at once observing that *she* was being watched. Neither of the men next to the table was the waiter. The new visitors were dressed in tailored but casual attire. It appeared like they had been someplace more formal but had taken off their ties and jackets. Their shirtsleeves were rolled up. Their slightly scruffy jaws couched charming grins.

"*Bonsoir*, ladies," greeted the one closer to Requiemme. The one next to her pressed in, leaning his thigh against the side of her chair.

"We noticed you both over here, looking much too tense." He tutted before lifting his drink, something in a highball glass that was a rose-gold color.

"As gentlemen, we thought we could assist somehow," his friend proposed.

Requiemme straightened her posture. She was dressed as plainly as Jayd, except that her shirt was green instead of black, which actually lent to her formidable aura. She always teased the woman about liking the color so much, saying Emme looked ready to take cover in the island bushes on a moment's notice, but tonight it made her friend look like a protective forest goddess.

"We are in no need of assistance," she said, her tone stiffer than a coastal pine. "Our gratitude to you both, all the same."

Highball Glass did that *tsk*ing thing again. "Come now. You must allow us to help, mademoiselles. Remy and I consider it our . . . mission . . . to do so."

"Mission?" As soon as the man made the word a special entity, Jayd pushed to her feet. "Why do you say *that*, monsieur?"

"Gervais," he corrected, dipping his face in order to directly meet her gaze. His eyes were dark blue or brown; she could not accurately gauge in the room's dim light. In contrast, his smooth smile was very white. Practically too perfect. "Let us spare the formalities of last names, yes? If we are to be... adventuring... together tonight?"

Again, the man's separation of one word from his others. Jayd sharpened her scrutiny at him, putting physical action to her intensifying instinct. "Adventuring," she repeated.

He stepped closer, edging in on her personal space. "Do you... like the sound of that?"

"If you are here on behalf of LaBarre, then I definitely do."

"Highne—errr—*Hildegard*!" Emme rasped with scalding syllables.

"What?" Jayd retaliated. "How do *you* propose we continue this exchange, then? With more cloaked codes and spy subtexts?"

"And yet that might be fun," Remy drawled. "Depends on what we might be... cloaking."

Once more with his word distancing trick—though this time, not from Gervais. It was not a coincidence. Jayd was sure of that now. "So LaBarre did send you." She bounced her gaze between the men. "But why?"

"Ahhh." Gervais wagged a finger that seemed more admiring than admonishing. "What a clever, clever girl you are, Hildegard. And LaBarre sends his sincere regrets, but he was... ehmmm..."

"Detained," Remy filled in.

"By what?" Emme was persistent, clinging to every inch of her open suspicion. "A business meeting? On a Sunday? Besides, the man has enough money to keep him in paint, clay, and canvas for three lifetimes. What *business* could he possibly need?"

"And so much for any more subtexts."

Jayd was past the point of withholding a punctuating giggle. When Gervais joined in with his own chuckle, she let some tension ease from her shoulders. By every saint in the everlasting, it felt good.

"So... ehmmm... LaBarre *is* actually nearby."

"What?" Jayd pounced toward the man as soon as he stated that much. She hoped her eager smile made up for her rude interruption. "Where? Why did you not tell us sooner?"

"Highness!" So much for Emme remembering the *Hildegard* part of this. "*Please*. We cannot attract undue attent—"

"He sends his regrets for not coming in person," Gervais interjected and flashed a pointed look at Remy. Jayd recognized the message. Evrest and Samsyn exchanged one just like it when they were children, trying to talk her into bug hunts. "But he is... allergic... to the velvet in the furniture here."

"Oh, yes," Remy concurred. "Allergic. Very."

"Then why did *he* pick it as our meeting place?" Jayd glanced to Requiemme, now starting to comprehend her maid's ultimate wisdom. Maybe she, too, should have started at paranoia—an intuition that gained validation with Gervais's flared gaze. Most cornered cats looked less intimidated.

"He likes it better out in the garden." Remy's explanation flowed with the opposite aura. A cat lazing on a sun-drenched balcony after killing every mouse for miles. "Not a stitch of velvet to be bothered with."

"Exactly." Gervais tipped his glass to his lips again, snapping into the same shaken-not-stirred energy. "Which is why, of course, he brought us."

"Just to fetch *us*?" Requiemme fired. "Rather than send a waiter or maître d'?"

"Free drinks."

The men were so synched about their tandem comeback, Jayd released a gale of laughter. No way could something like that be so perfectly rehearsed. The assurance spiked her trust—and then moved her feet.

"What are we waiting for, then?"

Requiemme caught her by the elbow as she checked her back pockets for her cell and spending cash. "Perhaps a texted confirmation from your fath—LaBarre—to clear our handsome escorts?"

"Fine." But Jayd half huffed it, giving Emme an eye roll in verbal form. She obliged the woman by yanking her phone out and punching in a fast message to LaBarre. But at the same time, she started walking toward the exit. If she stood here for a moment longer, knowing her father was just some easy steps away . . . Impossible. She would get to him faster than the message itself.

She was determined now.

And trepidatious. And so damn nervous.

But nothing eclipsed her biggest sensation of all. Excitement.

What would he be like? Look like? Would he know her at once, despite how she'd changed her appearance to fool the press? Would he be welcoming and loving, grateful for the chance to finally meet her? Or would he be bitter and brooding, angry about being paid off to stay so far away from her? She would understand that. She would listen and commiserate about his frustration. It was everything she felt too.

Holy Creator. She was feeling so much . . .

Just when she channeled all that anticipation into a faster pace toward the door, she was grabbed by the elbow from behind.

"We, ahhh, forgot to tell you, ladies," Gervais stated. "LaBarre is in the *private* garden. My deepest apologies for the oversight."

In spite of his court-worthy overture, Jayd tugged out of his grip. She was no stranger to people physically at events, but this was no event. It was a life milestone, and it was turning her whole body into blown glass. One wrong touch and she would shatter.

"A private garden?" she prompted. "I do not recall them having one."

"Neither do I," Emme charged.

"It's new." Remy drained his drink before setting it down. "Very exclusive."

Requiemme grimaced. "Perhaps we *should* wait on that text from LaBarre."

"It is literally just outside," Remy insisted.

"Come. I'll show you the way." Though Gervais offered a gallant elbow this time, Jayd was skittish about accepting. No. This feeling was beyond that. Emme had done right by her with the paranoia osmosis.

But damn it, manners also prevailed. They had to. Since she was two years old, they had. She gulped hard to push past the fear—and then curled her fingers around his forearm.

Right away, Remy tucked Requiemme's hand under his own elbow. Jayd fought not to focus on the stiff set of her maid's spine as they walked past a busy prep kitchen and then out a small side door. By then, her heartbeat was so strong that her whole body shook—but she was not certain the excitement was causing it anymore.

Because beyond the door, there was nothing but a narrow passageway. Stone walls rose up on both sides of the alley, which was no more than two meters wide. It was barely wide enough for flower boxes.

It certainly was not a garden.

But by the time she realized it and pulled in a breath to scream, Gervais clamped his free hand over her mouth. Remy had already flexed the same control over Emme.

Terror pushed at all her pores at once. A stiff wind cut down the passage and turned her sweat to chills. Then ice.

So cold ...

Ohhh, no. What have I gotten us into?

She wasted no time waiting for an answer to that. Instead, she wrote her own solution and drove her knee straight upward. But Gervais, with a sixth sense too frightening for coincidence, caught her by the thigh and slammed her back against the wall. The brunt of the force knocked her windless. During the critical moments in which she choked to regain breath, the *bonsun* in front of her became the same one pinning her down.

"Not a word from you now, my sweet *Hildegard,*" Gervais crooned, his thighs like torture chamber restraints. "Or I shall give Remy clearance to do very painful things to your friend."

A mewl erupted from Emme's throat. Her eyes were wide and flooded with mortification. Jayd stared back, visually pleading with her beloved maid. Remorse was now her personal wraith, creeping through her with regret and anguish. The grief worsened as Gervais circled around, pulling out the silk tie she suspected him of ditching earlier. He deftly doubled the fabric back on itself and then pushed the midpoint between her lips. She nodded at him, giving a nonverbal acquiescence to his challenge, though hated herself through every moment of it.

Just as quickly, she ordered herself away from the mental noose. This was no time for self-judgments. No time to be wallowing either. No turning back any clocks. This was the world of now, not a week ago. She was not wandering the coastal paths outside the palais, with her only stress being how to entertain her nephew for an afternoon, or which designer she would commission for upcoming press tours.

Right now, she had to think with logic despite her terror. With clarity through her misery.

Conviction that sparked her with a new idea.

If she gave Gervais the impression that she was petrified with fear—not a huge stretch at this point—this might end up in her and Requiemme's favor.

She hoped.

Dear Creator and all the angels, she prayed.

If just one of the bar's employees came out to take a break...

If Louis LaBarre finally showed up and asked others if they had seen her...

If she could scramble enough of her brain together to actually remember what Samsyn had taught her about tactical fighting... about how everything around her could become a useful weapon in a time like this...

But this moment, all she could focus on was Remy, with his stovepipe neck and bulging forearms, pushing Emme into a filthy corner next to a large green bin. As a fearful mewl erupted from her friend, Jayd's breath came in constant slices of ruthless pain.

But the extra agony was also her new energy. Galvanizing comprehension.

The giant bully intended on harming Requiemme, no matter what Jayd did.

Not all right.

Before the resolve was complete in her senses, she skittered her gaze to the side. A few seconds were all she needed to consolidate her plan, because it was a damn good one. She visualized every stage of the scene, almost as if the universe wanted her to have an exclusive sneak peek before it materialized.

Her arm flicking out. Her fingers stretching.

Those fingers curling around the neck of an empty wine bottle—a quality Cabernet, with droplets still gleaming inside—before she lifted it in a high sweep. Then lowered it for a violent crash.

Then the satisfaction setting in. The grim joy of watching the smashed glass across Gervais's head, sending shards across his face and into his closest eye.

"*Putain!*" he shrieked, doubling over and grabbing his face. "What the—"

"G?" Remy demanded. "What the fuck?"

"I'm fine," Gervais snarled, raising his head with a ferocious jerk. "Stay where you are. I've just got a feisty little bitch here." As he smirked, blood puddled in several crevices in his jaw. "But she'll obey if yours does—and luckily, I like to fight as hard as I fuck." After sweeping another empty wine container out of the trash, he smashed the bottle against the dumpster's lip. "Do not fret. I can take it, darling. What about you?"

More than anything, Jayd longed to stab the asshole with

an equally insolent smile. Instead, a scream crawled up her throat. She forced it down in time but could do nothing about the thunder of her carotid. If she still had all her hair, its length might have hidden the telltale throb at the side of her neck. But if she still had all her hair, these two monsters would likely have recognized her by now.

"*Mon ami*." Remy, despite being built like the bull to Gervais's pony, actually produced the more reasonable tone. "Can you keep it in your pants another minute, damn it, and listen to me?"

"No, goddammit." Gervais twisted an ugly scowl. "You went first the last time."

"Fuck you. I said *listen* to me—just like you should have been listening to these two for the last fifteen minutes."

"Huh?" Gervais grunted.

"Inside, mine called *yours* 'highness.' And their accents . . . not completely American. Especially this one's." During that, he rammed a hand beneath Requiemme's sweater. He massaged her breast as if analyzing a melon in the market. "Hmm. Just as I thought. Expensive lace."

"And you're going where with this exactly, Inspector Clouseau?" Gervais charged.

"That maybe they're good for more than just some thrills."

"Which means what?"

"That they're used to being kept in style. That wherever that money exists, there is bound to be more."

Jayd seethed so hard, she worked her tongue around the gag enough to form mangled words. "Bein' *keppp*?" she spat. "Becaw we cannaw kee *ourfelves* as such?"

"Hawness!" Emme exclaimed. "By dah Cweatah's toes!"

"Ah!" Remy flashed a triumphant leer. "You get it now?"

If Gervais had a response revving, Jayd squandered no moments in cutting his ignition short. She did not even tarry with a rebuke for Emme, nor the comfort of knowing her maid was probably already flogging herself for the slip.

Instead, she focused. Intensely. Right to the center of her body. She funneled her attention on bucking out and then up, determined to be the mongoose that unseated this snake.

As soon as Gervais swore again, caught aback by her burst of violence, she twisted to the side and away from the dumpster. For heartbreaking seconds, her equilibrium swam. She mistook the eddies of a puddle as the thin line of sky over the alley. As she righted herself and continued to stumble, shouts ricocheted up and down the looming, dirty brick walls.

"*Putain!*" Gervais's shriek split the air again.

"Christ," Remy gritted. "What now?"

"My nuts! Shit. I can't move!"

"Well, don't let her go! She's obviously the highness in all this."

"Did *you* hear *me* now? I can't move!"

"Highness!" Requiemme's scream was an urgent slice on the air. That could only mean one thing. She had yanked her gag free. And if she had done that—

"Highness! *Run!*"

Too late.

Remy had let Emme go to chase and capture Jayd. And succeeded.

She flailed, but the man really had to be half bull. He was barely breathing hard to secure her, while binding his arm around her at the perfect angle to push at her lungs. She only had enough air left to get out a defined shriek.

"Emme! Get out of here. Now!"

"No. *No*," Emme sobbed. "Not without y—"

A new scream on the air. Jayd was certain she watched as it shook some plaster loose between the bricks, but she could not be certain. She *was* sure that it did not belong to Requiemme. It definitely had not burst from her either.

Then who . . . ?

Really?

She slammed back against a wall, bringing knuckles to her forehead in shock. Was she truly watching this happen?

It seemed so.

Unbelievably, the screech belonged to Remy. She confirmed that because he erupted with it again while being hauled to the opposite wall by his back collar.

And his new handler?

Absolutely not Gervais.

This human was too big. Too mighty. Too daunting. A T-Rex to Remy's bull. A beast who persisted in shoveling the naughty puppy treatment at the man. Remy only had time for a dazed grunt before the man hurled him against the bricks like he'd peed on a Persian rug. The bastard's broken form crumpled along the wall before collapsing into a puddle of strange yellow liquid. No more snorts or growls from him now. Instead, the bastard spilled a string of slurry French pleas, plunging both hands over his crotch. Understandable, if the man feared what fate the force of nature might deal to his family jewels.

Not that his opponent noticed. Or cared.

Jayd was conscious of her mouth dropping open as the interloper paced over and twisted a hand into Remy's greasy hair. Remy whimpered as T-Rex forced him back to his feet.

Their new position turned them directly beneath one of

the wan alley lights. In the tube of that ghostly glow, the force of nature smiled down at Remy. Though the look was feral, it only strengthened the man's rugged beauty. A crescent of brilliant white teeth. Deep creases that ran at right angles to his formidable jaw. A gaze of deep cobalt brilliance, glittering with primordial-grade power. He was raw. Savage. Mesmerizing.

And why was she noticing all *that* about him?

She had no traceable idea.

Maybe considering his attributes above his shoulders was easier than watching what he did with the body below them.

How his massive shoulders rippled as he re-secured his grip on Remy. How his equally huge thighs flexed as he employed them for the action. How every speck of him was so ideally served by his formfitting dark-blue Henley and black denim bottoms.

No, she told herself. *No more.*

But what else was there to focus on? The man was all the way across the alley but might as well have been right there in her personal space. She breathed in and received his incredible scent—yes, even from here—all cloves and cedar and suede. Even Gervais's swearing and stampings were insignificant in the shadows of this forceful giant.

And who was she kidding? *Forceful?*

This man was more than just force. He was . . .

Ions. Atmosphere. Oxygen. Carbon. Subliminal but elemental. A nucleus split a million times, then formed into a human being.

If he even *was* human.

What. On. Earth?

There was the question she could not evade—the demand that thundered, over and over and over again, as the stranger moved again. The one way she prayed he would not choose.

With one hand still on Remy, he turned. And stared right at her.

Into her.

Rendering her eyes incapable of blinking. Her nerves helpless of all feeling. And her mind numb and incoherent. Paralyzed...

Until Emme's shriek broke open the air once more.

"Run! For the love of the Creator, Jayd! *Run!*"

CHAPTER FOUR

Shit on a fucking shingle.

The line erupted from the spaces between Brick's teeth like broken glass. Appropriate, considering the matching texture of his bloodstream.

He hated foot chases. Especially in cities like this, filled with the remnants of streets built by triple-digit civilizations. Kind of like Baghdad. And Kandahar.

But despite how well the princess had laid down the first of these douchebags, Gervais seemed determined to stumble right after Jayd Cimarron and her screeching maid.

"Goddammit," he snarled, pivoting back to the asswipe still trapped beneath his hand. He'd been looking forward to having some sport with the gnat before setting him free and watching him run, but his friend had dashed that hope. "I hate it when this happens."

"M-M-Me too," the asshole stammered.

"Shut up," Brick snapped.

The guy snorted. He got a few points for that bravery, though Brick retracted them as soon as he spoke again.

"Come now, my friend. We were only after a bit of fun. You understand, *oui?*"

"Not one fucking bit." Brick cocked his head and kicked up one side of his mouth. "So there's my liability disclaimer."

"Lia . . . bility?" The bastard's nostrils flared, adding to the bovine breadth of his features. "Disclaimer? F-F-For wha—"

After Brick cracked his head back, the dickhead went down with a grunt that'd be anticlimactic in other circumstances. After bending over to ensure that he hadn't actually opened up the guy's skull—though the universe might've actually thanked him for it—Brick settled Bull Face against the wall and wasted no time in sprinting toward the alley's open end.

Toward the rat's maze into which Jayd Cimarron had disappeared.

Followed by a predator who, at any second, could piece together her true identity.

"Fuck," Brick muttered. And ran faster.

When the alley opened onto the bar's loading dock, he skidded to a stop.

Shit, shit, shit.

Three other passageways branched off the area, as well as the driveway that led out onto the delivery access road. The driveway was only slightly wider than the alleys but still seemed like the most obvious choice of an escape—which was why he knew the princess hadn't chosen it. She was smarter than that. He knew that already. Regrettably, a predator like Gervais probably did too.

So which way *did* she pick?

His answer remained a frustrating blank, even as he identified the continuing spurts of Requiemme Farre's shrieks. Following the sound's trajectory wasn't as simple as it seemed. Not in a neighborhood with centuries-old architecture. Montmartre's plentiful trees and twisting roads were no help. In short, with these acoustics, the women might reach Belgium before he found them.

But that meant Gervais was facing the same odds. With

a partner in crime who'd be unconscious for a good while longer.

Brick hoped he wasn't facing the same jam. As he jogged toward the passageway to the far right and pulled out his cell, he might have even prayed it.

The same way he prayed like hell that Ozias wasn't using a burner phone and would still pick up on the call Brick placed to his regular Queensland line.

"You know you're just supposed to show up here, don't you, mate?"

Yesss. The big guy upstairs *was* still listening.

"Yeah, well, a funny thing happened on the way to the safe house." He didn't bother hiding the jumps of his voice due to his hurried pace. Though he was beyond tempted to race down the lane as fast as a human dart, he didn't dare risk the chance. Right now, listening was the most important part of this tracking. If he took a wrong turn and had to double back, it might mean handing the women off to Gervais.

Not going to happen.

He pledged it fervently beneath his breath while waiting for Oz to respond. The Aussie didn't take long.

"Something happened like what?"

"Like I found a certain somebody we're looking for."

Before he was finished, he was grimacing. *Somebody* we're *looking for?* Where the hell had that possessive come from? And so naturally? But it was one word and easy enough to fix once he saw the princess safe and sound with Oz and Jagger Fox. This whole episode would just be a footnote in his musings about the trip. He'd all but stumbled into the situation, and he could damn well stumble back out.

But not yet. Especially not as Oz's guttural croak shook up the line.

"Shut the fucking front door," his friend blurted.

Brick snorted. "Well, I could, but we can't waste time."

"How? Where?"

"A few blocks from you. At the Très Particulier. From what I could lift from ten feet away, she was there waiting on LaBarre." *And being the world's most gorgeous princess pixie in the doing.* "But I learned that part after a couple of player barflies swooped in. Wasn't a chance to grab her alone. The assholes had her thinking they'd brought Daddy Dearest and had him waiting outside."

"And she fell for it?"

"Hook, line, and sinker."

"And you *let* her?"

"Because she was going to believe *me* more than *them* . . . why?"

Oz's answering rumble was a kinda-sorta version of agreement. "Where is she now? Is Requiemme with her? Don't tell me she's still with the wankers?"

"Okay, then. I won't."

"But you'd be lying?"

"Not exactly that either."

"Shit."

"*Ssshhh.*"

Brick pulled the phone away by a couple of inches, needing the space to listen to the maid's new outcries. It sounded like they'd cut left somewhere, but this warren was still a collection of audible fuckery. For all he knew, they'd looped around and were behind him. His feet scuffed on the pavement as he spun around, perplexed. When the shrieks suddenly stopped, he swore under his breath. The silence was more unnerving than the ping-ping acoustics.

"Brick, you wanker! Talk to me. What's the full dope?"

"I have no idea. Why do you think I'm calling for backup?"

A strange cough from Oz. Okay, not so strange, considering the guy could count Brick's backup requests on one hand. The situation wasn't exactly Brick's comfort zone either. But that shit had vanished when watching Gervais and his buddy slather on Jayd and Requiemme like teenagers on supermodels. And again when he'd burst into the alley. And again when he'd left the alley, having to acknowledge he'd lost them.

"All right. Where are you, man?"

He looked up and around, attempting to pinpoint some unique landmarks. A window with a red awning. A broken parking ticket machine. Graffiti in a few shades of blue, the assorted French words formed of bubble letters.

But he didn't tell all that to Ozias.

Something about the significant knife in his face probably had to do with it.

The long switchblade wielded by a delicate but determined hand.

That small appendage leading his gaze down the attached slender arm—and finally out to take in his visitor's glowering face.

Holy shit.

That face.

Those huge, irrepressible eyes. Those cheekbones, the noble architecture surely descended from Cleopatra herself. And that mouth, lush and determined, set with equally regal pride.

Jesus. Christ.

She was so goddamned gorgeous, even this close.

Especially this close.

And yet, not nearly close enough.

The thought, not her blade, had him jerking backward. But the bold beauty wasn't having his retreat. Not by an inch.

"Do. Not. Move." She twisted her wrist to make the streetlight glimmer on the long blade. "Or I shall be forced to filet your testicles."

Brick would have laughed had he not been so certain she'd make good on the threat. Her stance was right; her grip was confident. With Samsyn Cimarron for an older brother, she'd probably learned how to gut a man before how to wear a bra.

And there was a thought he did *not* need. His cock was already seething at him for contemplating the woman's gorgeousness from the neck *up*. No way could he go there, considering what the rest of her succulent curves were like, though her tight T-shirt and pants weren't helping that particular war effort.

An apt comparison. His honor and his libido were Caesar and Mark Antony, ready to burn each other alive. On the outside, he kept up a neutral façade. He had no idea *how*, but it stayed in place even as the beautiful little warrior closed in on him with a half-hitched grin.

"On the other hand, perhaps I like that idea better," she murmured as the gleam in her gaze turned the color of opals in the sun. "The gutter cats will adore me. I am sure your balls go well with grime and trash."

"Hmm. And a nice Cabernet." And here it came. The sarcasm was more a default than a decision, his version of a shaky knee or a nervous twitch in situations that had descended from bad to worse. But it was better than the panic. Anything was better than the fucking panic.

Still, he frowned in confusion. What the hell was so bad to

worse about this? This hot water could be cooled at once with a simple phone conversation. The one he already happened to be having.

"Disconnect the call. Then throw down the phone."

Well, shit.

"You don't want me to do that... Princess."

For the first time, her blade wobbled. So did her breath.

"Who the hell are you? And how—"

"Do I know who you are?" he supplied, making sure their gazes locked at the same second. "Why don't you stow the blade so I can answer that properly? While you're at it, maybe you can tell me where your friend went?"

He edited himself this time, deliberately not mentioning Requiemme by name. Didn't help that the woman's mute button was still engaged. Though he'd found their key target, he already knew Jayd wouldn't comply with any plan before knowing her maid—*assistant*, whatever—was safe. He had no idea *how* he knew, but he did. Just like he knew, before the princess betrayed any new thoughts across her face, exactly what she was going to say next.

"That is no business of yours, Pura *prispoul*."

"I'm not Pura." He underlined it with enough authority to make her gaze bug wider. The tiny tic in her proud jaw announced that she noted the purposeful set of his. "Though if I were, you'd have just given yourself away, Your Highness."

Her nostrils flared. She swallowed hard. He saw why, as soon as her stunning turquoises lit up with a telltale sheen. "Shut up."

"I'll consider it once you tell me which way Requiemme ran." He said it mostly to buy time, subtly pivoting his wrist and tapping the button on his phone for a video connection to go with the audio. No way would Oz not be on top of the change. Hopefully, he'd be able to determine their location and get his ass over here.

"I said shut up!"

"You want help finding your friend or not, Princess?"

"No more questions!" Her punctuation, a practiced flick of the blade, was the first move he hadn't predicted. As Brick glanced down and gawked at the small gash in his Henley and the corresponding nick in his sternum, Jayd Cimarron reset her stance. This time, she had her elbow cocked and the knife ready to plunge. "*I* am asking the questions, *bonsun*. And now *you* will answer me!"

"Jayd?"

The summons was strange. It came from a distance but not blocks away. After a second, Brick recognized the source— from the device in his hand.

"Jayd? Answer me!"

The princess looked around with frantic jerks of her head. The alley light played over her choppy hair, making it shimmer with shades of purple and amber. "Jagger? What—how are you—"

"Ripley! By the Creator, talk to me!"

She snatched Brick's phone out of his hand. Her eyes got wetter as she peered at the screen. "Is it really you? What beneath the angels is going on? Why are you on this man's—"

"Because I'm working with him." Brick sucked up his nerves and just blurted it. By now it was pretty much the truth, and they had no time for a real tea party about this shit. "My name's Max Brickham. Most people just call me Brick. I met your friend this morning. He relayed his urgency to find you, and—"

She shook her head with adamant violence. "I—I do not understand. Find me? Why? Jagger, where *are* you?"

"Here, Jayd," he said. "Just as Brickham told you. I met him this morning, and—"

"You met him *here*? In *Paris*?"

"Yes." He pushed out a rough breath, clearly losing patience. Brick was comforted by the commiseration. "I got here yesterday."

"But why?" As her posture stiffened, her blade arm drooped. That was an even better bonus.

"Because Carris is here too."

The switchblade clattered all the way to the pavement. The woman's arm, along with the rest of her body, was limp and trembling. Brick kicked the weapon away—but not too far—before stepping next to her. If she was going down, he swore to be there for the catch.

"*Desonnum*." Fox's face on the phone screen was tight. "I am sorry, my friend. I did not want to tell you this way, but we must get you to safety."

"But Requiemme—"

"Her too," the Arcadian vowed.

"But even *I* do not know where she—"

"We will find her. I promise. I will make sure of it. Right now, you have to trust Brickham. Listen to him. Every moment that you are out there and exposed—"

"Well, I'm liking the sound of that."

She snapped her head up. This time, Brick was right there with her—before he spat the F-word in a growl to rival Geralt of goddamned Rivia. Yeah, yeah, fantasy computer world bruisers had bad days too—but that's what the Exit Game button was for. No such magical switch like that here. This was real life—complete with yet another interruption that he didn't need but never ruled out.

"Gervais. I have that correct, oui? Good. Well, *bonsoir.*" He sidestepped over, ensuring the bastard wouldn't be able to eyeball Jayd without confronting his chest. "You know what that means, douchebag? That happy hour is really over—especially for you. I know, I know. That's like shitty action movie lines on the bartop trivia machine. But you get the picture, right? You're not doing this tonight, man. At least not with her."

Gervais squared his stance, tossed his head back, and cocked his brows. "Because *you* are? Because you were so fast on the draw back at the bar, right?" He curled up one side of his lip, as knowing as Elvis Presley before a hip roll. "Oh yeah, asshole, I saw you there. I also watched you listening and leering at everyone like a goddamned pervert."

"Not everyone," Brick asserted. "Only dickwads that looked ready to pull shenanigans as soon as I took a second to pay my tab."

"*Ferme,*" the guy spat. "Remy and I made our moves like proper gentlemen!"

"Ah, yes. And then escorted us out to the alley, like 'proper gentlemen.'"

While the princess couldn't be blamed for her attack, escalation was the last thing this encounter needed. Before Brick could convey as much, Gervais shifted forward again.

"Now there's that sexy, sassy mouth I like so much."

Well, shit. Then there was that.

"Look, man." With a heavy breath, Brick pulled up every peacekeeping move from his practiced playbook. He was calm and cautious, counteracting the asshole's wired energy. The guy was ready to fight or fuck. Maybe both. Probably badly. "There's nothing for you to gain here—"

"Nothing!"

"But getting into some trouble and pain," he went on, as if Jayd hadn't been trying to sabotage her own rescue. "If you don't believe me, talk to your unconscious friend in the alley behind the bar."

Gervais sneered. "My *friend*? You think I give a rat's backside about that fucker?"

Brick sighed. Nuclear catastrophe wouldn't kill the human race. Stupidity would. "Whatever. Just move the hell on, Gervais. The night is still young."

"Yeah?" the idiot spat back. "And so's my left hook, dickwad."

Stupidity. Human extinction. Period.

Because the dumbshit had just handed his war plan to Brick on a silver platter. Before Gervais was finished with the threat, Brick had shoved Jayd aside and ducked the asshole's sweep of a left hook. But Gervais was investing a lot into the movie star move, including his full weight. When his fist met nothing but air, the jerk stumbled forward and tripped. Down he went, landing on his face with a bone-on-brick *crack*.

"What the? Ass. Hole!" the bully screeched, choking on the blood from his busted nose. "This is not okay!"

"That much is very true," Brick muttered. In an okay world, he'd be able to stick around and show this choad what happened to pricks who lured women into alleys for "good times." In an okay world, he'd be hauling up Gervais by his balls and then ensuring the guy prayed for mercy every time he took a piss.

But this wasn't that world.

And he had to make a smarter choice.

To get Jayd Cimarron out of here.

He leaned down, roping one hand around her wrist while jamming his phone into a back pocket with another. With any luck, none of the commotion had disconnected the call to Oz and Jagger, and he'd be able to give them a better report once they were out of Gervais's crosshairs.

But the world wasn't ready to be okay for him yet. And the idiot bully wasn't ready to be done with the chase.

After an outraged roar, Gervais was on his feet and giving them steady chase. Brick didn't glance back to confirm the fact. Not necessary. The shithead was as subtle as a pig in heat, swearing and growling and stumbling.

But despite his noise, the asshole was fast.

Brick cussed beneath his own breath. They had to get out of sight somehow.

The alley curved a little, buying them a few seconds of invisibility from the guy. Those moments were enough for Brick to look up and spot a small symbol that was stamped on the glass over an ornate black door. Other than the round insignia, which some might mistake as a bicycle gear or Celtic clan symbol, the entrance was completely boring.

But it wasn't unremarkable to Brick. And that round, three-part emblem was inducing him to anything but yawns in this moment.

This moment, with Jayd Cimarron's wrist in his grip... and her eyes, now pleading him so fully for her safety...

She picked *now* to get wise about trusting him?

He couldn't waste time answering that. He had to simply accept it. For the moment, he had what he needed from her to get this shit done.

He lunged forward and pushed open the door.

Safety.

Or so he assumed.

In the split second before yanking Jayd all the way through the portal, Brick glimpsed movement around the bend in the alley. Movement too significant to be a scuttling rat or feline.

It was human.

Fuck.

It was Gervais—observing exactly where they were taking shelter.

CHAPTER FIVE

"What on earth?"

The wonderment had assaulted Jayd's mind at least a dozen times in the last hour. This was the first time it breached past her lips. She was justified. The acceleration of her pulse told her so. Her mind refused to tame the throb, spinning into a strange storm of reactions as Max Brickham dragged her down a narrow, tiled hall. She was nervous but consoled. Furious but grateful. But strangest of all, she used the freedom to admit and examine all those things—which meant, in her most vital intuitions, she also felt safe.

So in actuality, she had gone insane.

That had to be it—because there was nothing safe about the atmosphere around her. The music was dark and moody. The air was thick and leathery. And then there were the shrieks and moans. Victims in pain, making her chest ache with—

What?

Sorrow? Anguish? Trepidation? Fear?

Only the last on that list was true, though it was not the same sensation she had always coupled to the feeling. She was afraid but not in fear. She was trepidatious but not terrified.

"Brickham?" she spurted as soon as they stopped in a round vestibule bracketed by a couple of doors. In front of them, a wide archway was filled by a black velvet curtain. The music was coming from somewhere beyond that, along with more broken groans and cries. "Wh-What is—"

He cut in on her with a harsh sound from his throat. "Quiet," he ordered. "And do exactly what I say. If your friend followed us in here, we'll need to act fast."

"That *bonsun* is not my friend!"

"And we are way out of time for semantics."

As he spat it back, the door leading from the alley was swung wide once more. Jayd gulped. Her fight or flight reflexes hit gridlock, leaving her limbs as paralyzed ice sculptures.

"Creator's mercy. What do we do now?"

Brickham grabbed something off a wall she could barely see and shoved it at her. "Put this on."

It was a mask of sorts. No, it was more a hood. It was made out of dark-red latex and made to cover someone's head down to the bridge of their nose. She was so busy making sure she had all the angles right before putting it on that she never noticed Brick altering his own appearance—by shedding his shirt and donning a black, burglar-looking mask of his own.

"Good," he said, nodding in response to her wide-eyed gape. "Now take off your pants."

"Excuse me?" She was grateful she sounded more scandalized than mesmerized, cloaking the effect of his new look on every heated ounce of her blood. Logically, she dismissed her reaction to spiked adrenaline and racing fear. Primally, it was not that simple.

Here, before her, stood a man.

Revision. A *man*.

Which had to be one of the craziest thoughts she had ever possessed.

She knew men. She had three grown brothers. *Men*. All three were as muscled and defined as Max Brickham. Though none of them had his dense but intricate tattoos, which nearly covered his pectorals and shoulders, the hardware underneath was similar terrain for her.

But in so many ways, *not* similar.

He was different. So very different. *Everywhere*. He was rougher. More rugged. Gleaming and mighty. Bigger and bolder.

A total stranger.

Which, so very oddly, only spiked her freak fascination with him. Especially as he bared all his teeth, which glowed more perfect and white than they should in this dimness, in a look that should have terrified her—but again, did not.

"*Princess.*" In the core of his croaked command, she found understanding. He was desperate, not dangerous. "Just do it, damn it. We've got to blend in a little better here."

But where was *here*?

She craved to voice that aloud. To get back just that spot of control in this mess of a night. But fate was not giving her even those ten seconds. She had less than that to make her decision here. A vital one.

Stay fully clothed and face Gervais, or trust Max Brickham to take care of her—in her underwear?

Before the dilemma finished taunting her mind, she had finished her decision.

And already leaned over to push down her leggings.

"Good girl. Thank you."

Though Brickham's voice was still a taut rasp, it flowed over her senses like honeyed praise. But when Jayd was about to reply with a trusting smile, she ducked and cowered instead. They had company. Not Gervais. Another man. He was nearly as tall as Brickham but did not come close in muscled stature or strength.

"Monsieur?" he prompted, flashing them with a suspicious look and a small flashlight's beam. "May I ... ermmm ... be of assistance?"

"You absolutely can." Brickham tapped a neon green armband that stood out against the man's otherwise black attire. "You the dungeon master here?"

Jayd gave in to a silent startle. *Dungeon* master? Where, under all the stars and skies, were they?

"I am," the man offered, his face tightening. "Which means I am obliged to inform you that all play must be consensual and safe at all times. Additionally, all scenes must occur in our private rooms, or beyond the velvet—"

"Outstanding." As Brickham extended his other arm, Jayd noticed the black leather band around his wrist. It was embedded with a silver medallion. He lifted it into the bright circle from the man's flashlight. "Glad to know you're about the essentials."

The man leaned in, examining the silver plate more closely. "This is ... a master's crest?"

"Yes. I'm affiliated with Bastille."

The greeter reared back with a popped gaze. "In Seattle? In the States? *That* Bastille?"

"Yes."

"This says you are also ... a founding member?"

One side of Brickham's mouth hitched up. "You could say that."

If they had more time, Jayd would be openly gawking at the man's respectful head dip. "Well then, it would be *mon plaisir* to waive your door fee, monsieur."

"*Merci.*" Max's murmur, in a flawless accent, was edged with impatience.

"Additionally, I am fully at your service, Master. Whatever you need for your play with us this evening..."

"Right, right." More restlessness from Brickham.

Master? What was *that* about? What, by the Creator and the saints, was going on here? How had Brickham turned this man from adversary to ally with a medallion and a few magic words? He was from a place called *Bastille*? A place named after a *prison*?

But the man catered to Brickham like he was royalty. She should know. But perhaps her qualifications mattered not now, considering she had no title or even pants to call her own. At this moment, she was merely the woman on the king's arm, not the center of attention herself. It was a surprisingly—perhaps shockingly—*pleasant* feeling.

All those ruminations did not block her from listening in on Brick's swift conversation with the dungeon master. As their host quickly rushed Brickham and her through two layers of the thick velvet curtains, she caught several parts of their conversation.

"... no need for a full station..."

"... any floggers, bindings, accessories?"

"... privacy and discretion..."

"... then an aftercare alcove?"

"By the Creator," Jayd whispered. She went unheard, thanks to her bowed head and the fact that they entered the area where the music was the loudest. Likely had something to do with the climbing din of her heartbeat too—which became a crescendo as so many of those words raced through her mind. Floggers? Bindings? What was a full station? Or an aftercare alcove?

Looking up brought her no clear answers.

Just hundreds more questions.

Ohhh...heavens.

They were truly not on earth anymore.

But they were not in the heavens she had just invoked either. But in the same token, it was certainly not hell.

She was at a complete loss for describing this place. It had to be some shameless debauchery den brought back to life from history. Or perhaps, had never died. Babylon? Zerzura? Sodom? Gomorrah? All of the above?

She had no point of reference except the truth of what her stare took in.

First, she realized how bizarrely overdressed she was. Most of the women, and a great deal of the men, were clad in skimpier attire—if they were clothed at all. But they were all comfortable with their exposure. She identified that in their eager and happy faces.

What she still had trouble identifying...was the rest of the scene.

Some people were bent over low stools. Some were tied to the wall or handcuffed to large devices. One of those was shaped like a tall X. Another was more like a mounted leather couch cushion, except for the rings up and down its sides. Other people were not using the equipment. They were in smaller, carpeted areas that overlooked the main floor. In many of them, there were just couches, chairs, and ceilings with groupings of large hooks. All the spaces were occupied by couples who were doing...*things*...to each other.

Things from which Jayd could not rip her stare.

Some of the men and women were deftly spanking or flogging their partners. Some of them were engaged in more carnal activities. *Much* more carnal.

She still could not look away.

It was all so frightening.

But it all seemed so ... right.

How she came to that conviction at once, she had no idea. She knew about this kind of lifestyle simply by listening closely at college parties. Well, maybe a little more than listened. She had been entranced, as if her sources were telling tales of far-off knights and wizards saving the day. Never did she imagine that those stories were real. That there were real people who enjoyed this extreme way of showing affection, gathered in special rooms like this to enjoy it.

But here they were. A lot of real people. Doing a lot of extreme things.

And here she was, standing and gawking, the rudest voyeur ever.

But only for another three seconds. On the fourth, Brickham again clutched her by the wrist. With the same rushed intensity, he hauled her to the darker shadows along the wall to their left.

Her head spun. Her stomach flipped. How "blended in" was the man planning to make them? And why did contemplating that answer make her breath catch like she was merely being pulled onto a dance floor by a boy she was crushing on?

But as fate had already established, Brickham was not a boy. Millions of kilometers from it. A couple of continents too.

No moment confirmed that conviction more than the next.

"Oh!"

She exclaimed it as soon as he swept her around and rushed her directly at the wall. Less than a second after she hit the ornate wallpaper, Brickham pressed in behind her.

By every star in the firmament.

This was . . . good. So very, very good. His torso was a wide shell across her back. His massive thighs framed both of hers.

"Fuck," he rumbled into her ear. "Did I hurt you, Pixie?"

"I—" Her breathing hitched but not from pain. *Pixie.* From his lips, it was the most beautiful thing anyone had called her. Sure, she had handful of nicknames related to her noticeable stature. Well, lack of it. Shortcake, Mushroom, Little Bit, Shrimp Dip. She was fine with them all, but never had they made her long to hear them again. Over and over and over again "I . . . am fine," she finally asserted, tilting a look over her shoulder. "How are you?"

For a moment, she thought she had said or done the wrong thing. His surprise was evident, even with half his face hidden by the mask. And for some reason, she sensed that manners mattered in here. Protocols.

"I'll be more than fine once we shake that asshole for good," Brick stated. "But that's going to mean obeying everything I say, okay?"

There was a smile in his voice if not on his full, determined lips. So Jayd gave him one of her own. "I understand, Brickham."

"Thank you," he repeated. "But my mandates start here, and the first one is no more talking. If you absolutely have to speak, you'll address me as Sir, not Brickham. I can't give you a full crash course in dungeon etiquette right now, but that one has to stick. You can speak to indicate you comprehend that too."

"Of course, I—I mean, yes, Sir. I understand."

As soon as the words rolled out, she wanted to smile

again. They all felt so real and right, especially when she felt the vibrations of Brickham's approving rumble.

With the same low warmth, he sidled closer to her. He kept one hand wrapped around the top of her hip while grazing the other one up her back, to the side of her neck. "*Very* good," he soothed, though he dug his fingers into her flesh with a new burst of force. "Now turn your head down, with your forehead pressing the wall. Place your palms to either side of it."

Jayd complied with swift readiness. The task was easy once she heard the cadence of Gervais's huffs between the placating murmurs from the man with the green armband. The *bonsun* was closer than she wanted him to be, though her mind could be playing tricks on her. But she did not dare look up to check. The latex hood only shielded half her face.

Brickham's voice, rough but reverent in her ear, was a perfect slice into her spiraling fear. "Don't focus on them," he instructed, eclipsing her wonderment about how he had read right into her thoughts. That no longer mattered. Nothing mattered but complying with him, briefly nodding so maybe he would speak again. Fill her ear with his warm breath. Consume her senses with his perfect strength.

Strength she desperately needed right now.

As soon as he spoke again, she was rewarded well for her effort. "Just stay with *me*, gorgeous girl." His voice was now aural cashmere. "For this to work, your world is only about me right now. None of the rest matters. Do you understand? Nod for me, Pixie."

She did just that once more grateful that he had not demanded more words. They likely would not come. Not with the lava that had once been her bloodstream and the starlight that had once been her eyesight. Right now, she did not need anything else. All her stresses and worries and fears slipped away, lost in the pulse of the music and the security of Brickham's proximity. She begged providence to make it last forever. Maybe, if she kept being his good girl, it would.

"Perfect." His voice full of more rumbling approval as he fitted his face into the curve of her neck. This time, there was no trace of Gervais's anger in the background—which crashed schisms of sorrow through her. If they had tricked the idiot and he moved on, was this the end of her sensual escape? "You're doing so beautifully, girl. Just a few more minutes. Our friend isn't giving up so easily."

"Y-Y-Yes, Sir."

The rasp was as natural as the air in her lungs and the vibrancy in her veins. But that was before she remembered Brickham's initial instruction—for which she got a swift reminder courtesy of the force of nature himself. His fingers, bold and masterful, slid beneath her underwear. His pinch, harsh and hard, dug into her backside. His anticipation, swift and sure, was ready for her reacting yelp. As his other hand clamped across her mouth, she broke into another high-pitched protest.

And just who was she kidding?

Not a protest. She was blatantly goading the man for more.

Holy heavens, how she wanted more.

"Under any other circumstances, I'd be swatting you for the deliberation, girl," he growled. "But we can't go there yet. *Fuck*." The rebuke was muttered, as if to himself more than her. "We can't go there at all."

"Why?" Again, a blurt she did not anticipate but could not control. She wrested free from his hand and pushed on.

"Brickham? Why not?"

A new dig of fingers into her bottom. A more ruthless clamp over her mouth. "Goddammit," he snarled against her neck. "I'll have your obedience, even if I don't have to ask nicely."

Another zap of fresh fear—though again, this was the good version of the feeling. The tingles that reached for more. The naughty need that scratched at her veins, craving to pry open the scary fortress of Max Brickham.

Craving Max Brickham, period.

What was happening here?

What was happening to *her*?

"And what if I do not want . . . *nice*?"

There was the answer to one question. None of this was happening to her because this could not be *her*. In the space of a few minutes, she had transformed into a completely different creature. A woman separate from the Cimarrons' little sister and the dutiful royal daughter. She was not even Jagger's bold Ripley or Emme's loyal friend.

She was simply a woman. Seen as such and desired as much. She knew that more clearly than the ire in Brickham's growl and the new tension in his massive form. She knew it with the sparkling awareness she had of both and the pleasure of knowing she was the cause.

And oh yes, she even knew it from the second that Brickham started rolling her T-shirt up from the bottom. She embraced the surety in full as he made a cotton roll out of the fabric and then worked the soft tube up, gently stuffing it between her lips. She rejoiced in it as he made sure her shoulders stayed bound by the part of the shirt she was still wearing, ensuring her new gag remained in place.

"Ask and you shall receive, little Pixie."

"Unnnhhh," she replied right away, the sound full of a frustrating ache. But not because of how he muffled her. It was because of all the new sensations he set free in her while doing it—and then, damn it, the sweet kiss he settled to her temple as he finished. Both were like fancy frosting on a decadent dessert he was preparing, only to simply stand there and gaze at his creation instead of taking a bite.

She hated it.

Hated being his showpiece. Being everyone's pampered, protected little froth. An oddity with no life. A princess with no crown. A woman with no worth.

She needed to be reawakened. But a magical kiss would not accomplish that.

She needed more. Like bites. And scratches. And punishments.

Right. The hell. Now.

She did not just think it. She put the intention into action, letting her instincts guide her. Another long moan into her makeshift gag. A new thrust of her chest, acknowledging the hardening points of her nipples against the basic cotton of her bra. Another shift of her weight down low, recognizing the need there, as well.

Oh, holy Creator. *The need.*

She wanted to stroke herself there. To circle and press the way she did when alone at night, fantasizing about being this bare and vulnerable for a man . . .

"Damn it." Brickham's guttural burst seemed spun from the core of those erotic visions, down to the coarse hunger in his tone. "You need to keep it down, kitten. Just for a few minutes longer."

Jayd replied by writhing with more force. She groaned again, louder than before, as the man sank his teeth into the top of her shoulder. It was brutal. And beautiful. And freeing. And fantastic...

"Christ on fucking toast." A long moment that made no sense because he moved a few inches away from her. Why would he do that if she was pleasing him? "You're...really liking this...aren't you, gorgeous? Oh *hell* yes," he commented, swiping his hand from her backside to her front. "You *do* like this."

Jayd gnashed into the rolled cotton between her lips. Hard. A sound erupted from the depths of her throat, beyond a moan but more strident than a scream, as Brickham began to explore her sensitive center. His responding grunt, as if he were being wheeled into surgery without painkillers, had her writhing against him with more need.

Yes. Writhing.

She was doing this. *Her.* Moving like this with such wanton need, with a person she barely knew. No. Not even barely. First name, last name, trusted by Jagger Fox, might come from Seattle. That was the extent of her knowledge about Max Brickham.

Except for the fact that he had already fought predators for her.

And was still doing everything he could to protect her, to take care of her. In ways he could have never imagined.

In ways *she* had never imagined.

But now, could barely imagine anything else. Could hardly think or breathe because of it.

How he made her burn.

How he made her quiver.

How he made her—

"Ohhh! Ahhh!"

—splinter and shatter and break and burst.

Dear sweet Creator . . . the bursting.

She was bliss and abandon. Fire and surrender. Vibration and light. An explosion that made everything so good and hot and right.

And the man who had brought it to her.

"Fuck. *Jayd.*" And his urgent sough in her ear.

"You're doing it, aren't you?" And his fingers, rubbing her core and pressing her most precious button.

"That's right. Oh yeah, that's right. Keep going, girl. Let me have all of it."

All of it?

Wasn't that what she had just done?

But Max Brickham, force of nature extraordinaire, was determined to live up to his nickname. Even now, before knowing he had it. Even now, *after* he had stroked her to one stunning climax. Even now, as he touched her in places she did not know about. In ways she had never known—but now, would never forget.

"That's it, Pixie. Almost . . . there."

There . . . *where*?

She almost demanded it of him, despite her cotton restraint. Because he could *not* be serious about making her—

But he was.

And now *she* was. All over again.

A climax even better than the first. An eruption so fierce and forceful, she swayed on her feet. But Brickham was there, steadying her. He pulled her back, closer than ever before, allowing her to rest her thighs atop his. Of course, that also brought the middle of her body flush to his. And ohhh yes, that meant being aware of the defined abdominal muscles that formed a perfect V to his own center. It also meant a sharp new awareness about the ridge where that V ended. He was pulsing there. Throbbing with vital need.

With lust.

For her.

Which made her even more dizzy. Brickham braced her again, his resilience seemingly effortless. She marveled at how he handled her as if he would an orchid bloom. As if she were the same weight. As if she were an equally special bloom.

Or... maybe not.

Her heart rate had barely come down before the man relegated their weight once more—this time, eschewing his tenderness for briskness and his sensual aura for a basic friendliness.

Yes... basic.

But none of what they had just shared was *basic*.

Why did he not acknowledge it? Or at this point, seem to know it? Even as he loosened her shirt and let it fall back into place. And yes, even as he accepted her leggings from the green armband man, who came over to relay that Gervais was good and gone, and deftly helped her get back into one leg of them.

As if he had extensive experience with helping a woman get dressed before.

As if he had done *all* of this, in a lot of places like this, before.

"You still okay, Princess?"

Her chest clenched. *Princess*. Not *Pixie* or *Gorgeous* or even *Good Girl*. Probably because he had used those endearments a thousand times before, as well. On other women he had taken to the stars and back. Other women who were probably better at this stuff than her.

Especially this part. Where she still had to stand in front of him, one leg out of her pants and a T-shirt with a large drool spot. Where she had to pretend like she did not know how all that had happened. That just five minutes ago, she was ready to take off more if Brickham had asked. That she would have done *a lot* of insane things had Brickham but asked.

But at this point, she could not even meet the man's gaze. "I—I am fine." Nor summon anything to her voice besides a rigid monotone. If she veered from that, it would mean certain disaster. Wavering would mean emotions, and emotions would bring tears. And were those going to help anything or anyone?

She was a grown-up, damn it. She had fled Arcadia from a desperate need to make that point, among others. And she had just been flown to erotic Eden as a woman, not a girl. She could not beg to be reverted back and held like a porcelain doll just because of her tender fallout from the experience.

Get it together, Jayd. You know *what self-composure looks like, even if you are falling apart on the inside.*

The new resolve was the perfect hit at the perfect time. With its help, she repeated, "I am *fine*, Brickham. And I can do this myself." She snapped the other half of her leggings from him.

"Wasn't implying you weren't." He was not defensive about it, though she had given him many excuses to be. Instead, there was an indulgent underline in his tone, reminding her of how Evrest had been with Camelia during the testier moments of her pregnancy. Those times had always warmed Jayd but also made her ache. Had her wondering if she would ever receive the same kind of patience from a man. She was a lot to handle sometimes and could be a mouthy, mulish princess due to holding her own against three equally obstinate siblings.

But she and Max Brickham were *nothing* like her big brother and his queen. No way had Evrest ever taken Cam to a place like this before. Or tried anything close to what Brickham just did. If he had, Cam certainly would not have reveled in it. Nor wanted so much more of it, all over again.

Oh, *rahmie Creacu*. What had she done?

More exigently, what would she do now?

Especially as Brickham stood there with one clear intent. He was fine with standing clear to let her get dressed, but not any further. Protectiveness seemed stamped into his very DNA, defining him like an aura.

A delicious, hard-muscled, all-male aura.

An aura she could not ignore as he stepped close again and spoke.

"We should get out of here. No telling if our friend might come back for another look around. The Dungeon Monitor told me about a loading dock out back."

Dungeon Monitor. The phrase, and all its adjoining context, struck her in visceral places yet again. Well, that and the tied-down naked people. And the flying floggers. But nobody really sounded like they hated being here . . .

"Jayd?"

"Huh? What?" She ripped her stare away from a man in leather pants and spiked boots, who also seemed to enjoy running spikes across the back of a pretty redheaded woman. From the gist of her moans and sighs, she liked spikes too.

"Come on, Pixie. Now."

She wheeled around, compelled by his gritty undertone. She did not protest when he reached for her hand and tugged her along the perimeter of the big room. As much as Jayd longed to stay for another hour and watch everything in here, it meant more to have Brickham's hand around hers.

So much more.

What was happening to her?

Never before had she been affected so fast and so violently by a male. To be honest, she had thought herself immune by now. That was what happened after being the tagalong for three of the most swaggering men on the planet. But things were different now. She could no longer be Evrest, Samsyn, and Shiraz's adored angel. Thanks to the Pura, she had become their iron albatross.

But at this moment, she felt like neither. No way could she be an angel with such wicked heat still invading every cell of her blood. But despite the molten weight of that fire, her mind and limbs felt as light as feathers.

The odd inner battle continued as they emerged outside and she breathed in the midsummer Paris air. The mixture of metro steam and night flowers was not enough to recenter her. She was quite afraid that nothing would, except maybe her own trip to a special dungeon again.

But damn it, princesses never got to go to the dungeon.

Only... she was no longer a princess.

For the first time ever, Jayd actually welcomed that thought with a full, real smile.

CHAPTER SIX

One step at a time.

One block at a time.

One heartbeat at a time.

Brick called up the familiar mantras as his personal flotilla of rescue buoys, letting them pull him along the streets between the dungeon and the safe house. No way were his legs and feet going to get him and Jayd there on their own. Not after the ordeal through which he'd forced them to keep him upright.

Oh, yeah. *Ordeal.*

He wasn't about to sugarcoat the description. Wasn't like his brain was going to let him anyway. It persisted with the invasions of memory, more hot and terrifying than any mortar shell or bombed-out building. No matter what else he focused on, the incursions kept coming.

The same way *he'd* wanted to come in that place. All over Jayd Cimarron's sweet, silken ass. Then her gorgeous, taut thighs. And then inside her too . . .

Holy shit, *yes.* With her walls shivering around him. Her arms wrapped around him. And her eyes—those turquoises that took him to such magical places—round and filled with nothing but him. Acknowledging the flare of their full fire together. The fire he was certain she felt too. She *had* to. *He'd* never experienced anything like it, that was for damn sure. It was a fucking *pull,* starting from the second he'd settled his stare on her in Tres Particular. That draw had become a psychological demand, and then an inescapable need.

And now a goddamned mess.

Because, of all the back-alley hideouts to duck into, in this whole huge city, they'd wound up against a dark wall with his fly against her ass and his fingers against her clit. And her passion in his ears. And her juices on his skin. So many fragrant, addicting drops . . .

Holy Christ.

One brick.

One step.

One heartbeat.

Sooner than later, thank fuck, they were climbing a narrow flight of stairs and then another, up into an apartment building situated between a vape shop and a florist. Ozias hadn't given him an apartment number, but he was glad to see there was only one unit up on the top floor. He wasn't quite sure what they'd do if Oz and Jagger were still out searching for Requiemme. What he *wanted* to do—press Jayd up against one of the faded walls and taste every inch of her lush bow mouth—wasn't happening.

Wasn't. Happening.

Not even as she paused, meeting his gaze with her own again.

Not even as she stared right the hell into him, boring with those unmistakable opals, until she surely saw every thought in his head. Including the illicit ones.

Damn it, that also wasn't happening anymore. Even if he had to scoop out his eyes to ensure it. The option was way better than trying to fight this feverish attraction to a woman he could never touch again.

The decision had nothing to do with the tiara that might

or might not touch her head again. There were many more walls of situational concrete between them. Barriers that had no chance of ever coming down. Most obviously, the half-dozen countries and thousands of miles between Seattle and Arcadia. Not so visible but twice as formidable: the differences between the two of them. She was struggling to connect with the right father figure. He'd never known his father *or* his mother and didn't care. She was a well-loved public figure. He valued solitude and secrecy. She looked at everything with eyes as open as island lagoons. His gaze had shadows that would never go away. Memories that would never conclude in anything but panic.

"Christ in a bathtub. Max fuckin' Brickham, you really pulled off this troppo hat trick." And here it was. Oz and his colorful sentence structure to the rescue when he most needed it.

"You think I'd call and make that claim just to mess with you?"

"Wasn't sure what you were after." Oz chuffed while stepping aside to let them fully enter the apartment. "Since your signal cut out in the middle of your fun little chase scene."

Thank fuck.

"So it did," he answered, checking his phone screen. "Though we might have to have a chat about what you're calling fun these days, buddy."

"But we're okay-golden with the *little* part?"

"Eat my nads."

"Sorry, mate. Don't fancy damp Seattle meat." Without giving Brick a chance to form a perfect comeback, he persisted, "So what happened? After you went dark?"

"Long story," he muttered. "Best for a different soiree."

Much different. He had no idea where Ozias fell on the kink-o-meter, and the last thing he needed to spill on an adrenaline rush was what he'd done with Jayd Cimarron in the middle of the Montmartre maze.

"Hearing that," Oz said, easing Brick's mind by a few more degrees. But not enough. The guy's tension was still too palpable. "Especially because we've got a bigger cock-up to deal with now."

And there was the explanation why.

Brick tensed again, signaling his readiness to his friend. "All right. What shit's on the line?"

Before Oz could answer, they were both shoved aside by a princess-sized rocket.

"Jagger!" Jayd launched herself at Fox like an almond out of a slingshot.

Fortunately, Fox was ready for the assault. The guy actually belly-laughed when catching Jayd at full throttle, leaving Brick to attempt a smile through jealousy-clenched teeth. It didn't help to remember that he had no reasonable claim to hold the woman like that anymore or that Fox's boyfriend still stood here in front of him. This was his stupid shit, and it'd be all over soon.

Too damn soon.

Oz and Fox had entreated him to help find a princess, and that was what he'd done. Delivery successful. After a few minutes to rest up and use the head, he'd be out of here for good.

Away, once and for all, from the woman who could derail his logic with a sole glance or movement. Or a lusty moan. Or an orgasmic scream.

Okay, it was really time to use his head.

Except not. Because standing here, witnessing Jayd Cimarron in the throes of utter happiness, had him forgetting any part of his own name now. The woman's delight filled the whole damn room. Her addictive smile. Her summer-sky eyes. Her iridescent laugh.

Not even Fox was immune, proved by his tender smile once Jayd stopped mauling him. "No worse for wear then, Ripley?" he queried.

"Last survivor of the *Nostromo*, ready to reach the frontier," she returned, validating the film reference that Brick already suspected. So she was a sucker for gory space stories. There was some unexpected trivia. It brought a dorky grin to his lips, imagining how that tiny girl would look in a dirty tank top with a space blaster in hand, lying in wait for the toothy monster.

"Good," Fox said. "That is *so* good. When we found Requiemme, we were afraid that—"

"Afraid? Of what?" Alarm instantly replaced her joy. "Oh, dear Creator. *Emme.* You found her? Jagger? What happened to her? You—you did not leave her out there, did you?"

"He certainly did not."

Brick joined her and Oz in looking past the diminutive kitchen into the shoebox-sized living room, from where the remark originated. Lying on the couch, beneath a lamp without its shade, was Jayd's maid. The woman's head was propped against the far end, while three large throw pillows were stuffed under one of her knees. Her pants had been cut open past that joint, which was swollen to the size of a small grapefruit. An ominously bruised one.

"Emme." Jayd's rasp channeled enough dread for the both of them, so Brick skipped his wince and led the way over to the sofa. Once there, he exchanged a fast glance with Oz while Jayd dropped to the carpet and seized her friend by the hand.

"I've looked at it carefully but could use a second opinion," Oz murmured to him.

"We have been trying to get ice on it," Fox added. "And I had some alternative herbs in my bag to give her."

"Hmmm. Everything is so much better with herbs." Emme sighed and then giggled, all but confirming Brick's supposition about the subject. Arcadia's balmy climate likely lent itself well to any number of interesting crops, including the ones that created the skunky-pine sweetness in this area of the apartment.

But Jayd wasn't having anything to do with a contact high. She gripped her friend tighter and demanded, "Jagger? What the hell happened?"

"Highnnnesss." Emme inserted a scowl along with the rebuke. "Wasn't . . . his faullllt."

"Then whose fault was it?" Jayd snapped. "Because I swear by the snake in the holy garden, I shall have their testicles boiled and then force-fed to them on a—"

"Stop." Only after Brick issued the order did he realize its impropriety. But to whom? Oz and Fox looked relieved he'd stepped in. Requiemme was blissfully high. If Jayd was his only concern, then he stuck by the dictate. "You're spinning yourself into undue rage. Settle down, Pix—your Highness—and listen before you leap."

Fox flared his gaze, communicating silent gratitude, before stating, "Ozias and I got to her just after the accident."

"Accident?" Jayd repeated. "What accident? And who on earth is—"

"That's me." Oz dipped his head with deference. "Ozias

Demos. Happy to meet you, Highness Jayd. I'm a friend of Jagger's, just here to help. But you can call me—"

"Oz," Jayd broke in. Her composure softened, if only by a little. "I can just call you *Oz*. Oh, I know who you are now."

Though Fox blushed by several noticeable shades, Oz practically soared to Emme's level of euphoria. Brick was psyched to see his friend so happy. Oz had logged more than enough hours in the service of good karma. He deserved to get some in return.

"When you and Emme got separated in the alleys, Gervais followed her footsteps first," Fox went on. "And obviously—"

"He found me," Requiemme broke in. "And grabbed me."

"Filthy *bonsun*." Jayd curled her free hand into a fist and twisted it into the couch cushion. "So vipers *can* wear silk ties."

"He smelled more like a mongoose," Emme rejoined. "Hmmm yes, a mongoose. One that hadn't washed his balls in days."

As the woman applauded herself with another long snicker, Fox took up the narrative. "Once the asshole realized he had nabbed the wrong prey, he tossed Requiemme aside—into the street."

"Oh, no!" A sob crept into the edges of Jayd's outcry. "My beautiful *bonami*." She lifted a shaking hand to Emme's pale face. "You were run over?"

Emme molded her fingers atop Jayd's. "Only a motorcycle, girl. Do not fret."

"Only a *motorcycle*?" Jayd retorted. "Do not *fret*?"

"The rider was responsible," Oz inserted. "He braked but had to do it fast. His back tire skidded out and struck Emme from the knee down."

Jayd unfisted her other hand long enough to tap her chest,

shoulders, and forehead. "Creator Everlasting," she muttered, confirming Brick's impression that it was tied into Arcadian religion. Whatever that was.

"So what now?" Brick took advantage of the ensuing pause to address Fox and Oz again. "Have you guys been able to assess anything?"

"Except that she's got at least two breaks and needs to be splinted right away?" Oz countered. "We were just getting to that special part of the evening. Well, Jag was. I've been on ganja distribution duty."

"Of course you've been," Brick gibed.

"Only to her, you gronk. Give me credit for a smidge of smarts."

"Okay. Maybe a smidge." Brick wasn't entirely teasing.

Fox stepped up, bracing hands to his hips. "I found a couple of spare pillowcases in the bedroom and yanked the towel rack dowels from the bathroom," he said. "If we're careful about where we break the rods, we might be able to set the bones ourselves."

Brick nodded. "Decent plan. But then what?"

"We're working on that now," Oz stated.

"Working on it?" Of all the princess's outbursts in the last two hours, this one took the top prize. "Decent plan?" she lashed, scrambling to her feet. "The woman was *run over* by a *motorcycle*. She does not need plans or people working on *then whats*. The *plan* is that we locate the nearest hospital with an emergency room, and—"

"No hospitals!"

He fired the rebuttal in perfect tandem with the other two men. Before they were all done, Brick stepped over to Jayd. There was already an argument on her lips. He cut it off with the sharp incision of his gaze.

"The second we register Requiemme into a hospital system is the moment your friend Trystan will know how to find you both."

Nearly immediately, he hated himself for issuing the borderline command. Not because of the answering fury across her features. Because of the exhilaration that it fired in every blood cell he possessed.

Not that she let him enjoy it for too long.

With too much sass for Brick's liking, the entrancing pixie tilted her head and lifted a leg. Literally extended her ankle until it was next to her ear. As Brick joined Oz in a stunned gape, Fox joined Emme in knowing chuckles.

With a few deft moves, Jayd twisted free the shallow heel of her boot. From the secret hollow inside, out popped a small roll of money along with a few plastic cards. She quickly flicked through them before holding one up between her two longest fingers.

"Then perhaps we do not give the hospital her real name, hmm?"

Fox stepped over, closely eyeing the fake French ID card. "Emerald Farrow," the man read out. "And do I dare ask what *yours* is, or how you even got these?"

"Oh, *Jag*." Jayd slanted up one side of her mouth. "Do you really want to know that?"

The Arcadian shifted backward, already communicating his reply. "All right, then," he issued instead. "How does this change things?" He rolled his shoulders and cracked his neck. "Or *does* it?"

"Of course it does."

"Of course it does *not*."

The first line burst from Jayd just as the second tumbled from her maid. Remarkably, Requiemme was the first to scramble a follow-up fight.

"Jayd Dawne Cimarron, *listen* to me."

"Requiemme Cyndir Farre, *no*."

"Damn it!" That had all of them, Jayd included, popping shocked stares. "You heard Jagger. He has found supplies to set my leg just as well as any doctor—"

"Not just as well," Jayd argued. "No offense intended, Jag," she added in a murmur. "But you also said there are multiple breaks, and that means the possibility of multiple complications. Do. Not. Dispute. Me." She wagged a finger at him with all four of the brutal syllables. "I spent enough hours in the palais infirmary with all three of my daredevil brothers. Breaks are rarely just a snap, in any form of the word. She needs X-rays, evaluations, and a proper cast."

Requiemme delivered her second gawk-inducer of the minute by scooting higher on the couch, using her bum leg to drag the pillow stack along too. "*She* has a say in what she needs," the woman protested past a tight grimace. "And *she* says that she did not survive a skirmish with one *bonsun* only to see you snatched by another!"

"Which will happen how?" Jayd returned. "I can remain here, with Brickham and Oz. Jagger—"

"Will not be able to do it alone," Fox intervened. "I can fashion splints from my supplies but not crutches. Emme cannot bear any weight on that leg, so it will take two of us to even get her downstairs."

"Fine, then." Jayd drew up her posture, clearly gaining steam from her friend's willingness to talk logistics. "So Ozias goes too."

Fox reacted with contemplative quiet.

Oz scrubbed a hand up his jaw.

Requiemme slammed a fist to her forehead. "Creator's toes. I am not comfortable with this."

Brick wanted to nod right away. Neither was he. Not at all. The mere idea of being sequestered in here, alone with the beautiful pixie princess, already had his mind racing, his blood sizzling, and his cock pulsing.

Not a temptation cocktail he'd had to fight in a long time.

A long. Damn. Time.

But was he going to be the one to negate Jayd now? Especially when she was right? He had all the necessary proof just by looking down at Emme again. Her leg was becoming a piece of abstract art, with shades of red, pink, blue, and purple blending into each other. The woman was wincing in pain more frequently, despite the copious ganja in her system.

At last, Oz said something again. "That leg really does need professional medical attention, kids."

"I am inclined to agree." Fox said it with enough apology to keep Requiemme quiet. "And we might have a fighting chance, even with security cameras, if we dirty up Emme's face a little." He looked at Oz. "You and I have a few days of hair on our faces. We can tuck our hair beneath caps."

"And you can pay the bill with this." Jayd pulled out Fox's arm by the wrist and then slammed her money roll into his palm. "No financial trail either."

"Perfect." Fox fanned the corners of the bills, which were all huge denominations. Since the Arcadian didn't question where Jayd had accessed so many euros at once, Brick decided he wouldn't either. That just left room in his brain for more dazed admiration of this woman, proving herself as brave and resourceful as she was bold and beautiful.

Not a thought he needed at this moment, especially when Emme groaned again. The princess abandoned her stubborn side to sweep a desperate look over them all.

"Please!" she cried. "Help her!"

The moment was a turning point. Fox and Oz blazed as impressively as a spec ops squad who'd rehearsed their mission a hundred times. Brick helped where he could, using some shoe polish that Jayd routed from a cupboard to add realistic "dirt" to Emme's face and neck.

In less than five minutes, they were out the door and into their rented A-segment. Brick watched from the window, struggling not to wince, as his friends eased Emme into the little vehicle. At least Oz had secured a four-door compact rather than one of the rolling soda cans favored by so many Parisians. He got hives just thinking of cramming into one of those glorified golf carts.

Though his existing circumstances were barely more than a step better.

Because here he was, cloistered with a human who captivated him more than ever. Who yanked the air out of his chest with every urgent step she paced to the kitchen and back. Who had him studying her with every pause at the apex of her path, a break just long enough to indulge some kind of restless action.

Some were basic, like her trademark finger taps on various surfaces. Others—the ones that arrested him the most—were more pronounced. A sweep of her arms toward the ceiling. A scratch of fingers through her haphazard haircut. A tiny hop-skip, as if she was preparing to play invisible hopscotch. Some of it was random and involuntary, but she was deliberate about so much too. Like a child dodging cracks to avoid breaking Mama's back.

She kept it up, back and forth and back and forth, for another ten minutes. Brick just let her. Though she'd set her own boat in motion with this adventure, fate hadn't promised her a pleasure cruise. If she needed the outlet of a good long pace, he wasn't going to stop her.

Because the alternative choice simply wasn't one.

Helping her take off the edge ... in *his* way.

Which was, of course, what consumed his mind as the princess suddenly stopped.

She stalked all the way into the kitchen and swung open cupboards. When she finally found a drinking glass, she made her way to the sink with it. But as she clonked the glass atop the hexagon tiles, her head sank too. She dropped it between her shoulders, which were a pair of palpable tension.

The observation jolted Brick to finally move his own ass. As he approached the kitchen, he was struck by genuine remorse. And yeah, that made as much sense as pickles in fruit punch, but it was his truth, front and center. The only choice he could make in reaction to how she was peeling her layers off for him.

Sob by heartbreaking sob.

Good Christ.

She didn't even cry like other women. She fought hard at the tears, shaking her head and sniffling deep. After the second, she palmed her forehead and cursed herself in raspy Arcadian.

Only after the third did she notice he'd stepped up behind her. "Brickham. I am fine. Honestly. Please do not feel you have to—"

She startled the second he cupped a hand over the ball of her shoulder.

"You think I'm here because I *have* to be, Pixie?"

He hadn't intended to slip out the endearment again. But it felt too natural to ignore. Too damn right. From the second he'd first seen her in the bar, this protectiveness about her had only gotten worse. And yeah, he meant *worse*. Because nothing good could come from this persistent, possessive fire—especially when it came time to snuff it out. That would only be in a few hours—tomorrow morning at the latest. Then Oz and Fox would be back and taking over again. As it should be. As it had to be.

But here and now, there were no had-to-bes. No shoulds or musts. Nothing but the comfort and strength he longed to lend her. And, to be brutally honest, the fortitude he drew from her too. From the stubbornness beneath her softness. The pride beneath her stance. Even the courage beneath her tears. Dear God, especially that.

"I just thought..." she murmured back, "that since you said you were working with Jagger..."

"That I was doing all of this for a paycheck."

She turned around by tentative inches. He hadn't given her a lot of choice about the matter, considering how close he'd moved in.

"Am I wrong?"

He dragged in a long breath. He wasn't sorry for not moving. "I don't need anyone's money, Jayd." He also wasn't sorry for skirting her query. It wasn't a lie. Bastille had been running in the green for a long time, and his bank account had gained a few zeroes last week alone, thanks to the op for Reece Richards.

Her forehead crunched. Her lips pursed. He couldn't decide which piece of tension he yearned to kiss away faster.

"So you dropped everything, just like that, just to help find me?"

He hitched a shoulder in a half shrug. "Yeah, pretty much."

"Why?"

"Honestly?"

She smirked. "Yeah, pretty much."

He ducked his head, using the tender motion for totally selfish reasons. It got his face even closer to those adorably smiling lips. "I hadn't even agreed to the task yet. After Oz and Fox asked me, I told them I had to think about it. I stopped at the Particulier because I'd spent several hours walking around, doing just that." He gave her a small smile. "In truth, *you* were the one who found *me*, sweetheart."

"I am not certain Gervais would agree about that." She joined him in only the briefest of chuckles before sobering and prompting, "So why did you give them that answer? What did you have to think about?"

Another huge inhalation on his part. Here was where the rubber met the truth-even-if-it-killed-him road. "I had to consider if I'd be able to stay personally distanced from you."

Her gaze flared. She dropped rough fingers atop his forearms. "But you did not even know me."

"But I had a feeling I would want to." He leaned in lower— yet one more way he shouldn't be tempting fate that was canceled by the feeling of her hands on him. He liked it. A lot. Too much. And damn it, he had to tell her so. *All* of it. "And my feeling wasn't wrong."

The air clutched in his throat as her fingertips tightened on him. "So . . . what do you know about me now?"

It was easy to answer her this time. Probably too easy, but Brick didn't care. "That you're much stronger and smarter than anyone gives you credit for," he said. "That you're sharp and resourceful, even in situations that would crumple grown men or shock a chunk of polite society."

He relished how her chest expanded against his, betraying the air she sucked in. He was referencing their time in the dungeon, of course—but more than that. She smiled again, seeming to understand that. It emboldened him to press a hand to her cheek, stroking her dark honey skin with the pad of his thumb.

"I also know how all that grit has ground away at you, bit by bit, until now. And that it's worse because you feel like crap about what happened to Requiemme."

Her huge blues welled up with new tears. "I was so stupid," she stammered. "I should have known my father would not waltz out to meet me based on a phone call and a few texts. I should have gone right to his house myself and left Emme back at the inn we were staying at."

"Which would have been the most damn fool idea of them all." Brick added the force of his fingers to his hold, ensuring he maintained her full focus. "You know that now, right? That if you're thinking that, then Carris already has too. That he would've been there waiting for you. Probably still is."

While his conclusion provided some much-needed personal assurance, it whipped Jayd into the opposite result. "Stars and saints," she sobbed. "Brickham, do you think that he would . . . do anything? Would he actually hurt—"

"Not a chance. I mean it, okay?" Compelled by an instinct he couldn't fully explain, he brought up his other hand to her face. "As far as that prick's concerned, your dad's the best bait for finding you. He has no other connecting threads to pull back to you. For now, that's how it has to stay." He drove in the point by stretching his fingers back into her short silky waves. "You hear that, right? And you understand?"

The woman nodded. But not right away, and not willingly.

Brick narrowed his eyes. Compressed his lips.

"Then say it," he ordered in a low growl. It was authority he didn't have and shouldn't assume. But it fit like a fucking magic slipper, better than it had in the shadows of the dungeon, and he wasn't exploiting it just to get his—or her—rocks off. There was a point to get across here, in the name of a vital cause. Her safety.

Because if the little daredevil decided to try another clandestine commando visit on Daddy Dearest . . .

No. Just fucking *no*.

"Look at me, Jayd—and say it, damn it. Tell me you really understand all of this. You won't reach out to LaBarre again, in any form, until Oz, Fox, and I give you the all clear—*after* we've gotten a complete handle on what Carris's plan is and where he's squirreling himself to plot it."

At once, he prepared for her retaliation. But the only fire in her eyes was from a newly warm regard. Her chin didn't shove into a stubborn pout. Instead, she regarded him with calm strength and a slight softening along the graceful ribbon of her mouth.

"So that means you shall be—how do you say it—hanging around for a while longer?"

Brick jerked back by a few inches. Yes, by choice. The space was necessary to process what he'd just heard in the woman's undertone—and now, what he beheld at the subtle edges of her expression.

Was this Jayd Cimarron's way of . . . flirting?

Oh, for fuck's sake. It was past time to toss that wad

of crazy. His wishful thinking was dangerous with a side of preposterous. If the woman had fled her homeland at the concept of marrying a vetted courtier who kept movie star hair *and* knew the difference between his soup and dessert spoons, no way was she giving second thoughts to Brick's skull cut, scarred body, and barely-better-than-street-rat etiquette.

"I'll give Oz and Fox my help for as long as they need it," he stated, keeping his tone to the right side of professional. "But if my hunch is right about what that entails, there won't be a lot of hanging around to it."

And now the woman yanked out a full pout. "Oh," she muttered, and nothing more.

"Hey." He didn't move back in but was glad he'd kept his hands in her hair. "Don't be wigged out. We're going to make sure you stay totally safe."

She nodded again—with that same strange reluctance. "I know."

"Good. And your part in all of it won't be hard at all. You'll just—"

"But what if I want it to be?"

"Huh?"

"Hard," she blurted. "Brickham. *Maximillian*." A new sheen formed in her wide eyes. Stunning sapphires that missed nothing. She slid a hand up, spreading her slender fingers across his calloused knuckles. "What if I want that? What if I am so damn tired of . . . soft?"

She had his full attention at her invocation of his proper name. But with the moisture that kept welling in her gaze and then contorting the rest of her face . . . The deal was sealed. He was riveted. "What are you getting at, Pixie?"

She swallowed. "You do not already know?"

"I think I'm getting a clearer picture," he grated. "But sweetheart, you're the final wipe on this window." He hinged his wrists, silently commanding her stare to an even keel with his. "I refuse to play guessing games. Tell me what you want, honestly and openly and fully. You'll get no judgments from me."

But she'd also get no softness—and he communicated that with every firm syllable. For once, the words came without effort. They were his second nature. The rock wall of his psyche that had saved his crumbling caves. Shored him up when he couldn't deal with life any other way.

And, if he was correctly reading Jayd Cimarron's face in this moment, it was the sure, strict stone that *she* needed too.

He waited as she struggled to vocalize it. And fuck, he'd wait all night if he had to.

"I . . . I want what I saw . . . back there . . . in the dungeon," she finally stammered out. "What I watched . . . the other people . . . doing."

Just like that, he was swallowing around hitching breath too. Wasn't a weakness he liked showing when slipping into his Dominant space, but nothing—*nothing*—about being with this gorgeous sprite was a normal thing. And that felt fine. More than fine. Holy God, it felt fantastic.

"And you want some of that . . . with me?"

More gulping on his part as the tiniest of smiles teased at her plush mouth. "Any and all of it," she whispered. "And only with you . . . Sir."

Fuck.

Him.

No more gulping now. His throat was too dry. His blood was too hot. His mind was too full of burgeoning comprehensions—and thundering conclusions.

The woman really had been flirting.

And then given her sincere truth.

And now was combining both—with heart-stopping resplendence.

It was no exaggeration.

His heart...

...n...o...t...w...o...r...k...i...n...g...

He staggered backward. His balance was gone. His senses were spinning.

Fate had either given him his fondest submissive dream or the one woman who'd dynamite his caves of sanity down to rubble. Perhaps both.

Probably both.

Right now, he didn't care about sorting it out.

He was too consumed with the words that flooded his throat and then tidal-waved past his lips. Words that had never felt more right to growl in his entire existence.

"Then get on your knees, sweet girl."

CHAPTER SEVEN

Jayd longed to burst into a grateful sob. It would be an extension of the joy that screamed through her heart, encouraged by the affirmation of her soul.

This was right. So very, very right. An answer to all the restlessness of her mind, anxiety in her soul, and insecurity in her psyche. A way to suck it all out, replacing her constant turbulence with the beautiful solemnity of ceding to this man. Oh yes, exactly like this. Surrendering herself to him. Giving him all of it . . .

"Good girl." His baritone flowed through her, strong yet silken as the hand he stroked over her head. "Stay like that, Pixie. Back straight. Eyes forward. Knees set at the width of your shoulders . . . for now."

For now? What on earth did he mean by that?

"Attention on me, Jayd." There was a bite in his tone, as if the thoughts had flowed through her brain and across his palm. "On *us*. On *this*. Understand?"

She nodded, but the thought flow was pushed back her direction just as fast. She was aware of his order before he even cleared his throat with gruff impatience. *Out loud, girl.* "Yes, Sir," she stated. "I understand."

"Perfect," Brickham soothed, and she yearned to tilt her head and rest it in his palm. She refrained as he spoke again. "Before we go any further, I have to ask you some questions. And again, I demand your full honesty for the answers."

"Of course. I mean—ermmm—yes, Sir."

"All right. The very beginning," he said, expelling a meaningful sigh. "Have you ever done this before, Jayd? Agreed to letting a man dominate you? Given him your willing surrender?"

"Are you jok—I mean, no, Sir. Never."

She was mortified when her stammering had him chuckling. She was more horrified when he would not let her hide any of her emotion, using his other hand to cup her chin and raise her stare.

At once, he was not laughing anymore. Also at once, she knew why.

His action brought her chin high enough to rest on the prominent rise in his jeans. And Creator help her, she reveled in every second of it. She could already feel the pulsing heat of him. The surging stiffness there, blazing at the confines of his crotch...

"Jayd. *Fuck*. What are you doing to me?"

She hesitated for a moment. "Do you want an answer to *that* one too, Sir?"

"No." He jostled his head. "Definitely not." And then pointedly cleared his throat. "Now you *will* clarify for me... You have never let a man spank your bare ass? Is that correct?"

"Yes, Sir."

"Or stripped you the rest of the way and tied you down?"

"N-N-No, Sir."

"Or used a paddle, or any other toys, on other parts of your body?"

"*No*, Sir." Her lungs worked for air as her core clenched with need. She was petrified and mesmerized in the same stunning moment. "Toys? What do *they* have to do with anything? At least in . . . the current context of things."

All too easily, Brickham burst with a fresh laugh. She didn't find this one so disconcerting. Actually, she was glad to be somehow pleasing him.

"They're called toys because the people who enjoy this lifestyle are fond of calling it *play.*" His smile, strong and determined, got a little wider. He fondled her chin with his equally mighty fingers. "After all, the results are supposed to be pleasurable. For *everyone.*"

Jayd allowed herself a smile too. "I think . . . I understand."

His face flashed with surprise. "You do?"

"I feel like I want to," she admitted. "But I can only relay what I feel right now, I suppose."

"Which is what?" Brickham's query was a soft husk.

"That when we had to leave that place earlier tonight . . . I did not want to hurry so much. And truly, it had nothing to do with the things *you* had just done to me—"

"At all?"

"All right, maybe a little." She giggled. "But in many ways, not at all." She paused again, letting him watch her frown from deeper consideration of the memories. "I only knew that I wanted to watch more. Learn more. *Feel* more."

"Of what?"

Stars and saints, the man was not letting her off any proverbial hooks now. He insisted on her thoughts even when *she* knew not what they were.

"Enthrallment," she confessed at last. "And bewilderment, I suppose—because of that. I felt as if I were watching a dozen perfect ballets. There was symmetry to it all. Beautiful balances of power, energy, surrender . . . stimulation."

She paused before that last impression because she

meant every raspy inflection. As she dreaded but also hoped, Brickham took notice. The surges in his eyes, intense as warning flares, told her so. But his answering words were soft as the flares' smoke.

"That's a wonderful way of describing it. Like a dance, with equal power to both partners. So many people see it as the Dominant exercising all the energy, but a Dom can only use what their submissive gives. They take all that magic and transform it into new, different power . . ."

"Like the kind they can display with toys." Though Jayd's pulse quickened as she spoke, she was grateful for Brickham's calm ocean veneer. She called it such because she knew the truth already. Oceans only *looked* calm. That was the case now. She could feel his excitement in the blood that pounded through his fingers. The palpable surge of the bulge so close to her face.

"Yes," he finally offered. "Sometimes they do."

"But not all the time." She supplied it because she sensed he would not. And because she needed—*needed*—to know . . .

"No," Brickham murmured. "Not all the time."

"Because they give the power back to their partner . . . in different ways?"

For a long pause, the pulses in his fingers ceased. So did the deep air through his chest. But other parts of him kept throbbing. Harder, swifter, and more unignorable than before.

"Yeah, Pixie. In . . . different ways."

"Tell me." A pair of such simple words—though they tore at her senses like talons and sliced her nerves open with equal cruelty. Her whole body shivered. For the first time, she swayed on her knees. "Please, Brickham," she begged, rocking her head back to search his face. But there were no more tender places for her to focus on. No more flares in his gaze to guide her the right way. "Wh-What is wrong?" she demanded. "Why will you not . . . tell me?"

She probably imagined it, but the man seemed to sway now too. As if seeking purchase from his fall, he twisted a hand into her hair with brutal urgency. Her scalp lit up with scorching pain. It was one of the most exhilarating moments of her life.

"Because maybe, Pixie . . . I want to show you."

★ ★ ★

Wait.

Wait.

Wait!

The command roared through him, over and over again, as Brick watched every captivating nuance across Jayd's face. How she blinked those luminescent eyes. The way she worked the plush pillows of her mouth together. The rapid rhythm of her breaths, shooting faster and faster from her nose, as she absorbed the full impact of what he'd just intimated.

Of what she could shut him down from doing, any second, with a single hesitation.

A *no* he still had to respect. As he had with so many other submissives, so many other times before.

But holy fuck . . . this time, it would kill him. He was sure of that.

Because this time, it was her.

The female he'd wanted to take to one of the dungeon stations from the second they'd entered that room. The princess who, ten minutes before that, was hissing at a bully in an alley like a kitten facing a gorilla. The woman who, ten minutes before *that*, had captivated him at that bar, eyes full of hope and head high with plans.

A pixie-princess-woman he still barely knew.

But in so many ways already did know.

Yes, this well. This wholly. Perhaps better than he knew himself.

Which did *not* make this a great idea. Likely one of his worst. Oh no, it was definitely his lousiest. He'd logged enough hours with Doc Sally to see that clearly enough. The last woman he'd "known better than himself" was another sprite who had more dreams than sense and enough fire in her belly to think she could make them all come true. Yes, even crossing a messy hot zone to get to him in the dead of night. Offering him all the afghanis she'd saved for five years in exchange for his help in getting her to a new life.

Asha had wanted to open a school for girls, focusing on entrepreneurship and independent life skills. After secretly teaching herself to read, she'd devoured her father's construction shop operations books. She'd told Brick she'd make him a table if the money wasn't enough. She'd even offered him other favors.

He'd refused the table. And the favors. And her money.

Fate had paid him back for the good karma with ten of the most horrific days of his life.

So what made him think things would be different now? *Especially* now? Even contemplating a risk this wicked with a woman like Jayd Cimarron.

The princess who still dutifully knelt at his feet.

Shit.

The captivating creature who gazed up at him with such

adoration and trust.

Shit.

The woman who was already such submissive perfection...

"Yes. *Please*, Brickham. Show me."

Shit, shit, shit.

Her words were everything. Soft entreaty. Erotic offering. Best of all, clear consent. That was it, right? At least the gateway for a good time? Safe words and limits could come with clear communication, something they didn't have a problem with.

But it wasn't enough. Not yet.

From her, *only* her, he needed...

More.

It was a bizarre recognition. This had never happened to him before. But it was as crucial as it was strange. He couldn't ignore the demand, which emerged in the form of a single word back to her.

"Why?"

Jayd slowly blinked her big turquoises. "Wh-What?"

Brick shifted a hand back down, wrapping it beneath her chin. "I want to know why, Pixie. Tell me why you were interested in the scene back at the dungeon. What did you see *there* that you're still craving *here*?"

She grew quiet, though remained engaged. He saw it in the attention of her breaths, the sustenance beneath her spine. And then she gave it to him in the silken steadiness of her voice.

"Escape, I suppose. The kind that comes from such complete surrender." More thoughts chased each other across her face. "Surrender...though it is not disconnection," she amended. "Just the opposite. I mean, there was a clear protocol to everything. Everyone was obeying such elegant manners. I suppose I noticed that more because I relate to it. But it was not like the etiquette at court. It was not so . . ."

"Not so what?" he prompted when she drifted for a few seconds.

"So . . . rote," she supplied. "Not so stuffy. So . . . meaningless."

Brick cocked half a smile. "You observed all that? Just during our brief time there?"

"Am I wrong?"

"You couldn't be more right." He tried to stroke away the new worry lines across her brow. "And I couldn't be happier about that."

A wave of warmth seemed to flow over her. "Then I am glad."

Brick moved his fingers back to the side of her cheek. *Christ.* She was beyond exquisite, but her beauty only started with Mother Nature's blessings. Her light came from the inside too: a glow that mesmerized him more and more as the night deepened. An addiction he was guiltless about indulging, knowing he'd have to be going cold turkey too damn soon.

"You really like making me happy, don't you, Pixie?"

She tilted her face into his hand. "You sound surprised by that."

"We met a few hours ago, Jayd."

"We did?" Though she kept her huge irises locked on him, they glittered with frissons of confusion. "Why is that impossible for me to believe?"

Brick couldn't offer her an answer. Why, indeed? Wasn't he racked by the same surreal disbelief? The same sense that every minute since their first glance in the alley had been, in truth, a day? A week? A month? And what was the difference when all of it was intended to lead to this? The rightness of her at his feet. The flawlessness of her gaze up at him, replete with such reverence and reliance.

Seeing him. Waiting for him...

"I want to make you happy too, sweetheart."

...to say exactly that.

He was expecting what that did to her. The wave of tangible excitement that coursed through her, making him wish she was already naked for his study of her flushed skin... everywhere. But instead of acting to make that happen, he paused. He was forced to, shaken to his marrow by a recognition just as deep.

As deep as the place from which his own vow had emerged. A part of himself that he'd written off long ago. The place in his soul that had first awakened with his need for Dominance and the corresponding longing for a submissive who understood the *exchange* part of Total Power Exchange. Over the last five years, many subbies had dropped to their knees and told him they understood—and so many times, he'd kissed them goodbye with a rueful smile. He'd simply wanted too much. Either that or fate was determined not to give it to him. Maybe it was part of the cosmic penance for how he'd fucked up Asha's mission.

But now, he saw the universe's larger plan.

He *was* going to get his perfect submissive. Just not for forever.

And maybe that was for the best too.

Maybe it was even better than the best. Beginning this moment, with the knowledge that they'd only have this small shell of stolen time, had him noticing everything with sharper vision, deeper appreciation. The sheen of the light across her silky spikes. The azure sparkles across her intense eyes. The sweet soughs of her breaths. The way her skin reminded him of the final seconds of a sunset, light brown and dark gold blended into one magical silk.

A fabric he longed to unravel more of. To explore in full. To bring to aroused blushes, and so much more . . .

"So . . . what do we do now?"

Especially after that exact question, from her rosy and parted lips.

A query that brought so many possibilities for answers— all filling his mind and swelling his cock. Yet he ignored all that to tug at her shoulders.

"Stand for me, please."

As soon as she was before him, her posture still regal and her face still upturned, Brick hauled in a steadying breath. It didn't help as much as he needed, but he couldn't find the focus to get in another. He barely saw anything else but her.

"What we do now, Pixie, is talk."

She blinked. "Wh-What?"

Brick brushed his fingertips in toward the base of her neck. "Not for long. Believe me, I won't last much longer than that."

She lifted a smile that looked like relief. "What do you want to talk about?"

He shook his head. "This part isn't about wants. We've got to establish needs. For us both."

"Such as what?"

"Such as the fact that I need to see you naked for all of this. And that I'll still need you to call me Sir. If you need, I can address you by another name too."

"Well, I really like calling you that. And I enjoy it when you call me Pixie . . . or anything else you want. Just *not* princess."

"Good enough . . . Pixie."

He murmured it while roaming his fingers along the collar of her T-shirt. Jayd's breath stuttered. She swallowed hard.

"That . . . ummm . . . feels very good, Sir."

"And it makes *me* feel good to hear you tell me," he replied. "Which leads to yet another important need for me, sweetheart. And this time, for you." He paused his caresses, making sure she was completely with him on concentrating. "We don't have time for a full playtime primer, but the core element of all this is *communication*. Not conveying what you think I want to hear or obeying my commands just to satisfy me. My fulfilment is tied into *your* fulfilment. Got that?"

Her parted lips and intense gaze weren't the response he expected. But they were sexy as fuck, especially when she added a curious kitten tilt of her head.

"Obeying?" she finally blurted. "Commands? Real ones?"

"Well, not beyond these walls," Brick explained. "Which makes them as real as we want them to be. But let's settle one point here and now." He pushed a hand up, bracing the expanse of her jaw with the wide U of his hand. "I'm a fair master. I won't issue any order that I don't reasonably expect you to handle and heed. If that does happen, then you'll speak up, and we'll discuss it before going further. Do you understand in full?"

The perplexity fled her face. Instead, as she lifted her stare to fully meet the lock of his, her breaths doubled. Stimulated tremors overtook her body.

So. Fucking. Hot.

He wanted more. So. Much. More.

"Pixie?" He prompted it in his steel shavings voice, already sensing it would tick off something for *her* needs list, as well. She proved him right with a gorgeous little whimper that coincided with a harsher shiver down her frame.

"Y-Y-Yes, Sir," she finally husked and swallowed with rougher emphasis. "I . . . ermmm . . . I understand."

"Good." Brick pushed his fingertips in by a millimeter, pinching the bottoms of her ears. "Then say it back to me." He lowered his mouth, hovering at heart-halting distance over her luscious mouth. "Tell me what you're going to do for me, sweetheart."

A blush flared her cheeks. But while Brick braced himself for the normal submissive stutterings, this remarkable female astonished him anew.

"I am going to listen to you," she stated without hesitation. "And then I am going to observe your orders. And I shall do it all because I trust you to meet my needs, Brickham. And because I want to meet all of yours."

Holy. *Freaking*. Fuck.

He almost said it out loud. He was halted by his convulsing throat, which his whirling mind already jammed full of other words. Her jaw-dropper deserved a friend to keep it company, right?

"Even if one of my needs is to finish this by feeling your climax around my cock?"

He wouldn't lie. Her flush, her gape, and her swift rush of breath were exactly what he'd wished for and better than he'd imagined. She was stunning. Beautiful. Beyond breathtaking. Even as she faltered a little while tentatively raising her fingers to his chest, then lifting her wondering gaze up to his. She searched him with endless aqua intensity, clearly seeking something from him. Approval? *Dis*approval? Encouragement? Permission?

Thank God she didn't make him wait to find out.

"Yes, Sir," she murmured, filling his sights with the resplendence of her smile. "*Especially* if you need that."

Now she was better than breathtaking.

She was his every fantasy brought to vivid life.

CHAPTER EIGHT

She should be afraid.

Why was she not more afraid?

Jayd had just given this man—this person she had met but a few hours ago—full agreement to control her body as he liked. To use her for his desire. To *command* her as he wished.

But few decisions in her life had felt more right.

Which did not make a stick of sense.

She should be on the couch in a fetal ball, dealing with the fallout from life's masochistic strikes today. The letdown of never connecting with LaBarre. The sick horror of being betrayed and assaulted by those two *bonsuns* from the bar. Then the fear of losing Requiemme in the streets, capped by the anguish that came with finding her. She had started this day with so many hopes but ended it with so many regrets.

Nothing about Maximillian Brickham felt like a regret.

Not from the first time she set eyes on him. Especially not in this moment.

This exquisite, extraordinary, completely consummate cataclysm . . .

That instantly made her crave another one.

And so many more.

More. Please, please, more!

She hoped Brickham saw the plea in her eyes as he bracketed her hips with his hands and slowly pushed her against the counter. At once, her thoughts were like butterflies in a eucalyptus grove, scattered but giddy. They took faster flight as the man hitched her up onto the ledge. In the same movement, he nudged his body between her legs.

Then dipped his head . . . and kissed her perfectly on the mouth.

Correction. This was no kiss. This was a *kiss*, flagrant and full and lusty. This was heat, force, and hardness she had never experienced before. This was a conquering, leaving no inch of her lips, tongue, and mouth unscathed.

This was every passionate dream she had ever cherished or imagined. And more.

At last, they had to break apart for giant gulps of air. But Brick did not venture far. Not at all. He made it easy to grip at his thick shoulders as he stayed thoroughly inside her personal space.

She reveled in the feel of him, her senses rejoicing in his obscenely masculine scent.

He barely blinked, fixating on her with his smoke-dark eyes.

"Good Christ." He sucked in such a harsh breath, Jayd started.

"Wh-What is wrong? Are you in pain?"

A subtle chuckle tumbled from him. "Torment, maybe. But not pain. At least not the awful kind."

She frowned. "Is there any kind of pain that is good?"

His features tightened. "Oh, yes. Sometimes there is."

The meaning beneath his words had her brain butterflies racing each other now. "Like what we saw back in that dungeon place," she said. "What those people . . ."

"They're called Dominants," he supplied.

"What those Dominants . . . were doing to their . . ."

"Submissives."

She jerked her head back. Fortunately, she did not go fast, since her crown bopped into a cabinet. "But I am not submissive."

As she finished that by wrinkling her nose, Brick responded with another laugh. It was warmer this time, making his eyes crinkle and his dimples deeper. "There's a difference between being submissive as a person and being *a* submissive for your Dom."

"Which is what?"

"Sometimes it's hard to explain." While his reply was as gentle as a breeze on the Seine, his features began to resemble the river's concrete walls. The incongruity was fascinating... and alluring. "Might be better just to show you, Pixie."

"Show me?" Now she was really afraid. But the jolt was also thrilling. It quickened every pulse in her body and ignited new fires in her blood. "You mean... to hurt me?"

"Not anything you don't want or can't handle. Just tell me no and everything stops. You still got that part?"

She was conscious of her own breaths, entering and exiting her in fast spurts, before she worked her mouth around words again. "Yes, Sir."

The fear lingered, but only its most exciting side, as she watched what her acquiescence did to the man. The intense indents on his temples. The hungry parting of his lips. The fresh, firm ropes in his neck—becoming determined curves as he bent in again toward her.

And kissed her twice as hard as before.

By all the saints and sinners!

Because ohhh, this kiss...

Who *was* behind it? The canonized or the condemned?

But did it matter? Why was she taking a pause for divine guidance, when she had Brickham's bold passion to show her the way?

And dear, beautiful angels, how he did.

She was lost beneath his ferocious, wet assault. A slave to the masterful whip of his tongue. A disciple of his decadent desire, filling her mouth with his taste as he worked his body tighter into the cradle of hers.

"Brickham!" she begged after he dragged free of her bruised and stinging mouth. "By the sweet stars!"

With hungry nips, the man kissed his way around the curve of her chin. "You mean the ones you're flying me to, sexy Pixie?"

"I—I think I might already be there."

As he circled his mouth the opposite direction, he openly bit at her skin. "Oh, darling girl," he growled into the hollow next to her ear. "We're just getting started."

"Holy...shit."

It was sublime to hear the man's breath catch in tandem with hers. "Well, well, well. My proper girl *does* like dirty words from time to time."

The growl with which he finished was an entirely new level of alluring. It fully emboldened her returning quip. "I grew up with three brothers, Sir."

A new rumble spilled from him. "Not a good time to remind a man of that fact, Pixie."

Jayd canted her head to the side while pushing a half smile to her lips. She slid her hand around until her palm spanned his broad jaw. Though her fingers still looked tiny next to his face, she set aside her awe in favor of dishing out a much-needed reality check.

"Firstly, my brothers are technically *not* that anymore. And secondly, even if they were, they would have every right to love me, not dictate to me. Not a one of them would even want that right. It would go against all the archaic doctrines they are fighting to change in Arcadia."

At first, Brick only reacted by shifting his hands down from her hips and onto the counter. Though nothing changed about his physical proximity, Jayd felt like it did. He seemed bigger now, if that was possible. More capable of surrounding her senses and consuming her every thought. Of scaring her in that deliciously amazing way . . .

"Is that another reason why you ran away?"

Or petrifying her in this whole new way.

"How does that matter now?"

She openly squirmed. Brick clamped her hips again, holding her still.

"It matters." He said it—and obviously meant it—as an order. "Number one, because I say it does. Number two, and most importantly, because it tells me a lot about who you are as a human and as a woman."

"One silly detail like that?"

"You think that's silly?" Brickham countered. "The fact that you were so concerned about your brothers, with the Pura forcing them to choose between your betrothal or their exposure, that you sneaked away to a foreign land on your own?"

"I was not exactly sacrificing a tenable situation," Jayd rebutted. "Evrest would have lost his throne one way or his sister's dignity the other. The only way out was for me to *get* out."

"So you did what you had to."

"I did what was best for everyone."

Brickham nodded, seeming to accept and agree with her claim, but Jayd did not surrender her pensive pout. What did anything about her tale have to do with anything between them now?

"You're a remarkable woman, Jayd Cimarron."

It was definitely nicer to hear him say *that*, but she was still flummoxed.

"But if you feel like *this* is also something you *have* to do..."

He only got that far before Jayd spewed with a chest-deep laugh. Just as quickly, she sobered. "What kind of females have you deflowered in the past that you feel you must say that?"

The cavalier approach did not fix things as easily as she wanted. "Females... I've deflowered?" Brickham's lips were stunning even when he twisted them—but not when he scowled on top of it. "Wait. *Shit*," he blurted.

"What?" she demanded. "What's wrong?"

"Damn it." He scraped a rough hand over his scalp. "So you *are* a—"

"Virgin?" She huffed as soon as he stalled. "Oh, Creator's toes. You can say it, Brickham. *I* just did. It is not a naughty word. I know what it means, and I know what I am doing here with it. What I am doing with *my* body and the free decisions I can still have about it."

His glower tightened. "Saying a couple of syllables is one thing, Pixie. Altering what the term means in your life—*forever*—is different."

"And I understand that too. But I am the exact same person as I was a couple of minutes ago, when you were growling such perfect things about your intentions for me.

Has your hunger for me changed that much? Does a thin membrane change all that?"

He growl-groaned. "Some—*many*—say that it does."

"And are any of them standing before you, entrusting you with all of it?" She spread her hands across the steel plates in his chest that pretended to be pectorals. "I am telling you that I want this, Brickham. More vitally, that I want it with *you*. That I have waited such a long time to do this because I wanted someone who would make it extraordinary. A memory to cherish for the rest of my life."

To her relief, the man's smile returned. Not as glorious as before, but it was a start. "Nothing like laying a little pressure on a guy, sweetheart."

Jayd cocked her head. "Would *you* rather say no, then? The consent extends both directions here, right? And I will not take it personally if this is difficult for you. Just do not expect me to pine for you if Trystan Carris finds me and decides *he* will be the first fork in my fruit."

She was poking the bear. She knew it before she finished her thought, but maybe that was what was needed to get through to the stubborn giant and his sudden attack of nobility.

She was so sick of nobility. She had eaten, drank, breathed it, and *been* it for twenty-four damn years.

Now, she craved other things. Wild things. Ferocious things.

She longed for the bear.

Yes, even in his openly incensed state.

"I should spank you for that."

And ohhh yes, even after he issued that. Maybe more now, as fresh fear flowed throughout her. But like before, she welcomed the apprehension. Its excitement in her marrow. Its uncertainty in her nerves. Its sizzle in her blood. Though she had experienced something similar after jumping onto that fishing trawler on Arcadia, this occasion was so much more different.

This time, the boat was about to go over a waterfall. And how sweet her drowning would be.

The anticipation shot her spirit with bravery and her lips with words. "Perhaps you *should* do that. Maybe, Sir, I even... deserve it."

The bear was officially jabbed again.

Her heartbeat galloped at her rib cage again.

And then exploded—as Brickham kissed her again.

This time, it was strict and sexual and brutal—but too damn swift. He shifted away too fast, leaving her lips parted and her senses unsated. Undoubtedly she kept that penury across her face, since the man took a long pause to simply stare at her. He was unnervingly steady about it, breaking the look only to let a smile break free. All right, it was more like a smirk with a curiosity chaser.

Ohhh, yes. Force of Nature knew exactly what he'd just done—and *not* done—to her.

He stepped back, continuing his maddening half grin while gathering her feet into one of his hands. Without deterring his gaze, he placed them on the end of the opposite counter.

"And now we get to the good part," he murmured. Such an innocuous collection of words, but delivered in his low and rough-edged voice, they became her aural crack.

Her senses were already spinning. Her body was already so needy. Her nipples puckered. Her breaths were shallow and stuttery.

"You... say that... as if..."

He leaned in again but kept the center of his form back where it was. He planted his hands on the counter next to her hips. "As if what, Pixie?"

"As if . . . your favorite part of a meal is coming."

"And that I'm past starving?"

He already provided that answer with more of his thick growl. It soothed some of Jayd's nerves. She could give speeches to huge rooms full of people but was at novice level with this kind of conversation. What did she say next? Or do next? Was Brickham still skittish too, even after all the justification she gave about her other skill level? What was the right move?

Fortunately—ohhh, so fortunately—Brickham made his first.

By hooking his index fingers into the waistband of her leggings and yanking hard.

"Oh!" The cry spilled out before she could help it. Brickham did not seem to mind. Maybe the opposite. His sharp catch of breath was like a whip crack in the kitchen's little space.

"Christ," he blurted, hurriedly tossing her leggings over his shoulder. Just as swiftly, he shucked his sweater and tossed it the same direction. "Yes. *Damn.*"

"Thank you, Sir."

"And those words, spoken so beautifully . . ." He dipped in lower, roaming his gaze all over her face as if trying to decide where to kiss her next. Also as if the fate of nations rested on his choice. "You're spoiling me already, Pixie."

Her cheeks heated. It felt magnificent. "I would be happy to keep doing so, Sir. I just—" She squirmed a little, riding another wave of what-the-hell-do-I-do-now. "How would you—*what* would you like me to do next?"

At first, his answer was only a darkness in his gaze and a pleased tilt of his lips. That did not last long. "Take your shirt off," he grated, emphasizing with a rough tug at the hem of the garment. The implication was clear. If she dallied about obedience, he would undress her himself.

As if she could think about tarrying.

As if she could think about anything else but the fire in her blood from the brush of his fingers. The shivers across her skin from the caress of his gaze. The need in her spirit from the authority in his growl. But it was not just his dominance. It was his blatant, prominent desire—all of it just for her. *Her*, as the woman she was to him. Not the princess who could aid his political standing. Not an illegitimate sister who had become a drastic liability. Not even as an exotic notch on his bedpost, a way of checking off the Island Kingdom Figurehead box for him. If anything, her social status was a giant red flag for the man, waving boldly between them even now.

It was time to rip that flag down.

It was time to strip away *everything* he perceived about her—except the needy flesh and soul-deep feeling that were truly, honestly *her*.

It was time to do it . . . *now*.

Jayd crossed her arms, grabbed the T-shirt by the bottom, and swept it all the way off.

At once, she trembled from head to toe.

At the same time, Brickham erupted with a new rumble.

She did not stop quivering. But she did want more of that sound. Ohhh, so much more.

One determined breath later, she reached up and then back, targeting her bra clasps. With double the purpose, Brickham seized both her wrists.

"Leave it on," he dictated. "If I see your nipples now, we'll never get to the best part."

Jayd managed a coy look. "I thought we were already there."

"That was the *good* part." His lips lifted. His gaze was smokey and his jaw was clenched. "This is the *best* part."

Her throat clutched around halted air. Stopping everything above her waist did bewildering things to the areas below it. Her intimate triangle, now bared to the night air and his rapt gaze, pulsed in ways she had never known before. She was soft but hard. Languid but aching. Naked and needing...

"The best part," she echoed with a dazed sigh. "Which means what?"

Tell me, Brickham. Please. But better yet ... show me.

"Keep your hands all the way up here, Pixie. Over your head. Grab these cabinet handles so you don't accidentally disobey."

"We could never have that." Though her tone teased, the effect vanished with her shivery exhalation. Could she be blamed? Even just looping her fingers around the handles was doing distinct things to her libido. Entrancing, erotic things. Her breasts pushed uncomfortably at her bra. The petals at her core were throbbing and swollen.

"Certainly couldn't," Brickham confirmed, using his newly free hands to pull open some drawers to her left. "Because the best part is also the funnest part."

"Which is why you have now opted for perusing the utensils?"

"More like ... treasure hunting. *Aha.*" His triumphant bark coincided with his roguish smirk as he removed a few items from a larger drawer. Jayd could not see any of them due to the man's broad frame but the clinks of colliding stainless steel were recognizable enough.

What in Creator's name was he up to?

Brick did not keep her in suspense. Which she wasn't sure to deliver thanks or confusion for, watching as he placed his "aha" stash atop the counter.

A rubber-paddled spatula.

A big pair of tongs, its steel ends cut into ridges.

A rolling meat tenderizer, its triangular nubs giving the device some terrifying new meanings.

"Oh, *my.*" She dotted it with a rough gulp, only to forget all about her trepidation as Brickham exposed the last item in his hands.

"A cookie cutter?" It was impossible to veil her perplexity, earning her the man's sleek smirk in return.

"Hmmm. Not just that."

"Sir?"

"It's a heart."

"But made out of steel."

He did not give her a quip for that. His demeanor changed to the very opposite of quipping. Suddenly he was all prowling heat, molten focus, mesmerizing confidence. Yes, even with a cookie cutter in his hand.

"Sometimes, steel hearts are the easiest to wreck." He held up the gleaming steel until they peered at each other through the open shape. "The hard stuff is only around the edges."

Jayd pinned him with a deeper scrutiny. It was not difficult to see what he had just given her. This unique revelation. The insight to *him.* She could no more ignore the gift than forget about it.

"But the part inside . . . is not that easy to fill. Is it?"

She meant it earnestly. Honestly. She knew Brickham understood that, even if he was not so easy to read now.

"Well, that depends." She was hit with more of his enigmatic energy, snagging her breath in unique ways as he leaned in again. His own throat clogged out loud from the second his crotch hit her kneecaps. "On what you choose to fill them with."

In a hot rush, Jayd already knew what he was talking about. A leap from the symbolic to the certainty. To the knowledge of exactly how he intended to use that cookie cutter.

The second she concluded it, Brickham confirmed it.

"Wrists," he directed, sounding like he was merely requesting she fetch a spatula for him. But they were not getting ready to make pancakes here. She knew it as soon as she extended her arms to him and he slid the big steel heart around her wrists.

"Oh." Her reaction came from her psyche as well as the naughty regions of her belly. Something had happened to her. Something visceral and sharp but spiritual and complete.

Yes. Complete.

Buried parts of herself, longing for this moment. Seeking this surrender. For the time when she would finally rest in this sublime trust. In him *and* herself.

"Now back up," Brick instructed, guiding her arms back over her head. With her wrists settled into the heart's humps, he used the upside-down point as a hook around one of the cabinet handles. "Feels okay?" he asked.

"Yes, Sir."

He grazed the side of her face before rubbing the pad of his thumb across her mouth. "That sounds better and better each time you say it, woman." He kept caressing her lips, tackling their corners with tiny but rough circles until he replaced his fingers with a long, dirty kiss. Once he had her quivering like a butterfly on a stick, he murmured, "Now I want you to say it while you spread your legs for me."

"Oh." She practically gasped it out. "Oh, yesss . . . Sir."

Most of it was a hissing mess, but it was a miracle she formed the words at all. Not after the demand he had made of her. Not as she realized how much she craved to comply with his command—and did. So swiftly. So eagerly.

Those feelings intensified as she watched what her acquiescence did to Brickham. How his chest rose and surged. How his gaze darkened and dropped. How he caused her stare to dip too, drawn to the part of him that had changed the most. The crux of his body was no longer defined by a broad bulge. She could see the outline of his whole shaft, pushing at his jeans like a living thing.

He riveted her. Fascinated her. But she was also frightened, not so much in that giddy, aroused way. By the heavens. Maybe he *had* been created from the elements themselves. As he freed the top snap of his pants, his arms flexed like magnificent storm fronts. His manhood continued to throb, equally powerful but dauntingly unknown.

What was it going to look like . . . when he freed it from its bonds? Would it be too huge for her? How on earth were they going to fit?

The questions hounded her so hard, Jayd barely noticed when Brickham shifted a little closer. Or that he had swept up one of the spatulas too.

But she noticed now.

As the man smacked the flat plastic to the insides of her thighs.

"Ow!" she snapped, wriggling.

The man himself was irritatingly calm. "Wider," he intoned.

"You could have asked nice!— *Ah!*" She shrieked as he did it again.

"Spread. Your. Legs. Wider." He emphasized each word with another sweep of the spatula, though reduced his treatment to teasing taps. Even so, as she merely thought about his stricter smacks, Jayd flinched again.

But flinching led to something else.

Clenching.

And by activating those muscles in her thighs, she clenched other things. Like the tender tissues between them. Like the intimate core there, already so slick with her arousal. Like the nub of need that vibrated harder as soon as Maximillian Brickham fixed his lusty stare on it.

"Sweet Creator on high." Containing her throaty words was as crazy as ignoring the sight of him. The spikes of his dark lashes, more prominent as he studied her splayed sex. The part of his lips, their firm pads wetted from his slow licks. And then the heavy flare of his nostrils before he spoke again.

"Sweet is absolutely right, little one. Every inch of you is that." He used the spatula's edge now, swiping it back and forth across her most sensitive petals. "But your creator? Not on high right now."

"Wh-What? What...are you..." More words she was unable to keep down, even as the man used his free hand to push her chin up.

"Your creator is right here," he stated, forcing her to confront the emphasis in his unyielding eyes. "Right here, right now, you're my clay. Mine alone, ready to be molded, painted, and then incinerated. To yield to my touch and be pliant to my pleasure. And when the time comes...to open for my penetration."

As he drew out that final vow, his voice like a dragon's sigh, he tossed away the spatula—and used his finger on her flesh instead. As Jayd cried out at the incursion, she reached to steady herself on his shoulders—recognizing, too late, that impossibility. Freeing herself from his ingenious shackle required being at a different angle.

She was really and truly at this man's mercy.

His to mold. To use. Perhaps even to hurt...

So why was she writhing even more than before? Excited in ways she had never dreamed? Wetter and hotter than she ever thought possible?

She was robbed of even a second to think about that. Brickham clarified that by clamping her chin harder. He expected her to be right here with him, mentally as well as physically. Not that he was making the mental part easy, with the steady pumps of his finger in and out of her weeping core. And soon his finger*s*, plural. Two of his digits, meaning twice the heady force of his invasion.

"That good too, Pixie? Answer me." His order was half an inch short of a snarl.

"Y-Y-Yes, Sir," Jayd got out with a gasp. "It is good. So, *so* good..."

His comeback was a tender but ferocious kiss. His tongue hunted for her tonsils as their teeth collided. When he finally released her, she was panting even harder. This time, she was not alone. Brickham's chest whooshed like a bellows. His neck was starkly corded.

But it was the look across his face, as if he had just found a rare jewel in a desert, that brought her a stunning epiphany.

He was *her* clay, as well.

He was trusting her just as fully, already showing her aspects of himself that had been buried for a long time. She knew that by noticing the little revelations. The tells that came in small, scattered moments. One of them came right before he slid his grip to the back of her neck, pulling her over as if to kiss her again. But he smiled instead, staring down at her with the full force of his arresting blues.

"Beautifully expressed, Pixie. Such a pretty little whisper." But then he dipped his head back in, growling so perfectly in her ear, "Now let's see about turning your whisper into a scream."

"Yes . . . Sir."

The words practically stuttered out of her, a frantic replacement for the expression that first sprang to her mind. A mind that Maximillian Brickham was deviously unraveling, moment by wicked moment.

By the sweet Creator.

CHAPTER NINE

Yes, Sir.

How many times had Brick heard that in his life, from how many beautiful and willing women? How many times had he savored the phrase, knowing exactly what it meant for a submissive to offer it?

But how many times had those occasions still felt so hollow? Nice, but nothing else. Frameworks for deeper meaning but never fully filled. He'd given up on anything different. The issue had to be him, not them. Something deeper than Doc Sally could get to, twisted into the panic that wouldn't dissipate and the guilt he refused to let go.

Yes, Sir.

But this time, it was different. With this stunning, sincere princess, it was very different.

Maybe it was the truth of their finality—knowing they'd have tonight and nothing else. Maybe it was the danger that had defined their every moment until now.

And maybe the difference was more obvious.

Maybe the magic was simply her.

Seeing him, nearly from the start, for what he really was. *Liking* him like that. Even pleading him for more. Trusting he'd give it to her. And wrapped in that trust, giving him more of herself too.

Christ. So much more.

To the point that she was bound, helpless, and nearly

naked before him. And, if her dripping pussy and flushed face were any indication, reveling in the experience.

Fuck. Her *skin*. And her *pussy*.

He was riveted by both, even wondering if he'd rescued a princess who was actually a magical witch. If so, was she a good witch or a bad witch? Holy shit, he hoped for the latter. He wanted to do some very bad things to her . . .

"Oh!"

Starting with evoking that very cry from her.

She erupted with it again, as he thrust his third finger into her tight heat. Brick answered her sound with a low and primal groan while twisting deeper into her waiting cavern.

"Good. Fucking. God," he grated. "You're drenched, Pixie."

"Yes."

"Your cunt is already soaked for me."

"Yes!"

He didn't miss what the filthier words did to her. The new weight in her stare. The way her irises darkened like a fairy lagoon beneath a moonless sky. That was good. Damn good. Without moonlight, he could move better in the shadows of her mind.

"This really is what you were begging for, wasn't it?" he murmured, suckling his way along the front of her neck. "A risk but a reward. Pain with permission."

He had no idea where the words sprang from, but they felt so right—as much for himself as her. Jayd affirmed the same thing, underlining his sentences with her needy little whimpers. Her lust was music for him. Sustenance. A necessity he craved to move on. Feedback he'd never needed from any other subbie.

"You have that permission, Pixie. Feel it all. Let it all in. Let *me* in. Fuck, *yes*," he praised as her inner walls softened, giving his fingers deeper penetration. "Damn it. So good, little one. Do you feel me inside you? Exploring your beautiful tunnel? I can't stop touching you like this. Invading you like this. And you don't want me to stop, do you? *Tell me*, Jayd."

He issued the demand when she only vaguely shook her head. Holy shit, the woman was already slipping into subspace. He still needed her mind right here, with him. He wasn't a wuss about accepting the gift of a woman's virginity. He *was* cautious about taking it when her head wasn't fully checked in too.

"Jayd," he prompted, embossing the syllable with command. "Stay with me, sweetheart. Tell me what you want."

She dragged her gaze open and swung it fully at him. "More. Just... all of it. *More*. Please."

He pressed a soft kiss to her slightly parted mouth. "More of what, Pixie?"

She licked her lips, clearly struggling for syllables. But focusing on them would keep her from flying off to the submissive stars before he could allow her to. "The pleasure. And the permission for it. And..."

"And what, sweetheart?" he urged.

"And the pain."

Jesus. Fuck.

He was supposed to be the one granting her some lusty license, but her husky plea was a flip of his own damn tables. An approval stamp for him too.

"Ohhh!"

He allowed himself to enjoy the hell out of her lusty shriek. He craved another at once, so he repeated the ruthless drive of his fingers into her shuddering core.

"Ohhh . . . Brickham!"

Perfect.

So damn perfect that he already forgave her the etiquette slip. Every muscle along her channel worked to massage him more, aiding his steady pumps until the air vibrated with the erotic, rhythmic slicks.

"How's that, Pixie?" he husked, lifting his head enough to watch her face. She was a fucking masterpiece. Her forehead was dewy with sweat. Her eyes were all the way shut, with her unearthly long lashes trembling along the formidable crests of her cheeks. But her lips were the most mesmerizing. Plush, red, and slightly parted. So damn tempting . . .

"Does it hurt, little one? Is this the pain you need?"

"Mmm." It was more a wince than a moan, ending in her pronounced hiss as Brick turned his hand over and used his thumb and pinky on the sides of her clit. "Shit!" she screamed as he pinched even harder. "Ahhh!"

"Want me to stop?"

"No!" she retorted. "It is . . . fine. I am fine, Sir."

"Good." Brick matched his snarl to the soft kisses he brushed across her eyelids. "Because the next part is going to hurt a little more."

★ ★ ★

As soon as his dark, decadent promise hit the air, Jayd fought what it did to every cell of her blood. The war of ice and flames, of dread and delight.

What the hell was wrong with her?

Why did she already know that this would be the singular

experience she remembered from Paris, perhaps even replacing the frustration locating her father? Why did she already know it would alter her for life beyond the membrane Brickham was about to break? Why did she already *know* that the mere thought of that act—being broken apart, by *him*—was the dirty secret at the crux of this conflict?

Because that thought should have her recoiling from him.

Instead, she was sighing and undulating beneath him. Hating him for the sharp pinches and invasive thrusts—before the next second came, and she adored him for what erupted in place of the pain. The stings. The heat. The sizzles. The *lust* . . .

"Pixie."

His voice was like molten rain, riding the wind in her senses. She could feel it on her skin but not catch it with her thoughts. They were rushed along on that storm too. And the whirlwind was so wonderful . . .

"*Jayd.*"

But there the man went again, tethering her down. "Hmm?" she snapped. "What?"

"Open your eyes. Goddammit, right now."

She almost thanked him for the dictate. She was just in time to watch as he withdrew his fingers from her, using them to pull down the zipper of his jeans. He made short work of pushing down the pants past her field of vision, likely to his ankles.

When he straightened, he carried his wallet in one hand, and his bare cock in the other.

Jayd choked on her own air.

"By all the saints," she finally husked—and meant it. Surely the saints *had* intervened when the angels were shaping this man, because the pillar between his thighs was the most magnificent thing she had ever beheld. It was dark and firm and proud, its length covered by indigo striations. Those veins pointed the way to a broad, shiny bulb, already wet with the milky drops that he captured with his thumb and massaged along its length.

"Not sure you want to extend an invitation to *them* right now, Pixie." His voice was coarse, its volume modulating in time to his self-pleasure.

"Sir..."

"Yeah?"

"You are beautiful."

He kicked up one side of his mouth. "Thank you, little one. So are you."

"You are also..."

"What, Pixie?"

"*Big*," she finally blurted.

"Which is why this is going to hurt."

He ended that by aiming his shaft straight for her entrance—but in the moment before Jayd would have fully flinched, he lifted his erection and rested it atop her lower belly. Why that made her breathe in relief, she had no idea.

"That's also why I'm going to ask you, one more time, if you really want this." He interrupted himself with a rugged grunt as his gaze fell to the same place as hers. To the sight of his swollen flesh along hers. The view that proved, more than anything, how drastically he was going to stretch her. How deeply he was going to impale her. "Speak up now, woman. Because once we get started—"

"I know." But she also thought they had *already* started, so maybe she knew nothing. Still, she pushed on. "I know, Brickh— Sir. And I want this." While a hard gulp thudded down her throat, she raised her stare back up to his face. The blue fires in his gaze made it easier to amend. "I want *you*. All of you. Inside me."

A strange expression washed over Brickham's face. She was clueless about how to interpret it until the man murmured, "A blessing from the fucking pope wouldn't sound better than that, sweetheart."

Warmth suffused her senses. It bloomed into an impish smile around her lips. "Flattery will get you everywhere, Sir."

"That's what I'm counting on, Pixie."

He pushed the promise deeper into her psyche by doing the same thing to her bottom lip. The slide of his thumb was a strict abrasion, digging so hard that he might have broken skin. Sure enough, when he pulled it back, the pad was smeared with crimson. Brick glanced at the stain, then back at her. Jayd did not shield her fascination, especially as he licked the blood away with languorous intent.

Her throat went dry.

She swallowed anyway.

But she refused to look away from him.

Even as the man pulled a foil package out of his wallet. Even as he held it up between them before sliding its edge into the seam between her lips. And yes, even as he rumbled out an order that jolted Jayd straight to her toes—including every trembling corner of her sex.

"Bite."

As soon as her teeth gripped the foil, Brickham twisted the packet up and away. Jayd refused to focus on how expertly he did it or how swiftly he handled the contents inside. Before she could blink again, he had the condom stretched halfway down his shaft. She watched, still entranced, as he worked the latex over the rest of his length. He grunted again, though she could not tell if the sound was from pleasure or pain. It was confusing to try reading him when she barely knew what *she* was feeling. Excitement? Anxiety? Fervor? Fear?

She trembled, dizzy and overwhelmed, when realizing it was all of them at once. The tidal wave struck harder when she looked down again. His cock seemed bigger now, straining at its thin sheath. Would that flimsy latex be all right? Would *she*?

Her mind could come up with no definitive answer. No rally cry of you-can-do-this, developed from years of keeping up with Ev, Syn, and 'Raz. But her brothers were thousands of miles away. Even Emme and Jagger were gone, likely hours away from being done at the hospital. This . . . was really only her now. Naked and spread for this man.

Rahmie Creacu.

Was this really happening?

Was he really going to do this?

"Time to be remolded, Pixie."

There was the answer to that question, at least. Not that enlightenment ushered in any shred of reassurance.

"Shit." Jayd gasped, unable to hold back the tears that clawed up her throat. "Oh, shit, shit, sh—"

A hand at her windpipe turned her final syllable into a helpless rasp. But while Brickham silenced her sound, he knew just when to ease off on her air. "Ssshhh, sweetheart," he soothed. "Breathe for me. We're going to take it slow."

He kept his hand right where it was, even as he notched the tip of his sex at the entrance of hers. As Jayd's heartbeat doubled, she figured out why. The feel of her pulse, hammering at the vise of his fingers, actually ended up in . . . sanity. Security. Like the steel around her hands, his grip was a perfect reminder that it was not her place to stay in control here. To be thinking—or stressed—about anything. Her only role now was to trust. To feel. To let go.

To be free . . .

As the recognition took wing through her senses, a sigh broke free from her lips. Brickham snagged that short too. His own lips, so full and ferocious, were the tools of his wanton handiwork. As he meshed and mashed and worked those pads against hers, she broke into a mewl. Even after he broke away, he suckled and nipped and bit his way down her neck, branding her with his scent and taste and marks, until she honestly had no idea where she ended and he began.

Though the impression possibly had something to do with *other* factors.

Like the fact that Brickham had pushed in his erection much farther than she thought.

Like the fact that it was not a wholly unpleasant feeling.

"Oh . . . my!"

Like the fact that as she erupted with the startled sough, Brickham cut loose with an unearthly groan. "Fuck. Holy mother of *all* fucks. *Jayd.*"

His massive frame shook like a haunted oak. Jayd's senses raced like a hundred butterflies seeking refuge in his branches. Only in this case, her hunger was not for his leaves. The butterfly begged the oak to do the devouring. To consume her whole with his ferocity and fire. To sweep her away in his violent, passionate storm.

"Is it . . . all right, Sir?" Five little words that stood for so much more. *What can I do to make it better? What can I say? Who do you want me to be?*

Because for once, for just *this* once, she wanted to be—

"Perfect."

How had he yanked the thought right out of her head?

"Perfect," he repeated, also seeming to know she had to hear it again. "It's better than all right, Pixie. This is...you are...god*damn*!"

Her high yelp coincided with his jagged oath—and his expanding movements. She was aware of him now, sluicing in and out of her quivering core, opening her wider with each of his rolling but gentle thrusts.

Though she wondered how much longer the gentle part was going to hold.

Or if she even wanted it to.

"Brick," she rasped. "Please!" She held back none of her lusty urgency. If that was what it took to make *him* trust *her* in return, so be it.

Brickham rocked his head back enough to put a couple of inches between their faces. "Please what, little Pixie?"

"Do not stop," she whispered. "Please...do not stop."

"Not unless there's an apocalypse, sweetheart." He leaned in and kissed her again. "No. Screw that. Even there *is* an apocalypse. Lady, we're past the point of no return."

Jayd allowed herself a small smile. She was not sure why. Just the idea of doing this while Armageddon raged outside... *Creator have mercy.* The heady visual made her even needier. How she reveled in him. His climbing passion. His hardening stalk. His heady scent. All his erotic huffs and growls and grunts.

Ohhh, hell.

Was she...falling for him? Beyond the square-jawed beauty and the too-good-to-be-true body. Beyond all the provocative ways he knew how to use that body?

No. By the saints *and* sinners, this was not a movie. Physical attraction, no matter how tumultuous, was only that. A biological reaction to primal level chemistry.

And ohhh, how they had chemistry. Enough to double the squares on the Periodic Table. Definitely enough that a person might mistake it for more. But she was not that person. Not anymore. She had this man all to herself for just this night, and she planned on savoring every last moment. Soon, she would not be calling them moments. They would be her memories.

She had to pay attention. To cherish every last detail. Yes, even the one that brought a defined knife of pain.

"Oh!" She stiffened as her inner walls kept screaming. She was stuffed full now, strained in ways she never imagined. It was strange but empowering to feel Brickham's hardness so far up inside her. Pulsing and stretching against her . . .

"Pixie." He swept his lips across the bridge of her nose. "I'd say I'm sorry, but I'd be lying." He dropped his hands to bracket her hips with his grip. The pressure felt even better than his hold at her neck. "Christ on high. I've jumped the line into heaven."

As he pressed his forehead to hers, he also yanked hard on her lower body—bringing the jolt that he still was not all the way inside her. Oh, sweet Creator. This was a doomed plan. They truly were *not* going to fit. Not at—

"Ahhh!"

Her shriek tumbled out in time to the scorching chain reaction through her breached core.

"Pixie. *Jayd*," Brickham groaned out. The exhortation came between his brutal breaths, despite how he sucked down full lungs of air. "Stay with me, sweetheart. We got there, okay? We got there."

"Got the hell where?" Because if this was the end, she was furious. Was this really what all the fuss was about? The "shooting stars," "wicked magic," and "carnal miracle" that she had heard about—ad nauseam—from the three women who possessed her brothers' hearts? On a mental notepad, she started in on some key talking points for Camillia, Brooke, and Lucy. Because this was, to borrow a favorite from Lucy, some king-size bullshit.

Or so she thought.

Until Brickham took over again.

With a rush of heated strokes, he ran his big hand over her waist, breasts, face, and hair. He stopped only when his palm engulfed her wrists, still caught over her head, and he was squeezing her there in time to his new kiss on her mouth... and his new pushes into her sex. Literally helpless to refuse both incursions, Jayd focused on softening for him. Opening to him.

And soon—so much swifter and hotter than she expected—percolating for him.

"Oh," she blurted, sounding—and feeling—as if she had just found the secret to world peace. Perhaps she had. Nothing in her life had ever felt this shockingly good this sinfully fast.

And moment by moment, it was only getting better.

Saints on high. What on earth was going on? Her lips were now fields of lightning. Her blood vibrated with mini rolls of molten thunder. Her mind was a storm of both. And her core...

Oh, what Brickham was doing to her core.

His rolling thrusts. Her hot pressure.

His extra shoves. Her extra zaps of awareness.

His careful, caressing slides. Her long, shivering vibrations.

"So good," he rumbled into the front of her neck. "Damn it, Pixie. You're so. Fucking. Good."

Jayd almost laughed. Was he joking? *Good?* This had gotten *good* several minutes ago. Or had it been hours? She cared not, nor did she even want to. All she wanted was more of his decadent kisses, full of his dark clove taste. More of his grip at her wrists and his glorious cock inside her body, branding every inch of her walls with his masculine dominion.

But the words had to stay locked in her mind. Somehow, all the wires between it and her mouth had been severed, then fused into the one gigantic nerve she felt like now. The massive, open exposure for this mesmerizing man . . .

The force of nature who dropped his hold from her wrists to her nape, doubling the impact of his command inside of two seconds.

Who splayed that hand along the back of her head, stretching his powerful fingers through her hair. Who held her in place with unignorable strength, filling her sights with nothing but his bold, hewn features and his burning, fierce stare.

He leaned in, kissing her fast and hard before gritting out, "You still with me, Pixie?" He inched up an impossibly alluring smirk in response to her frantic nod. "Good. That's really, really good."

Jayd was on the brink of rolling her eyes, except for two hard facts. First, the man's swagger was built on a base of raw sexiness. Second, his cocky ruggedness was ten times better when he was clothed only in her.

After seeming to read item number one straight from her mind, the man was swift about delivering the second. By lifting his other hand and palming it over one of her breasts.

"Oh!" she cried out.

"Somebody's got stiff, juicy nipples," Brickham murmured while peeling back one of the thin cups of her bra. As he continued to tease her aching peaks with one hand, he used his other to reach between her legs. "Somebody's also stiff down here. And quivering. And wet."

"Brickham." She panted. "Oh, *Sir*. Ohhh . . ."

"Oh, lady," he husked between increasingly fast breaths. "What this sweet little clit is telling me . . ."

"The same thing my cunt is telling you?"

He had turned her into one giant live wire, and now she jabbed back with that exposed electricity. And oh, how she gloated through every second of it. She even added a coy shrug, once it appeared like the man was swallowing and breathing normally again.

"Brothers." She was confident it would do as an explanation.

"Hot." Brickham jumped on the shorthand trend too. Well, it was *their* trend—and right now, no other craze or fad or fashion meant more to her. She doubted any of them would for a very long time to come.

A morose thought for a different time. *Much* different. This moment was only about connection, celebration, and completion. About basking in this unexpected bond with this unforgettable man. About cherishing as much about it as she could.

Including the part where he circled a knowing finger across her distended button . . .

And then again . . .

And then—

"Brickham!"

She arched up. He bore down—hitting the spot at her center that needed him the most. She moaned and sobbed and struggled to keep her body in one place. Any instant, her skin was surely going to shatter like glass and fall away from her in blissful shards. No mortal shell was capable of containing this ecstasy.

"Sweetheart."

His new growl was a blast of perfect flame in her senses.

"Need," she begged in return. "*Need.*"

"What?"

But while Brickham husked the inquiry, he lifted his hand away. She writhed and shrieked and glared. Did he not know the agony she was in? The frustrating brink to which *he* had taken her?

As soon as her mind supplied those answers, she huffed. "Fuck!" And spat that even harder.

For a second, Brick's whole form locked up again. But he recovered faster from the snag this time, which smoothed his way toward a lascivious grin.

"You insisting, Pixie?"

Jayd notched her head back, scrutinizing her lover through slitted eyes. Didn't make the man any less stunning, though it shored up her courage enough to speak again.

"Fuck."

This time, she was not flirting around. She was still half a Cimarron, and that part was the perfect helper for hurling out serious decrees.

Very serious.

"So my little one is insisting."

Thankfully, despite the silky pleasure in his voice, Brickham was too. She got the message, loud and clear, as soon as he seized her hips again. And hauled her forward again. And groaned with erotic abandon once he impaled her again.

"Fuck!"

Brickham joined her for that loud and lusty iteration. And hot. So damn hot. His cock ignited a thousand flames in her womb. Though he still rolled his hips on every stroke, each of those thrusts were different now. More drawn out. More decided. Definitely more stimulating. So very much of that. He was not just a force of nature anymore. He was several of them at once. She saw it in his stormy eyes and felt it in his Richter-worthy thrusts. Tremors that vibrated beneath her thighs and even sent tingles between her butt cheeks.

Seisms she started to feel in other places . . .

Along the length of her that still squeezed him . . . and stretched for him . . . and hurt for him . . .

And never wanted to stop.

Especially as she began to explode for him.

CHAPTER TEN

"Brickham!"

Her gasping scream would be engraved on his mind forever. Even so, Brick craved to hear it again. As in right the fuck now.

With one minor twist.

"Call me what you should, sweet one, and you can have all of your orgasm."

The woman flared her big turquoises, officially registering herself as the eighth wonder of the world in his book.

"All of it?" she stammered. "You mean *that* was not— *Oh!*"

Brick kicked up a grin as he readjusted his angle, making sure more of his pelvis rubbed along hers. Her answering whimper soared through him like a damn angel's song. No shit, considering her body was a heaven he never wanted to leave.

But their time together would soon be ending—a realization that sealed his dedication to two new aims.

One, to imprint as much of himself on her from the inside out. He was well on the way to honoring that with every purposeful lunge into the paradise of her sex. Two, he swore to memorize all the details of how he affected her. Every damn minutia. The incessant, erotic pulse in her neck. The way her arm muscles bunched every time his dick bottomed out in her tight, torrid heaven.

And speaking of that . . .

The woman's pussy was getting a memory book of its own.

A tome to withstand the ages, bound with chunks of his soul and filled with as many of these moments as he could fit onto its precious pages.

She was worth it. A female he'd never forget. A princess with courage that stunned him and boldness that inspired him. Who had nerves steelier than most dudes he knew but embraced her softness and submissiveness like a kitten with its first taste of cream. Who had no viable reason to trust him, but had—and still did—with so much of her honesty, intensity, passion, and surrender.

Christ. Especially that.

How she squeezed him. Soaked him. Milked him.

Moved him...

He could no longer deny the recognition. It was the fucking truth, and he'd have to accept it. Later, he'd unpack the whole mental mess it came with. The *why*s and *how*s and *what the hell now*s.

Right now, there were more urgent needs for his system to unload.

"Sir."

So much more urgent.

"Please...*Sir*."

She spoke it like a wish laced with worship. An appeal but a demand. Likely ruining him for anyone else who'd speak it again. Like he fucking cared about that right now.

"Pixie." His own voice was filled with the building pressure through his body and mind. He wasn't going to last much longer. His balls were wads of lava. His dick was a goddamned branding iron. And if the quiver of her clit was any indication...

"Oh! Yes! Please, Sir..."

And what an indication it was.

"Come for me, Pixie girl. All the way, my sweet Jayd."

"Oh . . . yessss . . ."

She flung her head back. The action shoved her breasts up at him. In a frenzied rush, Brick shoved the satin away from the swell that was still covered. He followed with his mouth. Sucked in her red, puckered nub with suction dictated by passion.

"Oh, by the Creator, *yes.*"

She was so close, but not all the way there. Not . . . yet . . .

Damn it.

Frustration and anticipation collided, blasting away his courtly control. Instinct roared in its place. The impulse had him biting instead of sucking. Pulling hard at the beautiful berry between his teeth.

"Brickham!"

As soon as her scream jolted the air, her pussy flickered around his cock. Her body surrounded his in wave after wave of undulating ecstasy. He knew exactly how to respond—by again grabbing her nipple and digging in like it was the best fruit he'd ever tasted. Because it sure as hell was.

"Wh-What is happening? What *is* this?"

"Let it come, Pixie," he grated into the valley of her chest. "Let *me* come with you."

"Yes." She would've sounded like a broken playback loop if not for the vocal sugar roughening her tone. "Yes . . . yes . . . yes . . ."

The gorgeous litany went on, a repetition between every drive of his aching autocrat of an erection, until her voice was hoarse and her thighs quaked. For one wonderful moment, Brick imagined stroking one of those thighs and fingering a mark upon it. His mark, branded permanently into her skin. No longer would she be his for just a night. She'd be his submissive princess forever.

Never to be.

But right here? In this incredible moment?

This was meant to be.

If all of Paris broke into flames then, he wouldn't have noticed. If aliens were suddenly skipping through Montmartre, he wouldn't care. There was nothing but her now. Nothing but her high cries in his ears and her succulent cunt around his sex. Absorbing every plunge from him. Taking every inch of him. Accepting every drop of him.

He couldn't get enough of her.

He sure as hell couldn't look away from her.

Not as she lolled her head back, scattering her dark bangs across her dewy forehead. Definitely not as the curves of her mouth fell open, making way for velveteen gasps that warmed his cheeks and lips.

She was spellbinding. A dream. Like a painting on a medieval fresco, meant to embody the wages of sin but secretly beckoning every male in the church to sign their soul over to Lucifer.

He'd be the first in line.

And why not? A long time ago, he'd resigned himself to the eventual direction he was headed for. She'd just make the journey worth it.

Already, she'd made *living* more worth it.

Perhaps more than that.

Holy mother of all hidden treasures. His Dominant mojo was back. No. It was *back*. He'd cuffed a perfect little subbie with a goddamned cookie cutter and then fucked her until she'd shattered, screaming his name. And he'd climaxed for her too. Given her so much, he wondered if his dick had any swimmers left.

That answer was yes.

Because he already wanted to do it again.

Even as he lifted her wrists to free her from his creative shackle. Even as he rubbed them, making sure he hadn't broken her skin. And yeah, even as he softened inside her, knowing it'd be time to slip out soon. But so many veins in his shaft refused to give up. They already gave in to more fantasies as he slid Jayd off the counter, with her legs around his waist, and carried her into the bedroom.

Unbelievably—thankfully?—the actions also provided distraction. Once he'd laid Jayd down on the bed, he was flaccid enough to peel off the condom. A trip to the bathroom meant he could properly zip up and grab a towel for cleaning her too.

Once he stretched beside her and started doing just that, the visions weren't so easy to avoid. The woman herself was no help, as she watched his every move with her endless aquas. Her whole body was still flushed and warm, giving off that elegant effervescence that was hers alone. It matched the smile that stretched across her face, turning the ribbon of her lips into a package he longed to bite open.

But not now.

It was time to chill shit out. To stop at his mental mountain stream and regroup his composure. Not a bad metaphor, considering a light summer rain began to fall outside. The traffic noises were quieter too. Montmartre never really slept, but there was a lull between the dinner crowd and the concert crowd, so the only sounds in the room were raindrops on the window and Jayd Cimarron's contented hums.

Christ, how he liked being the master of those hums.

How he wished he was the master of so much more.

Her sighs and her cries, her whimpers and her screams . . .

What about "not happening in this lifetime" aren't you getting here, dick for brains?

There was only now. These last few minutes with her. He was going to savor every second, even if that meant looking on while the woman fell asleep on him with startling speed.

Brick chuckled, accepting it as a compliment. Her exhaustion had been blatant from the moment she sat down in the bar, and nothing about the last few hours could exactly be called a break. Now, at least to her subconscious, she was warm and protected.

And to him, that was all that mattered.

He'd barely completed the full thought when a shrill scream knifed the air.

"What the—" he blurted, preparing to jolt from the mattress and assume a full battle stance—until identifying the source as the woman sleeping next to him. No, that wasn't right either. Not the screaming part. Or the woman part. The fucking *sleeping* part.

Holy shit. *He'd* nodded off? Okay, what alternate universe had he tumbled into? Because in the one in which he'd woken up this morning, he was still *him*. A guy capable of showing a woman the stars without tossing her into the sky along with them. A kink club owner who'd accepted that the Dom dream just wasn't meant for him. And definitely *not* a guy who fell asleep on watch duty without backup. Not when there was a prize this precious to guard.

The prize who, thank fuck, was still here.

A closer look revealed that Jayd was barely awake too.

She blinked and pushed up, gazing toward the window. The rain was softer, but the crowds on the streets below were heavier. Brick glanced at his watch. Half past ten. Thank fuck. He hadn't been comatose all night. On the other hand, he had no idea if Jagger, Oz, and Requiemme were still at the ER or half a block away.

A secondary concern from the second Jayd cried out again.

"Pixie. Hey. It's only me. And you're only dreaming. Sweetheart?"

Her eyes fluttered open. Not that it mattered. Her face was still clamped down with terror. Brick had seen all the signs before, from his own mirror, to label it differently.

He leaned in carefully, stroking her cheeks with his knuckles, until she blinked a bunch of times. A shaky sigh left her before she husked, "Br ... Brickham?"

"I was the last time I checked."

Another hit of relief, as she pushed out a groggy laugh. "It *is* really you."

He lowered a kiss to her nose. "In the flesh."

"Such nice flesh too."

He didn't fight his king-of-the-world smirk. It vanished as soon as she reached up and palmed the center of his chest. Brick gulped before scooping up her hand and gently bussing her knuckles. And now, yet again, he wanted to do so much more. Take this affection further ...

He had to get her dressed again. Hell, he had to put his own shirt back on.

"You okay?"

"I ... think so."

"Hmm." He frowned. "I don't."

"Huh?" she blurted.

"You're parched." He confirmed it by sliding a thumb across her bottom lip. "Stay right here."

He rose and headed for the kitchen. When he returned with a glass of water and all her clothes, the princess was standing next to the window, which she'd just finished opening.

Brick growled. "You know what stay means, don't you?"

She arched a pretty brow. "And you know what I'm hot means too?"

"That's a given, Pixie. But right now, your delectable little self can be hot over here."

"If I stay over here, do I get spankings?"

"No. You'll get a long lesson in topping from the bottom."

"Sounds like fun."

"And then a lesson in orgasm denial."

Well, that took care of her pants-free dawdling. Fortunately, the window ledge hit her high at the waist, and the pane itself could only be rolled out a few inches. Still, Brick handed over her panties and leggings first—along with a don't-even-think-about-saying-no stare.

Without a word, the smart little sprite started putting her clothes back on.

For long minutes, Brick didn't say anything either. He parked himself on the lounger in the corner and appreciated his last few views of her nudity. In the subdued light of the bedroom, her skin glowed like warm caramel. Her movements were efficient but exquisite, a ballerina's by any other name. Until...

Christ.

"Hey. You're still shaking." Not as violently as before, but enough that he noticed.

"I am fine."

"Bullshit."

"Brickham." No chance she'd be correcting herself to Sir this time. "It was just a bad dream."

"Says the girl who just attempted to yell the roof down? This time for all the wrong reasons?"

A cute snicker from her lush lips. "And you *are* the one who would know the difference."

He pulled up one knee. Rested an elbow atop it. From across that new trajectory, he was able to inject her with a harder stare. "I've had some experience with crappy dreams. Even more with the monsters who can cause them."

And there was the line that sank a hook into her. Though he'd half expected it, the tense frown was no easier to witness— or address.

"Who's your monster, Jayd?" He took care about the probe, wrapping it in a silken tone. Nevertheless, he betrayed his split nerves by rapidly running his thumb against his forefinger. "Anyone you've … met recently? Maybe someone who can be a bit domineering? And if so, maybe that certain person can help by talking things out with you?"

His fingers froze as soon as she erupted with a reaction. Her laugh was a brilliant burst on the air, full and free—and as riveting as her orgasm screams. He practically preened at being its inspiration, though he was confused as hell why.

"To be very clear, you were not the monster in my dream, Brickham." She said it as if merely commenting on the rain instead of lifting the anvil that had been parked on his chest. "If anything…"

"What?" he prodded, as the anvil lowered close again.

A blush tinged her cheeks. He couldn't say the same

about the blood rushing his cock because of it. "If anything, Brickham...you were the one in my dream who was saving me."

Now it was time to shatter the damn anvil.

Except for when his better sense crashed down in its place.

"In case you haven't noticed, Pixie, I'm not the guy who likes coming to your bower and waking you up with a tender kiss."

"And in case *you* have not noticed, Sir, it takes more than that to wake me up."

Well, that sure as hell wasn't helpful for the chaos beneath his fly. Still, something else sliced through his senses. A feeling so rare, he barely recognized it at first. "More? Like what?" Hope was such an odd commodity, he needed more validation for it. *Her* validation.

"Like...spankings with spatulas, maybe."

She averted her eyes, but no way could she shield her darker flush. No way did Brick want her to.

"Go on," he directed, now wishing the lounger was a dungeon throne. Hell, even a regular throne. Fuck it. He'd settle for a regular kitchen chair.

"Maybe...heart-shaped handcuffs would work too." Her tone wasn't so awkward. From any other woman, at any other time, he'd be celebrating that perception. But as she turned and took a step closer, still clothed only in her leggings and bra, he hit the opposite end of the spectrum. She was coming closer on a clear track of thought. He had to derail her from it. Quickly.

"And then spreading your legs for a near stranger?"

So shoveling more fuel into the engine was helping his cause...how?

"Not a stranger." And neither, damn it, was her tentative touch across his knuckles. Her fingertips were like butterflies on his skin—and hornets along his dick. He was so swollen. So ready to be inside her again. "You were the good guy in the dream, remember?"

"Right," he scoffed. "The good guy who likes cuffing you, stripping you, and then fucking you."

Her touch became a full clasp. She curled her fingernails in, gouging his palm on purpose. "The good guy who made at least a hundred of my fantasies come true," she whispered. "The *very* good guy who taught me there is nothing wrong about them, either."

At once, a frown took over his face. "Who made you ever think you were wrong?"

"Well ... everyone." She said it as if he'd just noticed it was pouring outside. "The world at large." With a fresh huff, she lowered to the foot of the lounger. "I am right ... *right*? Nobody normal is supposed to *want* their sex like that."

Brick lowered his knee but kept clutching her hand. "Like what?"

Yet another heavy sigh. "You know what I mean, Brickham."

"Pretend I don't." He pushed at her backside with his calf. Damn, it was nice to have her so close. Only thing better than her between his legs would be *him* between *hers*. "It wasn't a request, sweetheart."

She pursed her lips, clearly debating what to say, if anything at all. "All right, fine," she muttered. "There are things we are all taught, especially as women, to want from our lovers. And I admit, all of those things are nice ..."

"But?"

"But I have always just craved . . . other things . . . too."

She rushed that part out like a third grader finishing a book report. But a smile teased the corners of her lush mouth, encouraging Brick's rejoinder.

"Other things. You mean, like what I did to you."

"You mean *for* me?"

Fuck, he enjoyed how her beautiful mind worked. "And what you did for me, as well. It was a two-way circuit, Jayd."

Her smile widened. "Oh yes, it was."

"But you've still been taught to think of it as wrong."

"Were you not taught the same?"

"Sweetheart, most of my education about my dick and where it belongs came courtesy of some softhearted hookers on slow nights in South Park."

Her brows knitted. "Where?"

"It's a suburb of Seattle." He didn't bother going into the gritty—correction: the grimy and reeking—details about that one.

"Seattle," she echoed. "A lovely city. I have been there a few times. On official tours with my parents and brothers, of course."

"Which is why you still think all of it is lovely."

A chill wafted over her expression. It was enough to convey she'd listened—and understood—him. "So that is your hometown?"

"If that's the word that fits, then yes."

"Is there another that fits better?"

Why he hesitated about responding, he didn't know. She might be phrasing the questions a little differently than other women, but they weren't new. He had more than enough experience with dodging them too. But there was the fucking rub. This time, he didn't want to. With this woman, who'd given him the brightest heat of her body and the scariest secrets of her heart, he didn't want to play duck and cover. He yearned to give her the same.

Okay, *some* of the same.

"You're asking that of a guy who doesn't really know what that word means, Pixie." The confession felt as awkward as it sounded, but he ordered himself to go on. "Growing up, *home* meant a corner of the living room at my aunt and uncle's place, next to a leaky window and a fire escape that was very popular for the horny cats on the block."

A small frown crumpled her forehead. "Your aunt and uncle? But what about your *maimanne* and *paipanne*? Your parents?"

"Not around."

He braced himself for her reaction. The same response he got from everyone, drenched in sorrow and pity, whenever he tried to shut down his revelation by just making shit simple. And yeah, Jayd did switch up her expression—but to neither of the intents he was dreading. Her reaction was different. Remarkably so. She actually seemed interested in what he was relaying. Curious, not condoling.

"So you were raised by others." Again, it was more a statement of fact than a token of sympathy. It was almost like she...understood. No. Beyond that. It was as if she'd been through the exact same thing. And maybe, in her own way, she had.

"That also might be a matter of interpretation." He pointedly cleared his throat. "But I think Roz and Jerry tried their best, considering they didn't know I existed until the call from Seattle PD." His shrug felt as stiff as it appeared.

"Couldn't have been easy for old Jer, dealing with a disappeared brother and a magically manifested nephew in the same night."

"Of course." She emulated his move, though it looked like her shoulder blades were wrapped in rebar. "Everyone does their best, do they not?" Okay, not rebar. Her whole torso was turning into a steel girder. Even her gaze favored the harsh shade of the metal. "But you can acknowledge that and still be sad about what you missed. Your own parents." She visibly gulped. "Your *real* parents."

Rebelling against all his wiser instincts, Brick's throat closed up tighter. Shit. He should've known that zinger would be coming from her. But now the conversational ball was back in his court. Time to move things forward. Wallowing had never been his thing.

"I got out of Roz's and Jer's hair in a few years anyway," he relayed. "Once I was strong enough to get some decent work, I did. Mostly it was just lugging boxes and cleaning out storage rooms, but a lot of times there were spare cots in those places. Many of those times, I'd be allowed to sleep over in exchange for cut pay. It was always just the basics, but it kept my ass from having to sleep in constant rain puddles."

"Go on."

Go on?

But now that he'd gotten started, he actually wanted to go on. It felt good to indulge the whole "talk to a stranger" shit, especially when said stranger was such a gorgeous and generous woman. It was also nice to notice that he wasn't inducing her to a pity party or completely weirding her out. But the expression that *was* on her face . . .

He couldn't figure it out. So now *he* was weirding out.

"So you were well-prepared for your military service, then."

Well, hell.

So that was what she was thinking.

Brick scraped his free hand over his skull, using the action to disguise his astonishment. This was unexpected input. Unexpected but amazing. A statement conceived by a mind that continued to blow him away. Nowhere in that mind was the woman thinking how he'd grown up in back rooms instead of marble halls, or that he hadn't rested his head on a clean pillow until his first night in boot camp. Instead of fixating on his past, she looked at what he'd done with the lessons from it. The strength he'd turned it into.

What cloud in heaven had this female been created on? He needed the mailing address so he'd know where to send his long thank-you note.

But that was on the to-do for later. Right now, he refocused on a gorgeous sprite who was clearly waiting for his response. "Yeah," he told her, managing to stick in a sedate grin. "You could say I was ready to work hard."

As a matter of fact, his first few weeks in Army Gruntville were more like going to summer camp—well, what he'd always imagined that would be. Hot food and showers on the regular, mixed between outdoors competitions and learning to work in teams. He was giddy, taking to the structure and discipline like GI goddamned Joe. After a few weeks, when they'd pulled him aside and asked about his interest in special forces, it was the easiest *yes* of his life.

He'd been so fucking young. So comically naïve.

Fortunately, Jayd didn't read that chunk of his thoughts. Instead, she seemed engrossed in another thought track. "So was that when you started exploring your ... proclivities? The ... alternative ... ways of doing things?"

He suppressed a laugh. For a female who had no trouble declaring personal sovereignty over her virginity, her new stammerings were damn adorable.

"Kink," he supplied with an amiable wink. "It's called kink, sweet girl. Or if you want to get more specific about the subset, TPE."

She tilted her head. "TPE?"

"Stands for Total Power Exchange," he explained. "And yes, it often goes along with its popular sibling, BDSM."

She nodded, indicating she was familiar with the more notable acronym. "So they go together?"

"Often but not always." Brick gentled his grip on her. Not a discussion to start with someone unless they had the option to break free. "For me, the dynamic isn't always about the whips and toys and bruises. I'm happy to give those to a consenting submissive, if that's what they need, but it's not the necessary component for me."

The princess shifted, facing him more directly. When he responded naturally, increasing his hold again, her stature actually eased.

"And what is that?" she murmured, as if he'd held her with the force of a shackle so many times before. Already epitomizing the strength of his one-worded reply.

"Trust," he stated. "Plain and simple. But not just what a couple of people give with their bodies." He cut in on himself with a chuff. "The physical elements are the easiest part."

Jayd canted her head by another inch. "Because that is the part everyone can see."

Brilliant girl. Amazing woman.

His new admiration made it difficult to restrict his touch, keeping everything to a gentle thumb stroke over her wrist. "Which makes the other shit easier to hide." *Screw it.* There was no huge harm in circling his caress up to her forearm. "The part of the connection that's even better than the rest."

He braced himself for what was likely next. Subbies loved this line for the obvious opportunity it afforded. Steering the conversation back toward *the rest* as well as what they hoped to gain from him out of it. He'd never understood all that, considering all the components of his body and mind that went into every scene he was a part of. Dom drop, while rare, was real—and enough of a factor that he'd gotten pickier about his scenes, as well as who they were with. Never, in his whole kink journey, had he met a female he wanted to tie up again so soon.

Never ... before now.

And as Murphy and his infamous Law would dictate, *this* woman only looked ready to continue with the direct subject at hand. "All the things that are going on *inside*," she commented. "Yes, I understand." She caught his skeptical glance but wasn't deterred. "It is about other kinds of communication, yes? Not just the unspoken things with your body. The ways you talk to each other with your mind and even your soul. It becomes about deeper intentions. Forging those unspoken connections ..."

Brick wasn't sure why she purposely drifted on that thought. But maybe that was just how profound truths were communicated in heaven. She'd picked up the trick from the angelic crew who'd created her in the first place. It was either that, or—

Crap.

Why'd his brain have to go *there*?

But it was definitely there. Blocking out the logistics with gusto. Logistics telling him that kink wasn't some magical land beyond Virgin Valley. That Jayd Cimarron wasn't the unwitting subbie he'd first assumed. Which was bizarre but kind of cool.

"That's all...pretty insightful, Pixie. And pretty damn right."

She basked as if he'd anointed her with an A on a book report. "Well, it is a familiar way of thinking for me."

Though Brick unclenched his teeth enough to speak, he forced his tone to the diplomatic straight-and-narrow. "Because you've been secretly exploring your own proclivities?"

And if so, exactly how had she done so? With some select friends back on Arcadia? What kind of friends? Helpers who'd gotten to see her naked? Were they male or female? And did that part really matter?

Fortunately, she didn't discern his private asshole rant. The woman was actually laughing now. Not the robust burst from before but stunning him just as fully.

"If you qualify prayer as a proclivity, then yes," she offered.

"Prayer." Brick echoed the word as if he'd never heard it before. There were words with which he was friendlier, like *hippopotamus* and *turducken*. Practicing the word was an even more bizarre idea. But this moment changed all that. A lot. "So...while you and I were out there, doing what we did..."

A new giggle from her, dancing all over his unwitting pause. "You mean making the earth move and the stars sing?"

"Not exactly how I'd phrase it, but yes." He wanted to grin but doused the expression while straddling the lounger and reaching for her other hand. "Are you saying that in your mind, it felt like...what? Going to church? Confessing your sins?

Paying penitence?" Well, shit. He was out of his depth but just realizing it. He knew nothing about Arcadian religion, beyond the Creator that she, Jagger, and Requiemme invoked.

"Hmm." Such a brief but telling sound. It gave away her earnest consideration. "It was not like any of those things, really." She winced, seeming to silently apologize for shooting down his suggestion. "It was not like what I do on the outside for the Creator, if that makes sense? It was closer to what I feel on the inside ... when I recognize feelings that are bigger than me."

Brick studied her closely. "So, your church feelings."

"Not just church. The Creator is larger than a building— the same way we are creatures with substance beyond our bones and muscles and skin. There is more there, yes? Our souls. Our spirits. The parts of us that are better shared with those we care about." She stretched her fingers out, wrapping them around his forearms. "And those we trust."

One long moment. Then another. Stretches of time he didn't know what to do with. But like an astronaut surfing through space, he didn't want to tug on the safety tether. Not yet.

"Brickham?" Her query was pitched high, as if more than a few minutes had gone by. "What is it?"

Her turquoises bore into him like lasers. But that wasn't what made him opt for raw honesty with his reply.

"You trust me."

The lasers softened as if they'd been pointed at a stuffed animal factory. "I do," she whispered, bringing her knees up beneath her.

"You trust me as much as you trust your Creator."

"Yes." She nodded, adding unexpected emphasis to an

equally startling answer. But now that she'd given it, Brick wasn't sure what to do with it—especially when she appended, "Yes, Sir. I certainly do."

Thank fuck he'd chosen not to tug on that space tether yet. Being weightless and groundless was really fitting for how he felt now—except for when he hit reality reentry because of the confused crunch across her features.

"Pixie?"

"Hmm? Yes, Sir?"

"You're not locked down on that one, okay? You can take it back anytime. Hell, you can take it back now."

Jayd shook her head. "That is not why—" She shook her head as if ripping herself out of a trance. "I am perplexed for an entirely different reason."

He leaned over, releasing her hands so he could cup her butt and coax her a little closer. No way could he resist, with her being so close and looking so cute. Holy shit. Her confused face was as captivating as her orgasm face. How was that even possible?

"What is it, sweetheart?" Because at this moment, he'd unravel the meaning of the whole damn universe for her. He hoped his tender peck to her nose conveyed that clearly enough.

"If trust is the key to making the TPE work, why do I think about other people I trust... I mean, I suppose, other men I have dated... and not imagine doing any of that with them? Nothing that you and I did, anyway. And certainly nothing like what we saw back in the dungeon."

Brick lifted his lips to softly brush them across her forehead, enjoying the spikes of her bangs against his lips. "Relationships are as complex and layered inside the kink world as outside it," he conveyed. "There are clear rules and boundaries about the dynamics, but beneath it all, there are still human beings involved. Personalities in motion." While carefully choosing his next words, he settled his weight back again. "There's a damn good chance you were just meeting men who didn't enjoy the kinky corner of the playground."

"You mean the kinky corner of the *island*?" She ended it with a ponderous sigh. "Which, I assure you, does not exist on Arcadia."

"Do you know that as fact?" Before the rebuttal was done, he cursed himself. "Have you tried asking? Or had Emme or Jagger ask for you?" And then a new curse, more brutal than before. What the hell? He'd never been into masochism but having her back on the find-a-Dom pro tips had to be angling his punch card for karma's cut.

But what did it say about his sadistic side to give the woman such a generous taste of her submissiveness and then cut her loose to figure out the rest from here? Nope. That was also in the masochism column. Just thinking about her surrendering to someone else, the way she'd just given herself to him, stabbed his blood with icicled rage and his mind with primitive wrath.

Fuck.

Wasn't all this supposed to be a hot but quick dalliance? An easy distraction for them both? Certainly not a hookup that would infect him with an ugly strain of alpha-hole resentment. And that clarified things to the texture of cheese soup. Her next words didn't help the mire.

"Arcadia is not like Seattle, Brickham," she stated, verbally underlining every word.

"I'm aware of that, Pixie." He exaggerated his own

emphasis, borrowing some of her irritation to mix with his strained patience.

"You have to imagine it in the same category as one of your American small towns," she went on. "If the news is more scandalous than a weather update or a runaway pet, it hits the gossip pipeline like a flash flood. If just one wrong person learned that a Cimarron was inquiring about a place to get tied down and spanked, the island would lose forests from the combustion."

Brick shoved aside his impatience. She'd communicated more than words with all that. Her frustration and sadness were palpable.

"It's not as simple a place as it looks, is it?" he murmured. "Your island. Your...kingdom." He cocked his head. "I suppose politics are politics, no matter if the country's got five hundred or five billion."

Her composure warmed, if only just a little. "My wise Sir Brickham is starting to get it."

A gentle chuckle spilled from him too. "Wise? I'm not sure whether to thank you or spank you for that, young lady."

"You know *my* preference on that, Sir."

He sat back a little, already recognizing the danger zone to which they'd started inching again. Goddammit, how he yearned for an updated sit rep from Oz. If Requiemme, Fox, and him were all still stuck at the hospital, he'd be rolling this little vixen over and giving her exactly what she wanted. Right. This. Second.

"Fuck," he spat, fighting his throbbing cock as much as her sultry stare. Fortunately, the same kind of comprehension crossed Jayd's face, and she pushed herself to the foot of the lounger. Though the distance helped for a second or two, he was sure that if the couch became a football field, they'd find ways to gravitate back together. At least the erotic fog was thinning from his brain, and he watched some clarity return to her regard, as well.

"You are most right, of course," she stated, revealing that all the ocean foam in her eyes had migrated to her throat. "Sometimes, I think Evrest would have an easier time governing a larger nation. He has already accomplished so much for Arcadia and is leading us toward many more opportunities for prosperity. The ideas he has for partnering with other countries in our region and beyond..." Her lips curved into a proud smile. "It is astonishing—and exciting."

Brick doubted he blinked while witnessing the transformation of her whole composure. Though her posture straightened, it was with dignity and not stress. An unmistakable gleam reentered her brilliant eyes. It led to the conclusion that he finally voiced aloud.

"You're proud of him. Your brother. King Evrest."

"I am not the only one," she asserted. "The vast majority of Arcadia's denizens have embraced the improvements to our lifestyle, despite the small changes they've meant for our land and logistical processes."

"The vast majority," Brick reiterated. "Which still leaves room for the pesky minority."

The princess swiveled around. Her chin was still high; her stare was intuitive but incisive. "I am not certain 'pesky' is an apt signifier in this case, Sir."

"Valid point, Pixie." He leaned back, supporting his head by curling his elbow up against the cushion.

"So you do know more about the Pura than their name."

"And so do you."

He prepped himself for a fresh fume from her. She was clearly dangling a line, hoping to reel in more intel about him than the scraps he'd been tossing. But when she averted her gaze, clearly more scared than incensed, his alarm gongs went off.

"Jayd?" He leaned forward again, not subtle about his scowl. "Look at me." Thank God she didn't fight him on that. "Now answer me," he instructed in a lethally low growl. "Have any of those asswipes, Carris included, touched you? Or... hurt you?"

"No." But her swift answer didn't provide him with full assurance. Perhaps the opposite. "Not yet, at least."

Oh, definitely the opposite.

"Which means what?" he bit out.

"Exactly that," she volleyed. "I am certain they are wary about even breathing my direction, especially because they are confident I shall be traded into their clutches soon enough. But Emme has heard stories from the other palais servants..."

"Stories about what?"

She averted her gaze and wetted her lips. "The *bonsuns* have... initiations," she confessed. "They make people... the women and younger men, at least... prove their loyalty to the cause in very specific ways."

"Fuck."

"Those are just the whispered rumors, of course," she inserted. "On top of their more public actions, like kidnapping Brooke and invading the Palais Arcadia itself."

"Brooke," he echoed, searching his memory for a clearer reference. "That's Brooke Valen, right? The daughter of Chase Valen?"

"She is now Brooke Cimarron." The corners of her mouth

kicked up. "If I did not clear that up, my brother Samsyn would have my head on a pike. But you have it right. She is the daughter of the senator from your country, once presumed dead at the treachery of Rune Kavill."

"The apeshit radical responsible for financing the Pura into existence."

"They have *always* been in existence," she chided. "But with Kavill's influence, they had the means to finally level up. One month, they were a few groups huddling in scattered basements. The next, they had uniforms, offices, computers, and stacks of burner cell phones." While uttering that, she inched her way back toward Brick. Along the way, she wrapped a hand around his calf like it was her life buoy in a flood. "And now they are demanding a seat on the Arcadian High Council."

"And access to the inner palais through marriage to their princess."

The second it spilled from him—and turned her gorgeous face into a collection of agonized lines—Brick winced too. Christ on dry toast, had a few years out on Whidbey watered down his aptitude for discretion?

His throat ached as he forced back a growl. *No way.* This had nothing to do with his skills and everything to do with this woman. How she made him entirely forget *himself.*

"Damn it," he uttered. "I'm sorry, Pixie. Talk about dousing the moment in acid rain."

Jayd shook her head while scooting a little closer. She dropped her hand back into her lap, as opposed to flowing farther up his leg. He should've been grateful. Instead, he gulped harder to suppress a string of profanity.

"I think we have enough rain around here already, yes?" she lightly jested. "And you are not exactly dropping a shocker on me, Brickham. To be honest, I was not completely stunned when Trystan barged into Evrest's office with his sleazy demand."

He narrowed his stare. "But the intel they dragged in with them . . . the truth about your true paternity . . . that had to be one giant dirty bomb, right?"

"No."

Her gaze, soft and sad, was now centered on his sternum.

"No?"

His reply, terse and stunned, matched the finger he nudged beneath her chin. The woman was unashamed about returning his scrutiny. She even lifted a hand to trace gentle swirls along his knuckles.

"I have sensed, my whole life, that I was different from my brothers somehow. I mean, there are the obvious ways . . ."

"The *very* obvious." He let his touch dip to the valley between her breasts.

Her face warmed in that irresistibly steamy way again, but she schooled herself enough to go on. "While the timing of Trystan's news was the absolute worst, it was not an absolute blow to me."

"And to your brothers?"

"Them neither." Her demeanor grew even more solemn. "Regrettably, as the four of us grew into adulthood, our parents' wandering interests became clearer to us."

"Well, that must've royally sucked. Pardon the wordplay," he finished in a mutter.

"Somewhat," she admitted. "But only that. Ironically, my *maimanne*'s infidelity was a direct result of our parents' arranged marriage—an embarrassing element of the antiquated system that the Pura are still fighting for."

Brick grunted. "That *really* sucks."

She sniffed, but the action was more dismissive than miserable. "I cannot even pretend to understand the Pura anymore. The blinders on their eyes are formed of Titanium and then welded onto their minds."

"Well, there's an image."

"And I want to forget it now."

"Me too." But no way could they indulge his first solution for that plan, which had his dick already pitching another tent in his pants, so he pushed away and swung to his feet. The only answer to not touching her was getting the hell away from her. "I also think we've spent enough time looking backward for one night," he stated, turning his sights out the rain-soaked window.

"Which means…what?" Luckily, Jayd sounded as relieved as she was curious. The woman was earning the acumen he first gave her credit for, picking up on the same conclusion he had. If they were going to have a reasonable conversation, they couldn't do it within caressing distance of each other.

"You'll have to help me out with that answer, Pixie." He hitched a hip high enough against the windowsill to casually fold his hands over his crotch. "How are you envisioning the rest of this trip playing out?" He absorbed the brunt of her perplexed pout before adding, "You've thought that far ahead, right? Past the reunion with your father?"

Which, by this point, stood about a ten percent chance of happening—though he wasn't about to rattle off those odds. If he was starting to fill out her personality profile right, she'd take those statistics and conclude she could bend them to her will. That might very well mean her bolting out the door before his head finished spinning.

For a long moment, it looked like she'd already jumped on that dizzying ride. She steadied herself by spreading her hold on the edge of the lounger and extending her legs out. Brick wasn't complaining. Even encased in leggings, the woman's legs were mesmerizing collisions of curves and grace. But he didn't fixate on the lust. Not when her face was still plagued with such anxiety.

"Well, I was hoping to stay here for a bit," she confessed at last. "Not *here* here. I mean, somewhere in Paris—at least until things blew over, one way or another, in Arcadia. I have already signed a lease on an apartment for a month, with the option of continuing longer."

Brick pushed all the way to his feet and nailed her with his urgent stare. "Please tell me you used an alias on that lease."

She rolled her eyes. "I am impetuous, Brickham. Not ludicrous."

"Good girl." He released an assuaged breath anyway. "So your plan was to meet your real father, then have some time getting to know him."

"My plan *is* just that," she countered. "Yes, you are right. That *is* exactly what I plan on doing."

He cocked his head, hoping it'd soften the critical bite of his reply. "Despite the real possibility that you'll walk right back into Carris's crosshairs?"

She blinked at him, confused. "Is that not why you, Oz, and Jag have joined forces?"

Oh, hell.

"Sweetheart." He straightened his posture. "We're not the *forces* of anything here. We bundled our talents for one purpose alone: to make sure the dickwad didn't get his hands on you in the first place. But if he does and can charm or bribe enough of the right brass at the PP and the airport, there's not a damn thing we'll be able to do for you."

She was quiet, absorbing all that. Too quiet. Brick hated the new squall that seemed to stall over the building, dumping rain like hysterical tears. He shifted his weight, wishing she'd just let out her own emotions, but when she raised her head, her face was frighteningly dry. Nearly impassive.

Which forced his hand like she'd whipped a glue gun. *Shit.* But one of them had to crack this conversation back open, so to hell with his comfort zone.

"Hey, I'm sorry," he offered. "That's probably not what you wanted to hear, but—"

"If everyone only attended things they *wanted* to hear, Brickham, the world would never get changed."

"Truth," he mumbled while watching her shove all the way to her feet. But beyond that, he was going to be shit for words for a minute. Maybe two. He already knew the woman was bright, clever, tough, and tenacious. But level-headed to the point of profundity? She was a *princess*, for fuck's sake. A royal darling who'd been raised on a remote *island*.

Two facts that were glaring reminders of a third. A tenet pounded into his head so many times, over so many years, he was dumbstruck it'd vanished for three tiny seconds.

The deepest truth about a person is the hardest thing to see.

It was a damn useful mantra on his list, constantly useful for keeping him neutral when interacting with assets. Though Jayd Cimarron was far from a basic *asset*, he'd gotten too damn lax about the principle. He'd slipped her beneath a whole handful of his unfair filters.

"All right, let's back things all the way up, princess." He applied the order to his own brain too. No more casting this woman in the hues of her rank, her title, or her last name. It was time to strip her from his expectations as thoroughly as he'd stripped her from her clothes. *Not* a comparison that necessarily helped right now... "If Carris wasn't a factor here, and you and Emme were still wandering incognito through the city, what were your eventual goals for that scenario?"

For a long second, Jayd didn't react. As soon as she restarted a strum of fingers along the lounger's headboard, he knew the question was at least getting some deeper processing from her beautiful brain.

"Perhaps that is also why I needed the time," she finally stated. "To figure all that out, I mean. To figure *myself* out."

But she wasn't even finished with the words before a harsh V formed between her eyebrows. As soon as her aquas turned the shade of moonless midnight, Brick broke back in. "All right. What's wrong with that?"

"What is *right* with it?" she retorted, flinging up a hand. "There are billions of people across this globe, suffering in awful and real ways, and I am standing here swan-diving into my navel, worried about 'who I really am'?" After gesticulating the air quotes, she turned her hand and facepalmed herself. "You hear it, do you not? That loud scream of how banal and privileged I sound?"

"Wait. What about how *normal*?" Brick returned. "Maybe even how human?" He landed the last part before she could push out her huff. "Okay, I get it. You're a princess—"

"*Was* a princess."

He narrowed his eyes. Rolling them would've been a waste of time and effort. "You were raised with the expectation that you'd be wearing a crown for the rest of your life. We can agree on that, right? But that doesn't mean that at the age of..."

"Twenty-four."

Shit. She was only twenty-four? Granted, he'd slept with younger, though it had all been legal and consensual—and so damn illusional. He saw behind all those girls' jaded façades, knowing the "maturity" was just an act. But Jayd Cimarron wasn't pulling an act. She really did have the sentience and conscience of someone older.

After the initial jolt of that extra intel, he embraced it for the logical helpmate it could be. "Right. Twenty-four. At the age of twenty-four, crowned or commoner, you're not expected to have the cosmic eight ball memorized. Hell, with the wild ride you've been on lately, I'd be surprised the eight ball *itself* wasn't rolling to the corner for some fetal position time." He reveled in her awkward little snicker, complete with a punctuating snort, before going on. "So, yeah. Fine. You've had the grace of education, enlightenment, servants, and space. But you also had advisors, administrators, handlers, and PR gurus, all feeding you ideas about who you should be. But as soon as your birthright got ripped out from beneath you, all those concepts got blown to shit."

Jayd wasn't giggling at him anymore. For several long beats, all she did was blink. Then for several more, she did it as iridescent drops rolled down her cheeks. "That . . . is *exactly* how it feels."

"Then cut yourself some slack for the rest," Brick murmured. "You're a human being, not a machine that can simply be reprogrammed."

She absorbed his assertion with a hesitant tug of teeth on her lower lip. He'd barely recovered from fixating on that hypnotizing sight, when more diamond-perfect tears appeared on her lashes. And that did it. So much for his brain supplying a superb grand finale for his pep talk.

Fortunately, the woman herself broke their stillness. "Well. I *was* right in the first place."

Brick approached her with slow but steady steps. "Right about what?" His tone borrowed from the small smile that twitched at her lips.

"About you being so wise, Sir."

With a gruff grumble, he hitched his hold to her hip. He repeated the sound while drawing her back against him. "That's not wisdom, Pixie. That's just some hard life lessons sticking to my thick cranium."

She lifted a hand in tandem with her soft, searching gaze. As she spread her fingers up from his nape, she whispered, "Well, I am thankful to the Creator for knowing you would need the extra layers."

He slid her a skeptical look. "That so?"

"Of course." She hit right back with a wallop of conviction. "They helped keep you alive, yes?"

"Along with my wily friends and my killer good looks? Sure, I'll concur."

"Well, friends and looks only take you so far." Her comment was as literal as how she'd taken his. It was so adorable, he couldn't summon the nerve to correct her. "The rest is completely up to you."

"I'll concur with that too." He infused it with genuine warmth before adding half a smile. Goddamn. This little sprite in her earnest mode... She was so endearing. Entrancing. Extraordinary. "Especially because I've been inspired by a certain pixie with a lot of gumption of her own."

He was happy when the edges of her mouth kicked up. He ditched the feeling when the trend didn't continue up into her gaze. That burgeoning sheen still dominated the aqua depths, threatening to spill out again.

"I am nothing to be inspired by, Brickham," she grated.

"And I definitely don't concur with that one, Miss Cimarron."

"Says the thick-skulled warrior to the crownless princess?"

"Which basically makes us He-Man and She-Ra."

"He who and she who?"

He shook his head and chuckled. "American goodness nobody had the sense to show you during college." He tucked in and kissed the top of her head. "I'll have to send you some video links when we're not standing in the middle of a three-way Venn chart."

She didn't demand an explanation for that one. There was full comprehension in the stare she raised to meet his. They really were in the tiny triangle at the center of destiny's three-way, unable to make a move until they could contain the threat from Carris, locate the elusive LaBarre, or get a clear decision on Requiemme's condition.

Since there was a next-to-nothing chance on any of those right now, Brick opted for the golden opportunity he *did* have. Holding her as close as he could, for as long as he could. And this time, making sure to remember every detail of how it felt. Her perfect pliability as she leaned into him. Her delicious scent, like honey and amber on a summer breeze, filling his senses. But most of all, the assurance of her sweet breath on the base of his neck, spreading that warmth through his entire chest.

This was definitely one for his lifetime hard drive. One day, maybe he'd be telling his grandkids about the night he comforted a princess in a shabby Paris apartment and how she made him feel a little bit more whole again because of it.

Grandkids.

Okay, there was the best joke of the day. Because that was ever going to happen, yeah? Because he'd have so much to offer the tikes, right? Not to mention, the tike who'd have to come before them. The kid he'd be lucky not to fuck up before kindergarten.

No. Just no.

He'd settle for making a difference elsewhere. In moments like these, with a singular human like this, with a life ahead of her that he could help improve in his small way.

Small things added to the good of the world too.

His own body, now thrumming with heat after the ignition of her breath, was living proof.

And a point could never have too much proof…

Or a fire too much heat…

Or an attraction too many kisses…

He couldn't get in the concurrence for that one fast enough.

The same way he couldn't sweep his head down too quickly or push his mouth against hers with enough urgency.

And then add his lusty moan to hers.

And then twirl his thirsty tongue along hers.

And fill his spread hands with her luscious curves. The gorgeous swells of her hips. The enticing globes of her ass. Where to next? He needed to feel more. He needed to feel it naked…

"Brickham."

Her sigh, vibrating the stubble along his jaw, betrayed that her thoughts were damn near on the same page. Thank fuck.

"Yeah, Pixie?" he rasped. "What do you want? Tell me."

She sighed again. The sound hit him like an angel singing Mozart. Christ, what she did to him, even with simple air running past her lips . . .

There was more music now. But it wasn't her next sigh. It wasn't even close.

Just as quickly, the French pop song snippet ended. Brick nuzzled his lips to his sprite's ear, hoping all she wanted to hear were angelic trumpets as well.

The tinny cell phone song started again.

Goddammit.

"Oh! That is *my* phone!" she exclaimed.

Brick groused the curse aloud this time but loosened his embrace and let her step free. Correction: she bolted free before sprinting into the next room. Along the way, she muttered something to herself. Not cuss words. Brick could recognize that much.

He should have tried harder to figure it out.

Because it was too late to do anything once he latched on to exactly what she whispered so excitedly, over and over again.

"It is him. It is *him*. Oh, *Paipanne*, you are truly calling me!"

CHAPTER ELEVEN

Once she located her burner cell phone, still tucked away in the crossbody bag she had tossed onto the kitchen counter, Jayd traded her excited mantra for a pained huff.

"Another text," she mumbled, though a fresh thrill jumped up her pulse as she opened the message from Louis LaBarre. In the meantime, Brickham emerged from the bedroom—with *no* extra thrills to be had in his demeanor.

"What does he want?"

She crunched a full frown. "Perhaps to be spoken of without a growl before a person has even met him?"

Her scowl could not compete with Brickham's. For now, she would let him have the win. She did grasp his point of view, after all. To him, her quest to connect with LaBarre had nearly landed her in a pile of garbage, losing her virginity to the likes of Gervais or Remy. And Creator have mercy, she had no legitimate stand there. He was right. Her enthusiasm had made her careless and then reckless. She was not about to chug that double shot of stupidity again.

But he had no way of knowing that. That was blatantly clear by his frown, which he had clearly borrowed from an eighteenth-century vampire hunter. But his tone was closer to civil as he prompted, "What. Does. He. Want?"

Jayd could not help a small smile as she read the message.

My beautiful fille, my deepest apologies. I

*had an unavoidable business matter, and
it ran late. I am beside myself with grief to
have missed you, my darling daughter!*

She turned the device, showing the message directly to Brick. "Wow. Beside himself, huh?" His snort was soft but derisive. "Well, that makes everything just fine, doesn't it?"

She pulled the device back with a fierce snap. "People do have real lives, Brickham. Lives that are filled with things like work and meetings and priorities."

"Sure they do."

It was not his swift reply that kept her on edge. It was the urbanity in his voice, so smooth and controlled—a total mismatch to the gathering storms in his eyes.

"You have not even met the man!" she fumed.

"That makes two of us, doesn't it?"

She glowered, already bracing for the argument he was prefacing. It would be all of Emme's contentions on repeat. Why had LaBarre not bothered to contact her himself for twenty-four years? Why had he been so easily convinced to shove off to Paris instead of staying in Arcadia to be near her? How had he not missed her? Wondered about her? Made any attempt to see her? Or had he done *all* those things only to be thwarted by some Arcadian red tape she knew nothing about?

Or something worse than that?

Had Ardent Cimarron, the man she had called *paipanne* her entire life, purposely kept her from the man who truly deserved the title?

She hated thinking that. Even more, she hated believing—*knowing*—that it was a real possibility. But she also recognized that she was leaping to many unproved suppositions, which were festering into outright judgments. Every story in life had at least two sides. That number grew when the tale was dirtied with politics, power, public images, and the daunting job of keeping a country prosperous.

"Unlike most of the world"—she jumped her brows directly his way—"I refuse to color in lines that haven't been clearly drawn yet."

"Then that makes two of us once more." Another answer that was too quick and sure for her comfort, especially because of the follow-up he obviously had at the ready. "The same salt you're tossing on prejudging him, I'm pouring on insta-trusting him." He fortified his stance, officially becoming the most impossible thing in the room to ignore. "That brings us to the fun zone of finding a magic middle ground."

Force of nature. The man earned every word of it, along with a new add-on, once he finished his directive with a nod at her phone—

Which jingled with a new text from LaBarre.

*I will never forgive myself if I cannot hold
you at last. 24 years is too long to wait.
Are you still available now?*

She did not dare even hover a thumb over the screen. While Brickham's mandate had likely been dunked in the stuff before it hit his lips, she was compelled to see his logic. Her blind credence in LaBarre's texts—the only form of communication he seemed comfortable with, after her many attempts at a phone conversation—were what landed her in trouble before. But if Brick thought she was going to let him run five levels of security on her phone before she even responded to her father, he had a glaring awakening coming.

Still, negotiations had to start somewhere. She kicked off theirs by pivoting the phone again and letting the gorgeous giant dip in for a read.

At once, Brickham's face tightened. She indulged in a few seconds of beguilement at the sight. The person who fought like a winter storm, kissed like a burst of spring sun, and screwed like a summer tidal wave was now the guy resembling a protective autumn oak from the Wood Between the Worlds. Never had she enjoyed a lesson about the four seasons so much—even when they got a new overlay of his prickly growling.

"I assume I'll get nowhere in saying this isn't a great idea?"

Preparing for the man's contention was a smart idea, after all. The groundwork made it possible to slip him a serene smile. "That is an accurate assumption, Sir."

Her spin on the honorific earned her his flared nostrils and pursed lips. That was before he took a looming step into her personal space. Her senses crackled all over again. Would he correct her about it now? And in what ways? He was now back within stomping distance of his unused kitchen toys . . .

"Tough toenails," he went ahead and bit out. "I'm saying it anyway. *Not* a great idea, princess." He barely snorted when she took a turn at the glare—as well as the temptation to fetch the tongs and the tenderizer for her own evil fun. "But it's not a totally crappy one, either."

"Brickham." She launched into the protest before he was done, rolling her shoulders back. "You have the right to register your views about this, but as I have made clear, I am a grown woman. Despite what everyone thinks, maybe even you included, I have the capability to think for myself. I can also—" Her hands, which she parked on her hips for all of three seconds, fell limp. "Uh . . . huh? Okay—it's—*what*?"

Goodbye, autumn tree. Hello, brilliant winter sky, so bright and blue in his eyes, as he flashed a congenial smirk. "I said that it's not a completely crappy idea."

"You . . . did?" She recovered quickly, folding her arms with take-charge energy. "Ah well, yes. Of course you did."

"Meeting with LaBarre sooner than later means Carris has less time to coordinate any interventions."

"True." She had rarely agreed with anything more. Besides, this was a good thing. Very good. The *middle ground* he mentioned them working for.

"And since Requiemme's safe with Oz and Jagger, I can be fully focused on watching over you."

For a long second, her jaw worked against empty air. "Errrr . . . You want to come with me?"

"Sweetheart, you're lucky I'm not demanding to go to the bathroom with you by this point."

And there was definitely one more for the *truth* column, though she refrained from vocalizing it. There were too many other logistics—good ones now—playing laser tag in her brain. Her father had not stood her up! He still wanted to see her, to hold her! Even better, she would be going to him with a one-man security team in place. Brickham was capable of filling in for at least four Arcadian soldiers. That simple confidence already raised her radiance. If she had to do this without Emme by her side, Maximillian Brickham was the next best choice. Perhaps better . . .

She shook her head fast, banishing the musing. Emme and her poor leg needed every good thought and prayer she could spare right now. But she could send her friend a heart brimming with love and still have enough to shower on her father. She even unfurled a wide smile Brickham's way, while holding her burner up with a lighthearted wiggle. "So what do I tell him, Sir?"

This time, the man received the designation with better spirits. Brickham quirked a corner of his mouth before offering, "That depends. Are you asking for advice, Pixie, or still seeking permission?"

"Is one going to get me a different answer over the other?"

"Probably." His smirk remained, but his scrutiny darkened, implying his subtext. *Definitely.*

"Then what would your *advice* be?" She winked while doubling down on the emphasis and welcomed a kaleidoscope of butterflies to her belly when Brick's gaze smoldered in return. But all too quickly, he was back to his all-business overlay.

"If you're determined to do this, then I suggest someplace public. A café or coffee house near a crowded public area. *Not* the Très Particulier again."

"Why not?" While she had glaring reasons to avoid the place for the rest of her days, she was curious about his adamancy. And on a selfish note, she was riveted by the man when he took his testosterone showers.

"For one, I don't want the remotest chance of again running into our friends Gervais and Remy," he replied. "Snakes have a tendency to slither back to the same rocks."

"Exceptional point." She nodded with practiced poise. "And secondly?"

"It's not ideal to give anyone a clue, however tiny, about where you're staying. That even includes your pops."

He accompanied the explanation with a walk across the

room. After stopping before the bay window at the other side, he braced his hands on either side of the aperture. With him next to it, the big window now looked like a dollhouse feature.

"Third, it's best to have an environment with a lot of escape possibilities." The whole line of his upper back, from one outstretched elbow to the other, visibly tensed. "If things do go sideways—don't freak; that's a big *if*—it's good to have a number of escape routes. Access to taxis or a metro line, perhaps a few restaurants with easy back doors..."

"Also exceptional points," she interjected. "For which I have the perfect answer."

"Nothing's perfect in this world except your orgasm scream, Pixie. But let's hear that brilliant idea anyway."

Once more, her mouth fell open and danced with the air. She waited for her aggravation to bloom into anger at the smug slickster, but all she could do was laugh.

"Well, brilliance is surely an aggrandizement, Mr. Brickham. But if we go with my idea, perhaps I shall be rewarded with a few fun sounds from you as well."

"Fun...sounds?" he uttered, banishing his smirk. "Is this where I start to be afraid?"

Another laugh trotted off her lips. "I said *fun*, did I not?"

"Woman, your idea of fun is hitching a ride on a fishing rig across the Mediterranean and then chopping off your hair so you can Jamie Bond your way into Paris freaking France."

"Then maybe you had better take a few memos, Mr. Moneypenny."

The man dug a foot at the floor—exactly as if he were kicking a microphone her way. Or maybe demolishing the thing? Either way, Jayd enjoyed her girl boss moment as the towering man returned her grin with a stare that nearly took her breath away. He was grinning now too. His twin blues sparkled, the color an arresting match to the glittering rain spatters on the glass.

"Christ," he finally laugh-mumbled, shaking his head. "Now I really am afraid."

★ ★ ★

Her suggestion was actually a good one. A damn good one. The Place Blanche, within walking distance of the apartment, likely would've made Brick's own short list for an ideal connection point with LaBarre.

Six streets converged in the area, which was one of two plazas along the wide and well-lit Boulevard de Clichy. It had its own metro station and even a Starbucks. But its most important feature was the Machine du Moulin Rouge, which ensured they'd be surrounded by a few thousand tourists who'd just attended the club's famous cancan performance. At least he hoped . . .

The tourists didn't let him down.

Nor did the colorfully clad hipsters in line for the dance club a block away.

Nor did the equally vibrant Moulin performers, still in their high feathered headdresses and flowing boa bustles.

Okay, so they had a lot of company. Too damn much, if Brick's nervous system were going to be consulted about the matter—which it wasn't. He shut that shit down faster than the frazzled mother who went rapid-fire feral on her child for running across the raised grate in the middle of the plaza. When that didn't work, the woman held the kid's ice cream cone over a trash bin. Shit. French mothers had girl-balls of steel. And now he wanted ice cream.

Instead of dessert, he promised his synapses something better, perhaps to the tune of a double whisky, when they were done with this party. Wasn't the same as one of his friendly little pills, but he'd only brought one with him at the beginning of the day and burned through it before connecting with Oz and Fox. The rest of the happy little fuckers were having a party of their own back in his room at the Ritz, where he didn't dare take Jayd tonight. If he were Trystan Carris and doing a kick-ass job of underestimating Jayd, as the guy probably was, the city's elegant icon would top the list of his stalking locations.

But for the next hour—maybe less, if he was lucky—it was his job to stay watchful, diligent, dauntless, *calm*. For now, panic couldn't be an operative word in his vocabulary.

Especially when his first priority was keeping up with a hyperkinetic sprite.

"JD." He'd deemed the initials necessary for addressing her in public, just in case someone recognized her. Thankfully, no one had even sniffed her direction yet. "This isn't a timed treasure hunt, okay?"

"Says who?" It was only half a joke, as her searching gaze and chilled handclasp told him. Nervously, she tugged him one way and then the next in front of the concrete riser at the plaza's center, until he brought her to a firm stop by gently twisting her fingers.

"Says me." He scooped an arm around her waist and secured her back to his front. He pulled her in even closer before sneaking an affectionate kiss to her nape. For one wonderful second, he closed his eyes and pretended they were just another pair of lovers out in the City of Light. He mentally changed his name to Pierre, and hers to Giselle.

A blast of Halsey from the open disco doors crashed him back to reality. Though he scowled and straightened, he thanked fate for the wake-up. This was no time for quixotic fantasy.

This was time for being watchful. Diligent. Dauntless. *Calm.*

So far, so good. He practically preened, acknowledging the controlled thrum of his heart rate and the steady steel of his gaze. He hadn't felt more present or alert for a mission since the early days, before the spec ops fun had turned into the black ops gore. But he wasn't delusional. This wasn't a happy patrol through Baghdad or Kabul. He wasn't here to play guardian angel for the recon guys. This was a much different gig, in which he was already two strikes down for advantages. One, he was only packing a boot knife and a borrowed meat tenderizer from the safe house's kitchen. Two, he wasn't keeping the sweep for a couple of trained soldiers who'd know what to do if they were ambushed. The princess, with her default of instant trust and her obsession with LaBarre, remained a prime candidate for predatory dickbags.

Not on his watch.

Contingent, of course, on him keeping pace with the woman.

How the hell was such a diminutive thing capable of going Mach 5 in those stilt boots? Every step she took was a new attack on Brick's soldier Zen. If they got through this without her taking a faceplant on the pavement, he might start believing in miracles again.

The great cyberspace gods must have read his mind, because Jayd halted the second her back pocket buzzed. She had to tug a little to get the device out, which gave Brick the ideal excuse to ogle her ass a little longer. He wasn't a shred sorry. This woman's pert backside belonged in the Louvre. Better yet, in his greedy hands.

Another explosion of music from the disco. Another reality blast for his brain. He took advantage of the mental reboot, ignoring flirty flashes from one of the Moulin dancers, before stepping up next to Jayd.

"Papa LaBarre?"

The question was practically rhetorical. Jayd nodded without lifting her sights from the screen.

"He says he is here," she rushed out, breathy with excitement. "He is at the pub on the corner of Clichy and Avenue Rachel."

"Down *there*?" He stabbed a finger down the street, past the Moulin's big red planters and famous windmill. His scowl earned him a similarly stubborn stare from the princess.

"It is but another block, Brickham," she stated softly. "But we did walk several of them to get here, after all the chaos of today." She turned and placed a tender hand over his chest. "I do understand if you are tired and need to take a—"

"I'm not tired," he growled, pushing aside what her compassion did to him. He almost wished she'd have gone straight to pity mode. That shit would've rankled him to the point of macho-stupid bravado, and he'd be already leading the way down the boulevard to the pub. "I'm fucking jumpy. You told him to meet you *here*."

"So you think that a block's difference adds up to a conspiracy?" Jayd snapped. "Or could it be as simple as him knowing the place and wanting to have a comfortable environment to welcome me in?"

Before she was done, Brick was snorting through his ire.

Even after what had happened in the Particulier's alley, the woman was openly campaigning for the lost lamb of the year award. She wanted this meeting to happen so badly, she'd follow any shepherd who promised it. Yep, even over a damn cliff.

Which meant, even if a bunch of her beloved saints flew in to back him up, he wasn't going to win this little skirmish.

"Let's go," he grumbled, grabbing her hand with a brisk swoop. His gait was defined by the same raging resignation, but Jayd kept up without argument. It took gritted effort to stay focused on their path up the street, including all the nooks and crannies in which Carris could be hiding, instead of the woman's resilience in matching his steps. He'd bet his left testicle that she looked damn fine doing it too. Those impossibly high heels, carrying those incredibly curvy legs...

Focus, asshole.

Nooks. Crannies. Alleys. Doorways.

Focus!

He kept them to the wide sidewalk in the center of Clichy's median, where he could at least cross alleys and doorways off his checklist. He also didn't have to worry about the tacky tourist gift stores that lined the street, either—though a couple of kinky toy boutiques certainly caught the corner of his eye. He was in paranoid recon mode, not masquerading as a monk. Thank God for that tiny favor from fate. But under any other circumstances...

But this wasn't any other circumstances.

Nothing pounded the point better than his nerve endings, battling to simultaneously stab through his skin as they hurried into the crosswalk in front of the pub. The place was loud and proud about its Irish theme, which he counted as a consolation prize from the universe. His whisky reward might be closer than he originally assumed.

But first things first. Like staying way the hell on top of his game to ensure this little rendezvous didn't go tits up. To make that happen, his job was to make sure a lot of other things didn't. Things like Jayd being recognized by anyone in the place—most of all, a certain Arcadian asshole on the hunt for his missing property.

He could've done without that thought, which had him seeing red all over again. More importantly, not seeing the situation—or Carris—as clearly as he needed to. In any other time or place, he even wondered if he and Carris would've been buddies. The brotherhood of warriors surpassed a lot of borders, branches, and flags on shoulders—until a soldier gave in and drank the Kool-Aid of radicalization. After that, all bets were off. One wondered if they'd ever see their friend on the sunshiny side of society again or watch them die on national TV after they took hostages to make their point.

Trystan Carris definitely had a point to make.

And thankfully—or perhaps not—Brick knew what it was. More accurately, whom the man was hellbent on using to make it. The knowledge brought him his greatest advantage but his hugest weakness.

This time, he really cared about the asset.

No.

He'd cared about her back when they'd escaped Gervais by taking cover in a kink dungeon. That designation had faded once he slid his fingers into her pussy. Then even more when he stroked her into a stunning orgasm. Then even more when she let him shackle her to a kitchen cupboard and slide his body into hers. And once he'd spilled himself inside her . . .

Yeah. Caring for her was just a starter ingredient in this crazy cake.

So what the hell was he calling the dough now?

And did he really have an extra five seconds, let alone the five *hours* he likely needed, to unpack that answer?

Thank fuck for excuses that were as well-timed as they were solid. While letting the gift horse gallop through his mind and trample the Jayd-themed mush, he reached for the pub's heavy door and waited for her to enter. Less than three steps inside the place—a predictable amalgam of dark woods, green trims, and Celtic signs—he was right back by her side. If he could've gotten away with ordering her all the way behind him, that'd be happening already, but he spared himself the effort. Some mission objectives were simply impossible.

He focused on chalking up the positives so far. It was Sunday night, soon to be Monday morning, a fact honored by the pub's mellow population. Secondly, Jayd wasn't taking advantage of the light crowd and tearing across the room in a this-is-twenty-four-years-too-late fervor. Not that she *wouldn't* be soon, but he could breathe easy for now. Of course, acknowledging his reprieve meant he'd probably just jinxed it...

"Daughter? *Ma fille chérie?*"

Jinx.

He was certain fate itself showed up to laugh the word at him, though Brick barely cared once Jayd broke loose with a similar sound. As one of the Irish slang signs on the wall said, *Savage.* Perfect fit. The woman's laugh *was* savage: a mixture of breath and volume capable of knifing through a man's guts until they'd bled their vitality down to his balls. Yeah, even in a situation like this. Even when said man stood by as said woman repeated the laugh for *another* man.

All right, so said *other man* happened to be her father.

And yeah, Brick jotted that mental note down in permanent ink.

One look at the man, even before Jayd stumbled toward him, was all it took to figure it out. The genetics were all there, so blatant they were startling. As daughter and father clasped hands and stared at each other for the first time, Brick used his imagination to add in longer hair, a high-end shave, and a pair of breasts for Louis. With those enhancements, it would look like the princess was peering into a mirror. LaBarre's prominent cheekbones were the same. So were his high forehead and tapered chin. Even the man's posture was similar to Jayd's, full of restless energy.

But all of those factors were runners-up to the ultimate revelation.

LaBarre's eyes.

It wasn't just their color, which matched Jayd's arresting aqua down to the opalescent specks. It was their settings, the deep wells becoming perfect cradles for ungodly long lashes and exotically tapered hoods.

But if he'd learned anything from years of deep recon sweeps, the first glance rarely counted as the right perception.

He didn't want to be right about that—but as Jayd hauled the man close for a tearful grip of a hug, he already sensed that he was.

It wasn't the certainty about LaBarre being Jayd's actual papa. It was everything else they were supposed to be accepting about this meeting. Factors like the man's insistence on this exact venue, when it seemed LaBarre hadn't been here before either. And why did the man look like he'd just crawled out of bed and thrown on clothes from the floor, when he claimed he had a business engagement earlier?

But the biggest tell, just like before, was what Brick observed in LaBarre's eyes.

Correction: what he *didn't* see there.

Like alertness. Or comprehension. Or anything beyond surface-level joy. No, not even that. The man looked at Jayd but didn't see her. He was standing here, but his mind was clearly parked somewhere else. Like Ohio.

But Jayd noticed none of that. And why should she? The woman had turned her life upside down and her heart inside out to make this moment happen. But she'd learned about LaBarre less than a week ago. To be fair, maybe he'd been fantasizing about this for nearly twenty-five years. The guy had the complete right to cash in his dazed and confused card.

"*Paipanne.*" It was barely a whisper, but Jayd stamped both syllables with absolute certainty. Her shoulders shook as she crumpled against the man, though Brick refrained from stepping over once she clamped her arms around LaBarre's neck. In true pixie form, the woman wept like a flower but had the strength of a rainforest vine. "Creator be praised. *Mon merveilleux père.*"

"*Père,*" the man echoed, as if forming the word for the first time. "*Paipanne.* That means . . ."

"Yes," she filled in, voice strangled with feeling. The wet spot on LaBarre's shirt started to grow. "That means I have finally found you. That *you* have finally found *me.*"

"Ah. Yes, of course." The man was definitely still back in Ohio, commenting as if confirming he wanted fries instead of onion rings. "You're so . . . pretty."

The compliment, despite its detachment, was a new turbo

switch for Jayd's tear ducts. But that wasn't the only punched button here. Brick flipped a knob inside himself too. One he hadn't twisted so high in a long time.

A switch labeled *Suspicion*.

"*Merderim, Paipanne,*" she said with laughing underlines. "You are quite dashing, as well."

Brick managed—barely—to pull back his bugged glare. Dashing? Was she kidding? More and more, he likened the man to a walking MRU packet. He was pale and thin, even for a dude who likely skipped meals during creative jags. His pupils were like dehydrated peas. His breaths were erratic, as if someone had just jangled a remember-to-inhale bell in his ear.

Clearly, Jayd saw none of that. Her massive rose-colored glasses were firmly in place. Would Brick have expected—or wanted—it any other way?

He didn't waste time answering himself. It was easier to put it into action instead. He did so by finally taking that step, which placed his chest flush to Jayd's head, and reached over with his palm extended. "Monsieur LaBarre. *Bonsoir*. Name's Max Brickham. Should I get us a table?" Though he wondered why the man hadn't snagged one already. If the pub was closing off that section for the night, why had the guy insisted they meet here?

No answers on that from LaBarre. He glanced over like Brick was merely a moth buzzing by. The man was fully fixated—or whatever his glassy eyes and simpering smile meant—on Jayd. He leaned closer to her, like *he* was the moth and she was his hypnotic light.

"You are ... really my daughter?" he murmured, barely audible even in this laid-back room.

"And are you really thinking with a full deck, man?" For that, Brick got a princess-sized backhand in the chest. But just when he thought Jayd might repeat the retaliation, she returned her grip to LaBarre instead.

"Yes," she rasped. "I really am. It is nice to meet you. Wait. *No*." She laughed out the negation. "It is not just nice. It is amazing. And wonderful. Oh, *Paipanne!*"

Her effusion washed over LaBarre like oil over water. How Brick wished the comparison was an exaggeration, but that wasn't the case. The man literally stood there like a dormant oil spill, slightly curious about why a thousand tears were aggravating his surface gloss.

"*Paipanne*," the man finally echoed. "That sounds so familiar..."

"It's Arcadian," Brick pointed out. "You probably heard a lot of words like it when you were there."

LaBarre blinked slowly. "When I was where?"

"Arcadia." Jayd supplied it this time, though she nearly extended it into a question. "You remember it, do you not, Father? Arcadia. It is an island. And while you were there—"

"Arcadia," LaBarre blurted, detaching his hand from hers to rub his temple. "It is...an island? I was on an island once..."

"Yes," she said, cracking something in Brick's chest with her blatant, desperate hope. "You were. And you met my *maimanne* there. The queen."

"The queen." He smiled, though he kept the kneading fingers at his forehead. "So that means you *are* the princess?"

She laughed again, though her emotion was strained. Nervous. Forced. "I—ermmm—well, yes, I am, at least still on paper."

"*Magnifique*," the man exclaimed. "Yes, that is good. A

very good thing to know."

"I suppose." Jayd tilted her head and crunched her brows. "But was it not something you knew already, Father?"

"I'll second that." Brick pivoted forward a little, saving the brunt of his incisive stare for Monsieur Peas-For-Eyes. "Do you really not know why they disappeared you out of Arcadia, buddy?"

La Barre jerked his head up. "They did what? To who?"

"Christ on sourdough."

"What?" Jayd countered, joining her father in the scrutinizing stare. "Brickham?"

He tugged her back by a few steps, not bothering to beg an excuse from LaBarre. He doubted the guy would notice, and he was right.

"Your father... I'm sorry, sweetheart, but he isn't right," he murmured for her ears only. "And I don't have a good feeling about it."

She made a dismissive hiss through her teeth. "Not right?" she spewed. "Just because he is not groveling before me or obeying royal protocols?"

He arched his brows. "Then that would land me in the same basket, wouldn't it?"

"Indeed it would."

He disregarded her coy smirk, focusing on the parts of his psyche that were giving him some damn weird vibes. Uncomfortable wasn't the right word. Even suspicious wasn't the right descriptor anymore. He'd leapfrogged to the next level—into outright unnerved.

"All right, this is feeling bad, Pixie." He contradicted himself by flashing an all's-cool grin toward LaBarre, just in case the man was more lucid than he assumed. He continued through his painfully gritted teeth. "You know it too. Don't you?"

The question almost wasn't worth tagging on. He already saw his answer, blatant across the gorgeous sprite's face. There was only so much of the man's behavior she'd be able to depreciate with excuses like nerves, anxiety, and the pressures of his day. That margin was thinning by the second.

"It is fine," she finally said, though her fingertips hadn't stopped pounding her thighs and her teeth hadn't ceased worrying her lips. "*He* is fine."

"Right," Brick mumbled. "Sure he is."

She folded her arms. "Do not sound so thrilled about that for my sake."

Before he could form a comeback about how he'd be more thrilled if they found an inconspicuous table or got out of here completely, LaBarre chose to zero in on his daughter once more.

"So . . . you are my daughter. And you are a princess."

"So she's already informed you, Monsieur."

He was terse but diplomatic, though probably more of one than the other. Jayd's fresh whack to his chest confirmed as much.

"I apologize, *Paipanne*," she stated. "Brickham has had a long day *and* night."

"Ah, yes." Again, LaBarre's reply was like lip gloss. Pretty for two seconds before it dissolved into a shiny mess. "I understand that part. Of course I do. Long days. Scary nights." His whole form shook with a violent tremor. "Scary, *scary* nights."

"Oh, no." Jayd swept back over to the man, not stopping until she had him in another tight embrace. "*Paipanne*. Is everything all right? By the stars, please do not cry." She swung her head around. "Brickham?"

The only answer he could muster was a half-assed shrug. He wanted it to be more, but he was confusion's bitch right now. She'd refused to heed his warning, but three seconds of LaBarre's maudlin turn had her boarding the something's-not-right train? But this wasn't a time for pouting egos, especially his. At least she was on the tracks with him now. He could work with that if this went sideways and he had to.

Fuck, how he hoped he didn't have to.

Jayd went on with her comforting chantings for her father, but it seemed like she was consoling the inconsolable. Yet just when Brick thought she'd abandon the quest for good, the man moved back by a small step. He gripped her shoulders with shuddering need and impaled her searching gaze with his red-rimmed one.

"You *are* a princess," he finally said. "A kindhearted one. I can already tell."

For the first time since they'd walked in, Jayd fidgeted with discernible discomfort. "I have done my best to be just a good *person*, Father. My title has nothing to do with my character."

"But it has everything to do with your gold . . . yes?"

Well, shit.

Brickham refrained—barely—from spitting it out loud. From the second he'd confessed his suspicions to Jayd, he'd started a mental list of subjects that could qualify for this-is-bad status. The Cimarrons and their royal wealth were up there in the rankings. But his preparation didn't diminish a speck of his agony at watching Jayd answer her own wake-up call about it.

"What does my gold have to do with anything, Monsieur?"

Monsieur this time. Not *Paipanne*. But again, not a victory for Brick. Just a profound wash of sadness, watching LaBarre slip from the pedestal she'd so carefully constructed. But that was the thing about shrines. They were usually occupied by statues, not humans, for a reason.

"My beautiful, miraculous daughter."

As LaBarre reached for Jayd's hands again, the man looked clear, connected, and present. Well, imagine that. Brick could only grunt out a retort since he *had* imagined. His visions were based in a solid chunk of reality. He'd seen this behavior over and over again. Once upon a time, he'd damn near *become* this behavior.

"*Paipanne?*" Crap. She was back to *that* already. "What is it? What do you need?"

The man had the decency to turn red, but not the dignity to stop his new plea. "I ... have an injury, princess. My leg ... I fell off a scaffold, you see ... and it gives me so much pain. My medications are expensive. But they said you might be able to help so I can afford some more. They said—"

"Who?" Jayd pounced on the interjection a second before Brick could. "*Who* said this to you, Father? And why can you not have your doctor presc—"

"Fuck my doctor!" The man dropped his hands and recoiled. "He knows nothing about what I am going through. *Nothing!* All he says is that I'll get addicted and eventually die. He has no idea. If I have to live like this, then I *do* wish to be dead instead."

"Stop!" Jayd stalked at him like a Super Hornet off a carrier catapult. "Wh-What are you saying? Do you *hear* what you're saying?"

But the man hardly heard what *she* was saying. The whole

time she spoke, LaBarre was a puddle of kowtowing smiles and forlorn whimpers. "Please, my princess. Please. I need you. I need you!"

As every second passed, it was clear what the man had really come here for. A sole purpose. To hit up his own daughter for only one thing. And as that minute developed into another, with Jayd battling her father's desperation with her own, a tidy pile of deductions started stacking up for Brick.

Too tidy.

He was silent and steady about inserting himself between Jayd and LaBarre. He was steadier—and unrelenting—about studying the man, if only to satisfy his own harrowing hunch about what had even gotten LaBarre through the door tonight.

He started with three simple words.

"What is it?"

LaBarre jutted his chin. *Good boy.* He was coherent enough to hear the difference in Brick's query as opposed to Jayd's. But he still stammered back, "Wh-What is wh-what?"

"Cut it," Brick snapped. "I've had some peeks into the hole, buddy. I know what it looks like." He rocked back on a heel, taking care that his size didn't intimidate the man into full silence. But he didn't hold back on folding his arms and tightening his scowl. "Tell me, damn it. What is it, LaBarre? Oxy? Hydro? Tramadol? Morphine? All of the above?"

He added the last of it when his list seemed to affect the guy like a kid listening to Willie Wonka's newest candy creations. But to his credit, LaBarre fought the allure with a coiled cringe—for the better part of ten seconds.

"I'm getting better!" the man finally protested. "I *am*." He scrabbled a shaky hand through his rat's nest hair. "I just need a little help right now." He lowered that hand by reaching out to Jayd with it. "Just a little help . . . to make it through . . ."

"Until what?" Brick spat. "Your next payoff from the Arcadians?"

He could've sliced out his tongue for the slip, which had no validation other than his baldest instincts. If LaBarre really had been shuttled out of the kingdom so as to stay quiet about Jayd's heritage, it made sense that the guy would've demanded healthy compensation for it.

"Excuse me?" Jayd's words were the stuff of etiquette, but her jolting glare wasn't. "*What?* A . . . payoff?"

"Ha!" LaBarre barked. "You mean the silence pittance? The scraps they have not changed for over a year now? When I have rent to pay, and supplies to procure, and—"

"Opioids to score?" Sometimes, Brick hated being right. And other times, like this one, he hated being so right that he got skewered with a beautiful woman's glower for it. But most of all, he hated having to watch as she started connecting all the details for herself.

"It is a misunderstanding," Jayd spurted. "That is all. That is what it *has* to be . . ."

But her voice faded as her father reapproached. And she really saw him now. All of it. The haggard hitch in his posture. The constant disconnects of his attention. The desperation in his red-rimmed gaze.

"Why?" she whispered, stepping away with her arms clutched to her middle. Her sadness was a scythe across Brick's guts too. "Why . . . why?"

"I'm sick," LaBarre blurted. "I'm sick, daughter, and I'm in pain. So much pain. But you can help me. I just need some cash. Surely you can share with your dear old *paipanne*? Just so I can feel a little better?"

Brick huffed. He'd had enough of this bullshit. "She didn't raid the castle coffers before hauling herself all the way here, LaBarre. She had to sneak out with a few hours' notice, using mostly her wits and brains, just to make it here. And you know why? Because all she wanted was to meet *you*. For exactly *this*. Don't you want any of that too? Don't you want to sit and talk to your own fucking daughter?"

LaBarre attempted to cringe again. His gaze wandered around the room, as if he'd find his missing feelings stashed somewhere nearby. When he came up empty, he simply swayed where he stood before slowly shaking his head. "I just . . . don't understand. You're a *princess*."

Brick winced. "Let's cut the repeat button on that part, okay?"

"You're a princess," the dumbshit spewed anyway. "And you're supposed to help me. They said you had money. They said if I cooperated and came, you would help me!"

Jayd jerked in place once more. Brick was damn sure he joined her. No time to enjoy the jinx-worthy moment, though—not when it was clear they'd been dunked into the same shocking ice water at the same awful second.

"*Cock de Creacu.*"

Not the foremost expression on Brick's brain, but Jayd's profanity captured the moment well enough. Yeah, down to the dawn of his nausea—and the new rise of his paranoia.

"They?" He spat the emphasis while wheeling back at LaBarre. "They . . . who?"

The man jerked up his chin again. But no resignation or remorse about it now. "*They* helped me," he spat, full of defensive fire. "*They* helped to stop my pain. To help me feel bet—"

"They *who*?"

Brick startled again. The roar wasn't his. He turned, stunned, in the same second it took for his spirited pixie to become a pissed-off puck, launching herself at her dazed dad.

"Damn it, LaBarre!" she gritted out. "Who have you talked to? We need names! We need to know—"

His mind all but typed in the predictive text that went there.

But his ears never heard it.

All they registered, in the three seconds after the brutal blow across the back of his head, was a string of terrified screams interspersed with some violent Arcadian swearing.

Swearing?

It occurred to him, on his way down to the floor, that he might have gotten that part twisted. It hardly mattered as soon as his skull walloped the floor, and he spewed with his own unthinking obscenities.

Until even those were ripped from him.

As a pair of gunshots tore the air open—

And left only blackness in their wake.

CHAPTER TWELVE

Everything was so black.

So hot and suffocating and black.

But Jayd refused to stop screaming. Not for a second.

Not as her captors cinched the hood tighter over her head, locking her in with the memories of their bullets striking between Louis LaBarre's eyes.

Not as they zip-tied her wrists after carting her to the pub's kitchen, with its greasy smells tempting her to throw up into the dirty hood.

Not even as they hoisted her off her feet, and someone jabbed their burly shoulder into her abdomen, and she was certain she would never take a breath of fresh air again.

She cared not.

She would use all the filthy air she could. Would keep screaming as loud and long as she could. Would keep fighting and pushing and kicking until—

"Unnnghhh!"

She was tossed onto a hard, brutal surface, though it definitely was not the ground. They had departed the pub. She knew that much from the change in smells and air temperature. But beyond that, her sense of direction was shot. Terror clawed the edges of her psyche, tempting her to give up and quiver, but it was easier to cling to the fury. A lot more of it.

She hauled in another huge breath. These *soldasks* had not heard the last of her screams.

"If you even think about that caterwauling again, I shall gag you until simple breaths become your blessings."

Jayd fell into silence like a cat in the rain. *Not* because the fear had finally won.

Because the rage had.

As the hood was whisked away, her disgust spiked. "Creator's tears," she spat and dropped her head. The padded truck bed beneath her gleamed as salty drops spilled from her own eyes. "I did not want this to be true. I did *not* want to believe this of you!"

"Believe what?" Trystan Carris's murmur was like a loose snake in the bed with them. Silken but shaky. She gathered silent hope from that, deducing that he had likely slept less than her over the last few days. "That I would find out about your little stunt at all, Highness? Or that I would take action to save you from your reckless adventure before things got completely out of hand?"

"Out of hand?" She jerked her head back up, igniting her full glower. "You mean like your Pura thugs gunning down my father before my eyes?"

Trystan bared his teeth before she was done. "Your father is Ardent Cimarron, girl. That is all the world knows, and all they will continue to know, as long as you stay the fuck quiet and let me clean your mess up."

"*My* mess?" Her retort burst out as sirens started wailing up the old neighborhood alleys. "*You* shot him! In a room full of witnesses!"

"No." Trystan raised a knee and braced an alarmingly casual elbow to it. Jayd would have snickered at his awful quest for the smooth spy look if she was not battling back a new surge of bile. "It was actually your bad bodyguard who pulled the trigger, my little *doulée*."

"Do *not* call me that. I am *not* your sweet anything."

"Just as well." His shrug was too casual. Too confident. "Endearments make things so muddy anyway. Good thing I learned the lesson by observation instead of experience. Your strapping American illuminated so much for me—right before he gunned down the strung-out drug addict who was harassing you."

"*Gros de grawl*," she countered. But he was full of more than shit. He was full of lies. "I was there, damn it. I watched your minions raise their weapons, along with everyone else in the place—"

"Who were all decently into their cups, yes? Which means their testimonies will already be a bit...how do they say it here...*infidèle*? And since the pub's security system was inexplicably broken tonight..." As he inserted another unnerving shrug, her crack of trepidation became a chasm of dread. "Well, there is that, along with the fact that bad bodyguard boy is now suspect number one, complete with the smoking gun."

Her trepidation crumbled. So did her dread. True terror crashed into her senses like a sheared iceberg. As soon as it hit, her tear ducts erupted in scalding protest. But the stinging flood, pushing up from her belly, brought something else with it. The moment the bile hit her throat, she dry heaved to the side. Her vision swam, and she clung to consciousness by the barest of threads. Something waved before her vision. A stack of paper napkins.

"*Prispoul*." She wadded the napkins and then hurled them at Trystan. "Use them for the innocent blood you have spilled!"

As he scraped the trash off his face, the *bonsun* swore

beneath his breath. At least that took care of the asinine spy charade, but the price was Trystan's fresh glower.

"What, in the Creator's fucking name, is your problem?" He vaulted across the bed, assaulting her personal space with brutal hands on her shoulders. "I have dropped everything to come here, fighting to follow your foolish, reckless tracks. I have even instructed Santelle not to break the news about LaBarre, in hopes that we could—"

"What?" She snapped up her head despite how the horizon itself careened. The effect was not helped by the *bonsun*'s leering proximity. "That we could what, Mr. Carris? Come to some kind of *understanding*? Is that your brilliant plan? Because you torched every chance of it ever happening when you shot my *father* in front of my eyes. And then . . . what you did to Brick . . ."

She twisted her lips, fully intending to spit in his face, but the risk was too great of ghost gagging again. Another wall of ice crashed into her head. And chest. And limbs.

"Creator's mercy," she whispered. "Oh, no. Oh, *no*. Brickham. Max . . ."

Max.

One little word she could not refrain from repeating. The syllable that ripped all remaining veils off Trystan's composure—revealing all of the ugliness underneath.

"Maaaxxx." His voice was a gloating croon, but his eyes were affronted fire. Their dark depths moved over her, furious and invasive. "Someone has been getting friendly with her bad bodyguard, hmmm?"

Jayd fought to scoot back. To avert her eyes, surely giving away her truth already. "I—I have no idea what you are talking—"

"The hell you do not," he snarled. "So tell me. Just *how* friendly, my princess?"

She pushed with her feet, trying to get farther away. It was never a fair fight. In one lunge, Trystan toppled her over, securing her with his superior weight. Though she kept her thighs pressed together, that resistance was also useless. Trystan pushed her legs apart with a couple of dogged grunts.

Saints and stars, how she yearned to set free the thousand screams that clamored in her chest. But the *kimfuk*'s gag order was real. She was absolutely sure of it. The man was waiting for any excuse to hurt her, in any way possible. That was why she opted for the opposite. She went completely limp beneath him. Turned herself into an acquiescent doll. She was still and silent, even as he ground his crotch against hers with one message above all others.

"Did he . . . try things with you, Jayd?" he taunted. "Did he try things . . . like this?" Though his lips twisted with barely disguised frustration, the heat in his gaze changed. The anger took on a suggestive gleam—in direct proportion to the bulge that abused the crux of her thighs. "Maybe *more* things than this? With fewer obstacles in the way?"

Jayd slammed her eyes shut. She could do nothing about the tears that seeped out and rolled down her temples, but they were a small expense in exchange for what mattered most: saving the sanctity of her memories with Brickham. That fight became her sanity, anchoring her senses to a beautiful escape even as the monster hooked a finger into the space between her wrists to force her arms over her head.

"Did he do something like this to you, Princess?" the beast asked as he did. "But ohhh, what's this?" He pulled in a long breath. "Creator's balls. He *did* do a few things. I can still smell him on you, Highness Jayd. Oh, wait. Perhaps it should be Highness Slut now?"

She remained still. Said nothing.

And remembered everything.

Flattery will get you everywhere, Sir.

That's what I'm counting on, Pixie.

"Did he screw you too, darling? Oh, I bet he did—and just like a good Puritan lad, nice and sweet and tidy. Did he ask you for permission to come?"

More, Brickham. Please.

More of what, Pixie?

The pleasure. And the permission . . .

"Never mind. It matters not anymore. The *soldask* did me a favor. Now, I shall have no worries about being gentle with you, slut. And I guarantee, once *my* dick is buried in your tight little *chanli*, you shall never remember anyone el—"

A shriek worthy of an animal broke apart the air. Somehow, despite the muck that was calling itself her mind, she knew it was not her own. She would have been mildly curious about it, but there was no time. Not after the astonishment crashed in.

The yowl belonged to Trystan. From what *she* had apparently just done to him. He was doubled over, hands cupped between his legs and face seething in her direction.

But he looked different now.

Very different.

His lips were curled and feral, exposing bleeding teeth. His eyes were wide and murderous, though they were eclipsed by the hideous welt between them.

"By the Creator!"

Had she done all of *that* too? Nothing else made sense, though she could not claim any joy over the triumph. Not a speck of the elation that usually came after practicing the same self-defense moves on Samsyn or Jagger. But this time, it was not practice. She was moving with pure instinct, driven by jabs of raw adrenaline between sickening surges of fear—especially when Trystan wasted no time in lunging at her again.

And capturing her.

"Bitch!" He spat it so hard, her face was covered in spittle as he pinned her down again. "You really want to do this the hard way? I shall be more than happy to oblige."

"*Ummmph.*" Somewhere between her brain and her mouth, her vicious *no* turned into that pathetic grunt. But that was her only moment of playing tame. Rage rose again, becoming her new best friend, as the *bonsun* spread her knees, crushed them beneath his own, and then clawed at the waistband of her leggings with his free hand.

She swore. And yelled. And bucked. And swung her bound hands up, ready to bash his face with both fists at once.

But Trystan Carris was lean, sinewy, and shrewd—and he knew how to work all three together, anticipating every move she made when they were just thoughts in her head. His deflections were efficient and virulent. His dominance was heartless and vicious.

He jerked harder at her leggings, scratching her lower belly with his fingernails. Her tender skin bloomed with bright crimson, but Jayd ordered the observation to the edges of her concentration. She commanded her sights not to veer from the monster's greedy leer. Yes, even as the *prispoul* stared at his gory handiwork like he had won the Tour de France, the Super Bowl, and the World Cup at once.

But Jayd was certain none of those event trophies had to

worry about their recipients' burgeoning erections. Or about those champions slicking fingers through their quarry's blood, flashing a savoring smile before they drawled new words.

"Did you bleed like this for him too, Princess Slut?" As the words rasped from his lips, the light in his eyes turned into a slimy sheen. He raised his hand, showing her his bloody fingertips before wiping them across her cheeks. "And did he show it to you after he did? The evidence of what he did to you?" He smeared the blood in small but savage circles. "Did he celebrate by tasting it too?" That made him smile better than another fictional trophy, though it dropped as he leaned and pounded on the truck cabin's back window. "Meh. It does not matter anyway. On our way to the airport, I will make you forget that limpdick. I am going to gorge myself on all your delectable flavors, darling."

I am not your darling, you preening pig.

But she only told him that with her eyes. Her chattering teeth and trembling lips made it impossible to push out anything more than disgusted huffs. Where was the force of real bile when she needed it? What would this *kimfuk* think of his little feast if it was covered in her vomit instead of his filthy intentions?

"Gervais!" His vicious bellow broke off her thoughts as he pounded harder at the window. "Creator's filthy balls! Why are we not moving yet?"

Gervais?

Her brain lost the fight against the awful connection. No wonder Trystan had finessed her so smoothly into this trap. He had procured help. The opportunistic, underground Paris kind. Gervais had probably given him a discount too, eager to have his revenge on the "feisty *putain*" from the Particulier's alley, along with her moving mountain of a savior.

"Sorry, buddy. Gervais didn't get your pings. Or maybe he declined them? I reckon your Uber rider score isn't very snazzy."

"Saints and stars," Jayd rasped. By this point, few new events in the night could astonish her more than the upset about Gervais—but she was ready to ride this pendulum swing.

As she replayed the joy, wanting to make sure all of this was still real, filthier fare burst off Trystan's lips. "What the hell?"

"Off the mark again, pal."

"Huh?"

"This isn't hell, buddy. Least not yet. But if you're eager for a ticket on that elevator . . ."

On the surface, Brickham's voice was a snarky quip—but she already knew better and heard more. Her force of nature was a vast storm hidden by a peaceful mist. She knew that as fact, having already experienced the lusty force of that gale. But from the moment the man rocking the whole vehicle with his next motion, one point was clear. Lust was not on Brick's mind this time.

"How . . . the fuck . . ." Trystan stammered. "You—you were on the floor of that pub! Out cold! Gervais—"

"Clocked me so hard it was like a gong or some shit? Yeah, I kind of know. I was there." But right away, Brickham swapped his sarcasm for virulence. "So let's clear some shit up for you, yeah? This isn't the movies, asshat. If you hire a thug for your unpleasantries, better be sure they're willing to get their hands dirty. *Really* dirty."

As he went on, his voice got even more treacherous. Maybe it just seemed that way since she could fully see his face now. Creator have mercy, *his face*. The thick dark brows, now looking like wings lifted in furious flight. The sharp grooves across his forehead, slashing toward the bridge of his nose, which was flared as if he had snorted raw sewage. The frightening jut of his jaw, which only emphasized his clamped teeth more, before he parted them to form more seething syllables.

"Mistake number one: you really should've killed me while you had the chance," he continued. "But since that point's as tired as your dick, let's jump to bad decision two. You choosing to represent your country by jumping on your princess like a sewer mongrel."

"And you represented yours any better by doing the same thing?" Trystan's snickering finish was not a relief for the twist in Jayd's belly.

But if the charge was a shock to Brickham, he showed it not. "You and I aren't the same in any way, shape, or form," he finally growled.

"Is that so, now?" the *bonsun* quipped.

"That's definitely, absolutely, so."

"And you are planning on elaborating the point, then?" Trystan timed his pause with ruthless finesse, making sure nothing got in the way of a fresh blast of sirens. "I am certain the magistrates will be—how do you say it?—all ears about your explanation."

Just like that, Jayd's middle torqued with double the pain. "Damn it," she muttered, and then repeated it. "Brickham. *Brickham!*" But when her plea barely flinched his thunder-dark focus on Trystan, she gathered her strength and yelled louder. "*Sir*. Please! He is not worth—"

"I hear you, Pixie." His interjection was like a nuclear

tank rolling up in the storm. Low, quiet, malignant. "But right now, you need to stay out of this."

And now the vile cooperated, slowly churning up her throat. Trystan's gleeful cackle only worsened the assault.

"'Sir'?" he sang out. "And 'Pixie'? Well, my, my, my, Princess Slut, you really *have* made the most of your Paris adventure."

Damn it, damn it, damn it!

She stopped the litany at the triplicate. Even a hundred times more would not help now. She was hideously sure of it for torturous seconds before Brickham snapped forward and hauled Trystan up by the back of his shirt. As soon as she was free of the monster's awful weight, she used her feet to scrabble back into a corner of the truck bed. But she stopped short of climbing all the way out. Though a glance through the window revealed a slumped and unconscious Gervais, what if the *imbezak* came to and started the truck? She would not abandon Brickham, just as he had not given up on her.

Even now, as she looked up to see the man with his full focus on another cause.

A purpose *not* boding well for Trystan.

Who was twisting and yowling like an animal that had been shot.

Who, she suddenly realized, *was* an animal that had been shot.

She could not deduce any other theory, after gaping at the smoking gun in Brickham's free fist and the crimson bloom across Trystan's knee.

"Eeeaggghhh!" The *bonsun* crumpled against the tailboard. "You—you—what the fuck did you—yeeeowww!"

Brickham barely lowered his hand after ensuring Trystan

would have a horn-sized welt from the butt of the pistol in his grip. At once, Jayd recognized the weapon. She had watched the Pura cockroach shoot her father with it.

"Major mistake number three, Carris," he snarled. "Deciding to leave the shreds of your humanity behind with your smoking gun."

"Fuck you!"

"Hmm." Brickham cocked his head, contemplating the pistol once more. "No thanks."

For a flash of a moment, Jayd allowed some girlish flips into her stomach in place of the bile. The aroused butterflies took a spin through her soul, as well. Yes, the same soul that envisioned how easily this man and his twisted humor would fit right in with her acerbic but adorable brothers.

But not now. Not ever.

Not with the men who were not even her brothers anymore—though at the moment, the core of her urgency was to get moving again. If she allowed Brickham and Trystan to stay in striking range of each other, Creator only knew what kind of a call Evrest would be getting next. She refused to be the cause of even more strife for him, Samsyn, and Shiraz— especially now, as red-and-blue lights bounced into the sky over the buildings.

"Brickham." She clutched at his elbow. "The police!"

Between hyperventilating, Trystan flashed a sweaty leer. "Who are going to be *so* interested in hearing why you found a missing princess but kept it a secret. Before, of course, killing her *paipanne* in cold blood."

He was not finished before Brickham aimed the gun at his other knee.

"No!" Jayd whipped around to directly face him, twisting

fists into his shirt. Her lungs pumped with air that felt like flames.

"Jesus fucking—" He bit off the end, his chest pumping madly beneath her grip. "Goddammit, Jayd. Do you know what I could've just done to you?"

"Or *him*?" she spewed.

"Oh, yes," Trystan crowed. "Do it! *Do it!*"

"*No*, Brickham! Do *you* not comprehend? This is what he wants!" She sprawled her fingers along his jawline. "Please. *Please*, Sir. We must get out of here. We must do it now!"

She added to the effort by stabbing her fingernails into his stubble too. At least that jolted his focus directly back at her. She did not waste the opportunity.

"If they find you, they will arrest you. And if you are gone, guess what license that gives *him* again?"

Beneath her grip, Brickham's jaw went rigid. Creator be thanked.

"You're right," he gritted.

Creator be *praised*.

Without a word, he stuffed the firearm into his waistband, flush to his lower spine. With his free arm, he secured her firmly against his side. As soon as his other hand was clear, he grabbed the side of the driver's cabin. After one powerful swing, they were both down on the pavement.

"You okay?" They asked it in tandem, turning and checking each other for dangerous damage. Jayd swallowed hard, determined not to let the sting behind her eyes become the hindrance to their escape. All she yearned to do was kiss the gigantic lump on his crown and wipe the sweat and strain from his face. Brickham's gaze was doused in a similar kind of concern, especially as he curled a fingernail under the lock of her zip ties, freeing her with a quick but sharp snap.

"Shit. Did I hurt you, sweetheart?"

"I will be fine," she muttered, wasting no time to let him examine her. The bruises were not going anywhere, but the police obviously were. The tumult up on the main road got louder every second. The matching alarms through her senses wailed just as horribly.

"We have to get out of here, Brickham. Now!"

"Hey! Over here! He is over *here*!" Trystan's shout overlapped with hers. Instantly her chest clutched. Her pulse rate tripled.

"*Rahmie Creacu*," she gasped out—but Brick got to the point much better.

"Fuck," he muttered, clamping her hand tight in his. With another powerful swoop of motion, he yanked her into a full run. Jayd was more than ready to keep up.

Heading toward Clichy was out of the question, so they sprinted toward the darker end of Avenue Rachel. With all the quaint shops closed up by now, the little lane seemed ominous to her. When they got to the end, she swiftly learned why.

The end of the avenue was not actually an end.

It was the entrance to Montmartre Cemetery.

"By every saint that ever shit."

As she added to the burst by wheeling around, Brickham stopped to scrape a hand over his head. It did not escape her attention that his hand barely faltered.

"Well, here's what you really call a dead-end mission."

By the Creator. Was he truly adding sarcasm to the mix too? She was baffled about whether to laugh or cry—or to just ask him for her own head contusion. At least she could join him in his bizarre reality warp.

But there was no time for her induction.

Not a second's worth.

Not as they ducked into a moldy corner, behind a parked moped, and watched half a dozen gendarmes swarm over Trystan and the truck. At the same time, a white-and-blue van raced up onto the bridge up to their left, screeching to a stop at the top of the stone staircase that would have been their only viable escape.

No. Not their only one.

Jayd swung her stare around, back up at Brick. As fear clanged through her senses, red-and-blue lights flashed across his rugged face. The face that told her so little yet so much. A face filled with so many stories—including the one they were creating together, tonight. Would he remember this tale among the others in his life's tome? Would he remember *her*? Because she would never, *ever* forget him—or give up on him.

Not even now, as those garish lights were joined by others. Portable ones. "Damn it," Jayd muttered. The flashlights were like a swarm of gleeful click beetles. How she wished they were only that, and she was watching them light up during a peaceful midnight walk on the palais lawn back home . . .

But this was not home.

And this was definitely not peace.

And they had no time to ponder playful beetles in the night-blooming flowers.

In a few terrible moments, they would be trapped against this wall, locked down by light beams and accusing shouts and a mob of men in uniform who cared not about the real truth here. Who would see Brickham's face and know him only as a criminal. They would not be interested in how he had rescued her from Gervais. They absolutely would not care about how he had accepted the trust of her body and mind and transformed them with the sorcery of his passion.

They would not care about anything other than their "facts." About the "evidence" that would look so conclusive. Undeniably damning.

"Creator help us!" Jayd whisper-choked. As she backed up deep into the shadows, her foot splashed in a rancid puddle. She avoided a slippery fall by reaching for the iron bars embedded into a window-like portal along the graveyard's stone border wall. She almost went down anyway since the rusty bar came out in her hand. Well, at least she had a weapon now. It was not the sturdiest of things, considering it had come right out in her grasp, but it might buy them a few seconds of time.

"Pixie." Brickham's dictate ushered her fully back to the moment—not that he needed to use it. Her concentration was full from the second he slid in between her and the rectangle aperture. "Stand back," he ordered, seizing one of the remaining poles for himself.

When it gave way as easily as hers, she stopped to cross herself with gratitude. Now they both had half-decent weapons—or so she thought. Before Brickham used his bar to shatter the window on the other side of the bars. Once done, he tossed it through the opening.

As the bar *karrang*ed on the floor of the office inside the building, Jayd shot the force of nature a stringent look. But he was too busy to notice. He was already ripping out the other two bars over the window.

As he did, full comprehension struck her. It came not a moment too soon, since he wasted no time in turning to her, hoisting her off her feet, and positioning her in front of the totally open hole.

With speed spawned by panic, she curled her legs up beneath her. No more than ten seconds later, she was all the way inside. She stayed crouched as Brickham accomplished the feat in half her time. The man might be as big as a jackfruit but moved with the ease of a palm frond. He was just as strong and smooth about latching onto her hand as he rose, yanking her quickly through the ink-dark rooms of the cemetery's operations cottage.

She said another prayer of gratitude when they got to the door that led all the way outside. It was not locked on the inside, nor did it appear to have any security fixtures.

But assumption was a dangerous thing.

As soon as Brickham cracked the portal to get a visual fix on the gendarmes, the building flared with stringent sirens. Jayd was fairly certain her ears would be screaming with the sound for days. Brickham nailed her with his own stunned stare, and they shared the worst what-the-hell-now moments she had ever known. Courtesy of her brothers and their outrageous pranks, she already had a healthy collection of those.

"We cannot stay here!"

She latched on to the initiative, yelling it as best as she could over the deafening din. Already, Brickham ticked an agreeing nod. She was heartsick about the tension that fed it. She was aware he had spent most of this evening under one form of stress or another, but this was next-level material. A strain that owned him. A ferocity that possessed him. A focus that showed him not a shred of mercy. If she could only take away that darkness from him . . . even for half a moment . . .

But it was a misplaced wish.

She knew it in the very *next* second, while watching him

close his eyes and pull in a deep breath. He was not stuffing or ignoring those forces. He was drawing them in, making them a part of his persistence.

Creator on high, how he inspired her. She comprehended so much of it in full now. How he had survived a childhood on the streets. How he had dug deeper to succeed at his country's top-secret missions. How he had gotten through everything tonight and was still so formidable. Nothing in his psyche was wasted. He used it all for resilience and survival.

That was what she would do too.

The affirmation—the *vow*—came not a second too soon. As she enforced its motivation in her mind, Brickham communicated through basic hand gestures. He told her they would be running across the main walkway, toward the tall tombs and crypts that were tucked beneath the blue lattice bridge that ran across this corner of the cemetery.

Jayd delivered a complying nod. The covered area was the best choice for finding a good hiding place, especially if the prefecture decided to call in helicopters for the manhunt.

They did not dawdle. With all the officers fixated on the cottage but unable to get through the locked gates at its side, the chaos was going to be the best cover they had. She was certain the gendarmes would discover their break-in point soon enough. Brickham was likely three thoughts ahead of her in that regard. But by the time that happened, she and Brickham would be out of their sights again.

They would have to keep moving, but she was no longer afraid of that. She was oddly calm, feeling in control. Being in the right surely had something to do with it, but there was more to it. Brickham knew what he was doing. His steps were silent and sure. His determination was decisive.

She trusted him in full. With every move she made in his wake. With every breath she took while doing so. With every beat of the leaping heart in her chest, the growing smile on her lips.

By the merciful Creator. They were really going to do this. They were going to be okay.

Until, in the flash between one moment and the next, they were not.

The alarms fell silent inside the cemetery offices. In the same second, every light in the building came on. Strident shouts crisscrossed the air. Jayd could decently translate most of them, but that was not necessarily a good thing.

"They found the window wreckage," she told Brickham in a fast whisper. "And now they are going to break up into search party teams."

"What else?" he demanded, already interpreting her fresh wince.

"They are ordering search dogs too. And a couple of helicopters."

"Only a couple?"

Though his sarcasm was undercut by tension, it worked wonders for her own anxiety. If he was still capable of cracks like that, he had to still be harboring a few schisms of hope. If he had hope, so did she—despite being pitifully out of breath by the time he made her jog under the bridge, between stone monuments of all shapes and sizes, then through a copse of thick maple trees.

By the time they emerged on the other side of the grove, the distinct rumble of copter rotors throbbed the air.

"Damn it," she blurted. "Did they have to be stationed that close?"

"Let them come." Brickham yanked her deeper into the vast graveyard. "We'll be well over one of the back walls by then. We just need to get out far enough that they won't be searching—"

He cut himself off with a hiss when a pair of flashlight beams sped through the trees. Then spewed another when one of the gendarmes claimed to notice something.

"Shit," Jayd rasped.

Brickham uttered something understandably filthy at the same time, though the oath never lifted from the volume of his breath.

When he did speak up again, it was not to deliver any more sardonic banter. "All right, back wall is out. At least for now."

"So what do we—"

"Back the way we came," Brickham asserted. "With a lot of fucking prayers."

At least she could help with that part. She kept up her inner pleas to the Creator with every step they rushed back beneath the trees, though she was increasingly certain the supplications were disappearing into a void—especially when more lights slashed at them through the gloom.

"Saints help us!" she cried, watching the beams flicker across the taller gravestones.

"I don't think they're listening any more than your Creator, sweetheart."

"Which means what?" She spat the words more from a need to do something, anything, rather than needing a whole answer. Still, the man who clutched her hand as it was fused to his was ready with a dark deadpan.

"Which means we really might be trapped."

No. Not a deadpan. An admission. A resignation. Perhaps even a surrender.

"No." She made the word her verbal fist, swinging it at her dismal thoughts. "No. *No.*"

"Pixie." Brickham pivoted and tucked himself over her. "I've been in shittier scrapes before. As long as we can call Fox and Oz and get you safely back to them, then—"

"No!"

"*Jayd.*"

"I said no, Brickham. That is not one of our options."

One of the gendarmes called out to his comrades. Something about thinking he saw something right where she and Brickham stood. There was more to it, but she was unable to think about translating. A thousand emotions were a damn tsunami in her mind. Fear. Anger. Desperation. Confusion. Resentment. And yes, more rage. So much more.

"Jayd. Sweetheart." He cupped her shoulders. "Listen to me."

"What part of *no* are you *not* understanding here?"

"Fine. You got a better plan?"

Cunning beast. That certainly shut down her *no* parade fast enough. But the man was clearly not indulging a personal gloat fest about it—perhaps because he already sensed that she did not like parades that got silenced, odds that got bad, or doors that got slammed.

To her, locked doors only meant one thing.

The challenge to find open windows.

She wrested free from Brickham, frantically scanning every their immediate area. Nothing within a ten-meter radius got overlooked. She paced the path led by her gaze, letting her fingers glide over intricate statues, grand stone edifices, and even the wrought-iron gates that guarded many family crypts.

Iron gates . . . that should all be locked.

Except for the one that was not.

"What. On. Earth?" Or in this case, what was *not* on earth—like several members of the Aider family, their inscribed names lost to her in the deeper gloom of the vault. It was not as cavernous as others around the graveyard, but it was not the smallest. Like the bears' house for Goldilocks, it was just right—at least for what they required of it. *Aider*. The family's name even translated to assistance.

Thank you, divine Creator. And thank you, Aider family.

"Jayd?"

Brickham's panicked husk made her realize how far inside the enclosure she had actually moved. Another blessing: the ornate iron gates were old but silent. Perhaps someone had recently oiled them and then forgotten to resnap the lock.

And thank you, negligent caretaker.

"Jayd? Goddammit!"

His demand, more a desperate croak, yanked her back out so she could flag him down. Though he sprinted over, his steps still barely ruffled the leaves—until he jolted to a stop in front of her and her new friends from the Aider family.

"What the f—"

More bellows and yells, courtesy of the Paris prefecture, drowned the rest of his charge. He would not get the luxury of repeating it. He did not look like he wanted to.

"Get in!" Jayd did not squander any moments either. As the words left her mouth, she shot out her hands and clamped his elbows.

And then frowned.

His arms . . . felt different.

Different to the point of strange.

Of course, every one of his magnificent muscles was still

in place. The sculpted striations were still rugged and rippled beneath her grip. But they were lax as ropes, simply dangling at his side. Gone was the man's patent vitality and discernible drive. For the first time since they met, there was no purpose in his stance or energy in his awareness.

"Brickham."

He responded not. Finally, she had to shake him as hard as she could. The effort only succeeded in shifting him by an inch on the outside, though his head jerked, and his gaze flared.

"Did you hear me?" she exhorted. "I said get in. If we close the gate and stay still, perhaps they will pass right by and—"

"I heard you." His interruption had her pausing again. Creator's mercy, *not* a wise move, but she had no choice. Not when a violent tremor emanated from the center of his chest and took no prisoners as it coursed down his towering frame. For a heart-stopping second, she almost thought she would have to cushion him from a full faint. "I heard you, damn it," he repeated from clenched teeth. "But I'm not getting in there."

She hissed, unable to shield her flare of frustration— until it ignited into something more. An outright explosion, courtesy of her dawning comprehension.

He was not being obstinate.

He was gripped by full terror.

And very awful timing.

Because several menacing light beams swung even closer—grazing the leaves he had soundlessly rustled less than a minute ago.

Jayd swallowed her petrified gasp. And just like that, flung out the rest of her proper princess programming. Futile fretting had no place in this dire moment.

It was time for more explosions.

But not just for *her* psyche and spirit.

It was time to blast out Brickham too. But no way would the man ignite his own fuse. She would have to do it for him—despite not knowing the first thing how.

Creator help me.

But unless the Almighty had that strength all grilled and ready to go, this fortitude was going to be her own responsibility.

She had to dig deep. She had to summon the inner dictator that Samsyn ordered her to find when they sparred in self-defense drills. This time, she had to take that chieftess seriously. She had to honor her. Empower her.

The explosions must begin.

"Brickham."

It was a damn good start. Her timbre was nearly as low as his. She delivered it from gritted teeth, clenching them to the point of pain.

"Fuck. You."

But he gave back as good as she had given. Fortunately, she was ready.

"Fuck *you, degan diktu bhutan!*"

In the half second he took to try to translate her slur, she seized opportunity by its stubborn horns—and succeeded. She yanked him another three steps before his senses came back online. It was far enough to pull the portcullis closed.

But as she finished the act, regret crashed in. It mimicked the mental airstrike that obviously bombarded Brickham now. The bombs that sparked a rasping litany to his lips. The assault that made him grab his skull with tremoring hands.

"Brickham?" she prompted, as loudly as she dared. "Maximillian?" She could not justify the switch to his proper name, except the unignorable feeling that he needed it.

Not that he acknowledged it or even seemed to be aware of her anymore. He continued his incoherent whispers, their incessant haze getting thicker as he paced to a corner of the crypt and slid to the ground there.

What the hell did she do now?

With sadistic timing, icicles congealed across Jayd's mental explosives. Of all the ways she anticipated this going, there was never a plan for her force of nature turning into a defeated ball in the dirt.

No. Not defeated.

She knew that once she boosted herself into motion, dropping to her knees in front of him. He had his own legs bent up, with his elbows meeting his kneecaps. His hands still straddled his head. His gaze was angled straight out. Even as she leaned in, he did not see her. Mentally, he was gone. Lost to her. Lost to *himself.*

"Brick . . . ham?" She deliberately broke it up while trying to get closer to him. But when she reached for one of his hands, he startled like she was made of fire. He flailed with the same violence, but she caught his wrist before he could backhand her face. "Hey. *Hey.* It is me. Only me."

The soothing seemed to penetrate his fog, so she repeated it. Then again. Then at least a hundred more times, letting him roll over her fingers so he clutched them in return. She did not give up on her consolation, even as he lifted his stare over the tight hills of their locked hands. Like before, he did not see her. He was still someplace far away and dark. Intimidating and frightening.

Saints and stars.

The words tumbled off her lips before a horde in dark uniforms and shiny helmets tromped by. But the searchers were not the reason she fell into gut-wrenching silence. Her insides were overcome by anguish of another ilk. Distress at a different level.

His level.

She saw it now. She felt it.

And while she absolutely did not believe it, she forced her mind to accept it.

Brickham was . . . terrified.

That fear was strong enough to kidnap his mind. It had whisked him off to a totally different place. A separate nightmare.

"*Rahmie Creacu,*" she spilled on a sparse breath, tenderly kissing each of his knuckles. No more flinches from him at that, which gave her some hope—until he started to heave in harsh breaths between rocking himself back and forth.

Jayd wrapped her hands tighter around his, praying she could let him ride out the terrible journey until coming back to her, but their pursuers were not going to be so cooperative. Another mob of them tromped over, sickeningly close to the "locked" gate at the front of the Aiders' resting place. The steel that had meant salvation for Brickham and her.

If that steel decided to talk with so much as a creak or whine, they would be finished. Brickham would be off to jail, and she would be—

No answer to that was even palatable.

But having to consider them was the perfect kindling for her new fire. The explosions, back just in time, making her release Brickham's hands so she could lunge all the way at him. Luckily—miraculously—he let her. His knees parted at her pressure, and she did not stop until they were chest to chest in a messy but perfect embrace.

The whole time, he never stopped rocking.

So she picked up the rhythm, swaying with him.

"It is only me," she said once more, punctuating with a gentle kiss to his ear. Beneath her lips, he got down a labored swallow. "I am here, Brickham. I am here."

His only answer was another brutal shiver. She wrapped herself tighter around him. Her limbs trembled as she fought to absorb some of his torment. "I am here," she told him again, fitting his forehead against her neck. "I am right here. Right here."

She kept the words soft, her strength solid, and her prayers continuous. But the Creator had used up a lot of attention on them already tonight, so Brickham remained a prisoner of his fear's alternate dimension. Nothing made her surer of that than the words that rasped from him next.

"Don't leave me." His rocking got worse. "Don't leave me." Then even more so, as he cinched his arms around her with painful force. "Don't leave me."

"I am right here." She pushed it out with the meager air her lungs were still capable of. "I am not going anywhere, Brickham."

Thankfully, that seemed to register with him. The pressure of his head against her neck was a rough, desperate push. His stubble stabbed through her shirt and scratched at her collarbone. She barely noticed. Not when his massive body surrendered to more violent shivers.

"Don't leave. Please don't leave!"

"*Brickham.*" At last, as the uniforms finally moved off to search another quadrant of the graveyard, she was able to growl it more than whisper it. She pulled back by a few inches, far enough to grip his contorted face. "Look at me. I am here!"

But he was not back. Not all the way. To him she might as well have been one of the ghosts in this place. "Don't do it, damn it. Don't leave me, Asha!"

She stiffened. That made sense when one's veins turned cold enough to suck the air out of their lungs all over again. She was not just a ghost now. She was battling the memory of one. A memory strong enough to make this vital man turn catatonic. But she could barely see her way straight to honoring that, instead fighting her way out of an emotional cesspool. A mire she had rarely visited her whole life, let alone dipped a figurative toe into.

Who the hell was she kidding? She was more than a toe's worth of jealous.

"Damn it." She gave up the spiteful ice for a steam bath of shame. This was ridiculous. No, worse. This was stupid. Brickham was the man in *her* embrace now, and he needed her.

But as much as *she* needed *him*?

Lightning could have struck the cemetery and blown her nerves apart less. But as she recognized the confession as her glaring truth, she was more clear than ever about what she had to do. For both of them.

CHAPTER THIRTEEN

He was shaking all over but unable to move. Burning up on the inside, but an iceberg on the outside. All his muscles were locked; all his senses were screaming.

Get out! Get out! Get out!

Exactly as they had in the caves beneath Bamiyan.

Just like then, it was dark and damp. He could hear insects scuttering against the walls and water trickling like some goddamned resort fountain. But beyond that, it was quiet. Too fucking quiet. Why was it so quiet?

Get out. Don't wait, damn it. You waited last time. You remember that, right? You waited on her—and nearly paid the ultimate price. The price you watched her pay...

"Brickham."

But if she had really paid that price, why was she calling to him? Was she trying to tell him something, from beyond the grave? If so, then what?

"No," he growled. *"No, damn it." I'm not listening this time, Asha. You need to just rest, girl. Please ... just rest ...*

"Brickham!"

Why wouldn't she rest? Why wouldn't she leave him the hell alone?

"Brickham, please. You have to hear me. You have to come back to me!"

And why did she sound so different now? Throatier. Tearier. A thousand times more terrified. Which made no sense. The only thing that had ever actually spooked Asha was the threat of a life without possibilities. Without freedom. But now, she sounded so desperate. So trapped.

"Brickham. *Brickham.* Do you hear me? I have nothing left, damn it. I have nothing left—but you have!"

What the hell was happening? She'd never said things like this before.

"Please, Brickham. I need you..."

And dear fuck, she'd definitely never touched him like this before.

"Good. Christ!" His own exclamation was his galvanization. And cognition. Could he be blamed? When a guy was being stroked in the crotch like this, the wise move was getting mentally online for it—if only to realign his shit and stop it. Because he didn't feel this way about Asha, nor would be convinced to. He'd made that clear with her from the start. So...why was she...?

"Brickham."

She was ready with another urgent caress along his shaft. Jesus fuck, it was impossible to ignore. But while his balls clamored for more, especially as she scooped down and massaged them too, his mind detonated in protest. This wasn't right. *This wasn't right.*

"Oh, no. This is very right."

Only her determined retort made him realize he'd blurted the objection out loud. All right, he'd just say it again.

But he could only babble like a hard-up booter on his first night off the base.

"I...can't," he finally managed. "*We* can't."

"But we very much can." Another perfect caress turned into another moment of torture as she pinched his cockhead.

How was she weaving such sorcery over him, even through his camos? "Please. *Please* just come back to me, Sir . . . and I shall show you how much."

Before she was done, Brick was jolting again. Hard.

Sir.

Like an asteroid hitting a warp jump, his whole being rushed back to reality.

Sir.

Every circuit in his psyche rammed back online.

Sir.

Every drop of his blood sizzled with fresh fire.

Because never, out of the thousand times he'd been addressed that way, did it mean what it did now. Never did it *sound* like it did, full of as much authority as penury, as much command as entreaty.

Never had he so fully liked it that way.

"Pixie." It spilled from him on a breath thick with relief—and rejoicing. "It's really you?"

At first, she only responded by kissing him. She tasted like tears and wind, with a hint of the wine she'd sipped back at Très Particulier. How had that been just a few hours ago? It might as well have been years. He truly felt that close to her. That replete with delight at rediscovering her.

"Right here," she said with a soft, sweet smile. But he knew differently. He *had* heard her, each and every time she anchored him through his darkness with it.

His darkness.

That was the best descriptor for it this time. He hadn't weathered an attack that severe since the first week after they'd found him in Bamiyan.

But something told him he'd be recovering much faster

this time. Unlike then, he had a damn good excuse to check back into reality.

The sooner the fucking better.

"Oh, Pixie…you certainly *are* here." He didn't bother sifting out the soft savagery from his snarl or the strict demand from his grip, cinching her waist with one intention. To position her core atop the hump in his jeans. "But I think here is better." With a rough jerk, he dragged her up. With a rougher one, he shoved her down. "And here."

He savored her stunned gasp. If he knew her leggings as well as he thought he did, the silky coverings wouldn't provide much cushion for her spread flower. That meant, any minute now…

"Oh! By the Creator! *Sir!*"

…she'd start to spill with succulent sighs like that.

After rocking her softness up and down his bulge several more times, he finally grasped enough self-control to speak again. "Sweet, perfect Pixie," he husked. "You've ruined that word for me."

She lifted a corner of her mouth with languorous pleasure. "Which one?"

"You know which one," he returned, sliding a hand to her thigh and pinching hard for good measure. When she reacted with a startled but sultry yelp, he dug the fingers of his other hand into the nip of her waist. "Say it again," he dictated, bucking his hips to give her proper motivation.

"Sir," she whispered at once, leaning in to seal her compliance with a respectful kiss.

"Again," Brick ordered, biting her lower lip to keep her mouth close and ready.

"Yes, Sir. Anything you want, Sir."

They tangled tongues with the next kiss. Their bodies began moving in carnal unison. As Brick hitched up, his perfect princess rolled down, then over and over again, until they were writhing in possibly the hottest dry hump of his entire existence.

And of course, he kept demanding the beautiful word from her.

"Again. Tell me you're still here with me, Pixie."

"Yes. *Yes*. I am here, Sir."

"Again. Tell me how you like riding me."

"I do like it, Sir. Oh yes, how I like riding you."

"Even if I'm pounding everything inside you? Hurting you?"

"Yes. *Especially* if you hurt me. Please!"

"Are you close now?"

"Yes. I am so close!"

"Because I'm fucking you? Hurting you?"

"Yes. Oh, yes!"

"Again. Tell me how close you are."

"Yes, Sir. Ohhh... it hurts, and I am so close, Sir!"

She wasn't lying. He knew it from the erotic shivers that began overtaking her. From the way she flung her head back, lost to her sensual rise. From the way she started gasping so hard and heavily, he had to grab her neck and force her back down for a wild consummation of a kiss.

Not a moment too soon.

As their teeth crashed and their tongues dueled, another small squad of Paris's finest came running by, seemingly certain they were on to something. But while Brick had tamped his Pixie's vociferous vocals, no way could he halt her incessant grinding. No way did he want to. He needed this as badly as she, but more than just a win for his cock. Marching back up the street and putting a bullet through Carris's heart was out of the question, but pleasuring the woman of his obsessions, right under the noses of the cops the bastard had sicced on them, was a very nice chunk of very sweet revenge.

But that wasn't the best part.

Nothing was better than watching this exquisite female chase her ultimate completion—and knowing he was the lucky shit who'd be giving it to her.

No. Not just lucky.

He was blessed, plain and simple, and this moment was another miracle in this crazy, calamitous, completely star-crossed night. Those gas balls in the sky were working overtime for them tonight; the least he could do in return was honor their effort—and, hard as it was, believe in their magic. After all, it wouldn't last forever. It couldn't.

But right now, it was the closest to perfection he'd ever get.

The feel of her in his hands, undulating over him.

The glory of her in his gaze, her profile etched in moonlight.

The miracle of her in his senses, vibrant and vital and bold. Bringing him back to life, even here.

But maybe . . . especially here.

Fate hadn't wasted a detail of the symbolics. He got it. Death was rarely a conscious choice, but hiding from life was. That included mental walls as well as physical ones. Emotional islands to match the real ones. And for the memories that wouldn't stay put in those confines: his psychological crypts were always ready, sealing away the fear and panic. Most of the time. On the occasions when his zombies rose up, intent on smashing his mental caskets and wiping out his brain, he had his pharmaceutical friends to watch his back. To keep him safe in his emotional graveyard.

The recognition slammed him like a falling sarcophagus. And filled him with just as much horror.

But now . . . just as much awakening. And conviction. And commitment.

Tonight, he hadn't needed the zombie prevention pills.

He had something better.

Some*one* better.

And he wanted more.

More of her light, her energy, her erotic glory. More of the flawless flames she was bringing to his pores, his blood, his cock. More of the urgent, magnificent passion he was giving her in return.

More.

More.

He issued the demand aloud then, stabbing it into every note of a savage snarl from his taut lips. The tone, and its lusty origins from deep in his belly, clung to his continuation. "Give me more, Pixie," he commanded. "Work me. Grind me. Harder. Harder!"

"Yes." Just one word of sweet obedience from her, but it was better than an entire novel of erotic poetry. A ten-foot-tall stack of porn mags. And every nasty video he'd ever seen. "Oh yes, Sir . . ."

"Hmmm."

It was more a growl than a hum, roughened by the arousal that rushed his senses, the pressure that pushed at his shaft. He wasn't going to last much longer. The time limit on his volume threshold was even smaller. The enticing whimpers and gasps from her lips added another layer to that concern. The cops hadn't bailed on searching the whole cemetery yet.

Obeying pure instinct, he wrapped a hand around the back of her neck and then tugged. "Come here," he instructed. "Give me your mouth, girl. All of it."

She was hot and ready with the acquiescence, plunging her warm, swollen lips into a lusty vacuum seal over his. Together, they hauled in heavy air through their noses while meshing their mouths in all the ways their bodies couldn't. It was fervent and fiery. Tight and wet. Wild and wanton. Illicit... and explosive.

Holy fuck.

Explosive.

He knew it as soon as the woman's mewls doubled in time. Then tripled. But then stopped completely, as she humped him with blinding abandon. Her hips rolled in ways he'd only ever fantasized about, with her downstroke hitting perfectly along the aching crown of his pulsing length. Then again, and again, and—

"God*damn*!"

If the gendarmes discovered them because of his groan, he'd go to prison a happy man.

No. Not just happy.

Deliriously drained.

Sublimely screwed.

Past the point of any and all erotic returns.

And absolutely a prisoner before they even cuffed him. That part had already been handled by one hell of a stunning princess. One incredible surprise of a woman. A female who, in the space of one night, had changed every night he'd know after it.

He hoped the shackles never came off.

Shit, shit, shit. The admission was definitely one for the emotional crypt. That much was already clear—and terrifying. But just for a while, just for *once*, he was going to just let that fact lie. Oh yeah, right where it was, out in the open, across his mind and soul.

Big mistake? Likely. Probably. But he literally had no fucks left to give about it. Especially not as Jayd breathed his name so gorgeously across his lips. And then again.

Brick jerked gently at her scalp, compelling her to meet his direct gaze. "What is it, Pixie?"

A troubled V crinkled between her eyebrows. "I . . . I do not know if I can stop."

He gave her a cocky smirk. "You asking for permission, sweet girl?"

The V stayed, though she cracked a little grin. "Are you granting it?"

He burst with a quick chuckle. "Yes, sweetheart. Your Sir is granting it." Damn it if his johnson wasn't already jerking back to some attention, making him buck upward in time to her naughty downward slides. "Come on, my hot little Pixie. Let it go. Give it to me."

Like the perfect little girl she was . . .

She did.

"*Ohhh!*" she sighed out, shuddering with audacious abandon. "*Faisi vive Creacu. Merderim, Hocatre. Merderim.*"

Her poetic little tribute, or whatever it was, only put Brick deeper under her sensual spell. She'd hypnotized him, and he couldn't be happier about it. Her pleasure was so full and free and sexy, especially every time she slid her quivering core along his swollen length. If this was a normal night and they were tangled in sheets now, he'd already be half-buried inside her again.

But nothing had been normal since he met this woman. And right now, even though they were postclimax cuddling amid stone angels, somber saints, and about seven members of the Aider family, he wouldn't change a single thing about it.

"Brickham?"

Except to add that tiny whisper to the scenario.

"Hmmm?" He drawled the reply with the same lazy tenderness as he stroked a knuckle up her spine.

"Do you think the Aiders will mind a guest soul in here? I am fairly certain I cannot move. *Ever* again."

He laughed again but then reiterated, "Hmmm." He reversed direction in the space between her shoulder blades, caressing back down before adding, "Well, that's too bad."

"Bad?" she countered. "Why?"

"Because I was just thinking, if we did this with access to a bed..."

She was on her feet before he could think of what witticism to end with. Brick didn't waste time indulging another chuckle, though as soon as he caught up with her, a sound kiss was in order. He bestowed the thorough smack to her lips as a pair of squirrels cheered with their soft chirps, which had Jayd breaking off with a quiet giggle.

Brick couldn't even be pissed with the little bastards. Their vocal freedom gave him an essential bead, letting him know the coast was clear for scrambling to one of the cemetery's side walls. Even if they had time to just get Jayd over and out to freedom, the risk would be worth it.

He grabbed her hand but let her use her other one to drag open the crypt's gate. But before he led her out of their hiding spot, he pulled her back against him one more time.

The embrace was too short but beyond essential. Just enough time for him to kiss her again, this time with fervent intent. Another moment to cup her cheek, and ensuring she gazed far and deep into his eyes. Oh yeah, all the way back to the place where all his secrets lived, and his soul was usually the world's most adamant hermit.

The hermit who stood up and spoke for him now.

"Thank you," the guy whispered to her, and she smiled back—but not for long. "Hey. What is it?" he prompted as soon as the inquisitive frown took over her face.

Before she could answer, there was a flurry of new yells across the graveyard. Noises that were too damn close.

"We need to go," Jayd muttered, clearly shelving her frown-worthy item. While Brick hated that she had to hold back anything from him, his worse aggravation was that *she* was thinking clearer than *him*. It wasn't a circumstance he was used to, and he didn't like it.

And he was more than ready to fix it.

"You're right," he said beneath his breath. With the same hard focus, he tightened his grip against hers. "Let's get the fuck out of h—"

More shouts now. So much closer.

Shit.

Then the damn flashlight beams—also perilously close.

Shit!

"Brickham!" Jayd's cry was nearly a wail. "They are—"

"I know." And he did, without the translation he'd cut her short on.

They were caught in too many crosshairs again. But he was determined to get her out. Him too, if providence smiled—

but that remained to be determined.

Right now, he had to shake off his postattack brain fog, shove down his lingering erection, and ignore the fact that he knew nothing about the logistical details of this place or what equipment they were being tracked with.

Yeah. Only all that.

Piece of goddamned cake.

The cake he fought not to choke on, before gritting out the only words that really made sense at the moment.

"Fuck me now."

★ ★ ★

In spite of Brickham inviting every catastrophe to rain on them between the crypt and the wall, the only precipitation they received was the real kind, in the form of a humid mist that dragged along ominous thunder. The wet was far from cold, but Jayd still shivered as Brickham crouched down and formed a foothold out of his massive hands. She could practically predict what he would instruct to her next.

"Step in."

Yes. Exactly that.

"Use your weaker leg," he went on. "You may need your stronger one to get another toehold. But mostly, try to use the ivy as ropes and hoist using your lats and delts. Got it?"

Barely.

But she kept that to herself, keeping her answer to a swift nod. As horribly inept as she felt about scaling this wall using muscles that sounded more like sorority house letters, she was ten times more terrified about staying in the cemetery. Outside the walls, they would have more options.

Starting her quest was not as daunting as she thought. The ivy was slick from the mist, but not impossible to grasp. As Brickham suggested, she gained leverage by also toeing the wall whenever she could. Before she knew it, she was halfway up.

"Creator be praised!"

She spewed sweat along with the rasp, but reveled in her salty taste of victory as her sightline grew to include a small street with offices, apartments, and even a little café. A cat on an apartment balcony gave her a lazy scrutiny. Creator's toes, she was even overjoyed to see graffiti on a wall.

"Oof! *Boktah salpu!*"

Brickham had left out the part about the descent—the *drop*—being the hardest part of all this. As she stood and gingerly rubbed her bruised backside, the knave himself dropped gracefully to her side, probably earning points from the damn cat in the process. Jayd did not surrender her glower, along with the darkly sarcastic commentary he was about to get an earful of.

Commentary she never got to give.

Words tended to die when a girl's tonsils were illuminated by a king-size flashlight beam.

She was learning that the really hard way.

"Goddammit," Brickham gritted.

Jayd spat the Arcadian version of it beneath her breath before seizing Brickham's hand. She clung as if their palms were slathered in ultrastrength glue, even as she swung around and faced their hunters.

"Go ahead," she spoke out, shocked by the strength in her defiance considering her limbs had turned to seaweed. "What are you waiting for?" she continued, hiking up her chin. "Do it, then. Arrest him. But you shall have to do the same to me!"

The officer attached to the spotlight took a couple of steps forward. "I don't usually squander my handcuffing skills on situations like this, Your Highness, but if that's the game you're after—"

"And there's the fucking money shot."

The expression was beyond her comprehension, but since Brickham laughed his way through every word, she dared to inhale again. But two seconds later, she cut the inhalation short—as her senses caught up to the full facts of the moment.

Fact: the officer had spoken to them in English, not French.

Fact: there was a distinct laugh in his line too.

Fact: the chuckle was not accompanied by a French accent.

It was Australian.

"Sorry, mate. My money shots are reserved for one human alone, and you're not him."

The quip transformed Jayd's hunch into hope. And then, as she watched three figures stroll closer, her hope into joy.

"*Rahmie Creacu!*" she exclaimed, rushing at them in return. "Emme!" She embraced the woman with careful elation. She did not miss the elephant-sized cast between her friend's ankle and knee, as well as the hefty crutches Emme was using to maneuver with the thing. "How . . . on earth . . . did you . . ."

"You and Brickham are quite the stars of the midnight news." Her assistant made a rare attempt at wry humor. It was washed out by the anxiety that coated her whole face. "We listened to the reports, and then Ozias took his best guess at what Brickham would do. After Jagger switched out our rental car, we came over and started praying."

"And it worked." Jayd gulped down happy tears. "The Creator is good."

"Yes. Good, indeed."

But the pleasant words did not match Emme's tired gaze. Jayd shrugged off her resulting discomfort. The woman had likely been poked and prodded in more ways than she wanted at the hospital, before having to ride along with Ozias and Jag on a wild goose chase for Brickham and her. No wonder her energy was not spiking to meet Jayd's adrenaline high.

"The leg is okay." Jagger supplied the information while stepping over, looking decently dapper in a PP officer's uniform. "The fractures are straightforward and easy to set. The bruising makes it look worse than it is."

"Creator be praised," Jayd murmured, though she basked in the celebration for but a few seconds. "But why are you out here, still putting weight on it?" she accused at Emme. "Jagger, you two could have dropped her off at the apartment and then—"

"Not an option," Jagger inserted.

Jayd cocked her head. "Is *what* not an option?"

"The apartment." Ozias supplied that part while pivoting toward them. He was dressed in a dark-blue uniform that matched Jagger's. "It's not anywhere close to an option. Not anymore."

Jayd zipped her stare between him and Jagger. "Do I dare ask why?"

Jagger stepped forward, jamming his hands into his front pockets. "After Emme was discharged, we had to go back to grab these standby uniforms—"

"Which you came by how?" Brickham inserted.

"Long story," Oz supplied. "I'll save it for the plane."

"The plane?" Jayd jumped in with her own query, hating its necessity as much as the dread that brought it on. Her instinct prickled, starting to fill in the likely reasons for Oz's wrencher of a revelation. "To go where?"

"As we were leaving the place, a horde of the city's finest descended on the building," Oz continued. "I have no idea how it happened, but we're well and truly blown."

Jayd cocked a look toward Brickham. As soon as their gazes met, they were on the same page about that answer. "Gervais," they declared together.

Emme echoed the *imbezak*'s name with a shocked snort. "You mean that piece of trash from the alley at Particulier?" she added.

"That *sneaky* piece of trash," Jayd clarified with a fast nod. "He was Trystan's getaway driver."

"Trystan?" Jagger spat, clenching his jaw. "You saw that *kimfuk*?" His gaze expanded more. "Wait. *Getaway* driver?"

She didn't bother nodding again. "He used LaBarre as his bait for me," she revealed. "But once Brickham and I made it to the meeting place—"

"Shit."

After Jagger and Ozias sliced her short in unison, it was Oz who went on once more.

"Bugger me. Things are really starting to make sense now."

"Sense like how?" Jayd pressed. *And what about the damn plane?*

"Like how Brickity-brack here really is all over every TV feed in the city, wanted for offing Louis LaBarre in cold blood."

"What?" While more ice attacked Jayd's bloodstream, every one of her nerve endings ignited in outrage. "Have they even asked any of the people who were there? The witnesses who saw *Trystan* pull the trigger?"

"We only know what is being broadcast across the city," Jagger stated.

"Crikey." Ozias swept the wedge cap off his head and twisted it in his fist. "I knew you didn't stir that shemozzle, mate."

"Fucking right I didn't." Brickham looked ready to tear up one of the roadside trees by the roots and hurl it into the cemetery wall. At this point, in spite of Oz's pledge of faith, Jayd was ready to help with the task.

"Damn it," she cried. "This is not fair!"

"Fair doesn't sell newspapers or link clicks, Pixie." Brickham's voice was disturbingly deep. His taut posture was equally unsettling.

"And every media outlet in town is rejoicing about the surge," Ozias revealed. "But in many ways, so were we."

"Which is why we have to get you out of here," Jagger asserted, indicating to Brickham. "The sooner the better."

Brickham wheeled back around, still stiff and tense. "Bugging out is definitely a necessity," he conceded. "But that shit's on me, my friend, not you." He pulled in a lengthy breath, making a noticeable effort to fix his gaze down the street. "I can also move faster if I'm on my own."

Jayd twitched. All right, it was more like a stunned jerk. That was not the clarifier that mattered, anyhow. That priority belonged to the agony slamming her chest and the sharp pain everywhere else. If he truly pulled up a tree and dropped it on her, the excruciation would barely compare.

But this time, her hesitance helped her. Instead of her lunging forward and calling Brickham five kinds of an idiot, Oz did it in a more considerate, but commanding, way.

"You're getting a walloping negative vote on that plan, mate."

Brickham's answering glower was so predictable, she almost laughed. *Almost.* "Wizard man, this isn't a pack of flying monkeys to zap out of the sky."

"Damn straight it isn't." To her shock, Ozias cracked a relishing smirk. "We've got much better wings waiting, anyway."

And *there* was her airplane explanation.

One that she was already half expecting—but now fully questioning.

"And that is going to work out how?" she charged, folding her arms. "If Brickham is now *ennemi du public* across all twenty arrondissements, do you think they will just let him stroll through security at Orly or De Gaulle? For that matter, even at Beauvais? And even if we get him onto a plane, do you think the Americans will just ignore the fact that Brickham is wanted for murder here?"

"*Wanted,*" Oz echoed, stressing the word hard. "But not *convicted.*"

Brickham squared his stance. "That's not going to matter, and you know it."

"Fully aware of the deets, mate. But now we're squabbling semantics, when we should be getting into the damn car before the gendarmes make another sweep this way."

"He is right." Jagger grunted. "More than you want to know."

Brickham clawed a hand over his skull, baring his teeth. "*Fuck.*"

Jayd pressed close to him again. With every new inch, his conflict weighed heavier in her own psyche. "We have to at least get out of this neighborhood, Sir." She weathered his irked side-eye for deliberately using the honorific. That did not stop her from dipping her forehead to his bicep, going for all the irresistible submissive points she could get. "We can do that faster in a car."

He growled again, but it was with half an effort at best. "Damn it," he bit out, for her ears alone. "Do you have to be so adorable *and* right?"

Five minutes later, they were holding hands in the second row of a silver SQ7 that seamlessly blended with the traffic through the north part of the city. Even past midnight, plenty of pedestrians were still out enjoying the summer night, with busy traffic to match.

Jagger, behind the wheel of the big vehicle, was going on about how the police would be hesitant to give chase with so many bystanders to worry about. Though he made valid points, Jayd also saw them for what they really were. A fact parade, delaying the details she was actually after.

When he paused to focus on navigating a busy roundabout, she readily jumped on the chance to change that parade's course. "So who is going to put on their grown-up underwear and inform me what the plan is now?"

When her initial response consisted of a tight cough from Ozias and the distinct twist of Jag's knuckles around the steering wheel, she did not know whether to cry or curse. As she brooded over the possibility of both, a cell phone rang. She ruled out her burner, still tucked in her back pocket and set to vibrate.

Oz was the one to reach over and yank the device from the breast pocket of Jagger's uniform. During the move, the boyfriends swapped a quick but significant glance. Once more, tears and growls fought for a stake on her composure. She shoved them aside as Oz tapped the green button but held back from saying anything. What was *that* all about?

"Sorry, man. He's driving. You've got Oz here." After no more than two seconds, he stated, "Affirmative. We found her. Yep, she's right here." No confusion about who he was referencing with that, since he bounced his sights right to her during the update. "Yeah," he went on. "Of course."

Of course what?

She thanked herself for keeping that scream inside, since Oz swept the phone toward her and then jiggled it. She would have likely shattered the eardrum of whomever was on the other end of the line.

"Your turn with the top banana, Princess *preesh*."

And now, she wished she had shrieked.

As soon as the Aussie wielded the Arcadian endearment, her curiosity about the caller was given a new coat of paint. *Not* a pretty one. It was probably a mixture of pale green and yellow, just like the acid churning again in her belly. She had room in there, considering she no longer wondered about why Oz and Jag were unconcerned with logistics and security for their upcoming flight. Those details snapped into place with alarming speed.

After accepting the phone from Oz—because refusing it was clearly not an option—she huffed into the device, "*What?*"

An answering grunt filled the line, and she cringed. Out of her three brothers, Samsyn would have been her last choice for this specific moment. While Evrest and Shiraz were as equally protective to the point of irritating, they could be softened in their own ways. But Syn had always been her growling hard-ass, a trait that had intensified since he placed a ring on

Brooke's finger. While Jayd was crazy about her badass sister-in-law, she was certain the woman probably fixed omelets of nails for their breakfast each morning.

Syn's new snort snapped her back to reality—as thoroughly *sur*real as it was. "*Fembla?* You are with Jagger now, yes? What is going on?"

"So very pleasant to speak with you again too, *rerda*," she rejoined.

There was a chance, a tiny one, that the oaf would pay attention to her subtext and abstain from his daunting dragon breath. His agitated huff told her otherwise.

"You get to have *pleasant* when you have sown some of the same yourself, Jayd Dawne. Do you have any idea of the hell we have all been through from your stunt?"

She gave back as good as he was dishing in the nasty-snarly department. "I did not disappear into thin air, *imbezak*. Surely Evrest told you that I texted several times."

"And after each time, you tossed your fucking burner phone."

"Like *you* fucking taught me, *degan soldask*." She drew in a long breath, making it a point to avoid Brickham's scrutiny. She did not have the energy to justify her language, which only reared its uglier side in certain situations. Cliffhanger plots. Abused animals. Her brother's stubborn temper. Yes, even now, as he fumed his way through trying to tame it.

"You are all right, then?" he queried, now surprising her with his earnest tenderness.

"Yes," she murmured. "Fine. I promise. A few bumps and bruises, but . . ." She stopped, praying to swallow away the sudden sting behind her eyes.

"But what?" Damn it, where was Syn's inner Smaug when she needed it the most?

"Nothing," she countered. "It has just been a long day and night."

"No shit."

She jerked up her head as Samsyn punctuated with another noisy sigh. "'No shit'? And you are confident about that *why*, brother?"

"*Fembla.*" Remarkably, a patient chide from him this time. "Your not-so-little incident has made the international news feeds."

"Fuck." Apparently, asshole media moves could be added to her insta-profanity list—as well as her connect-the-dots-to-the-truth rubric. "Wait," she stammered a second later. "*My* little incident? How does anyone even know—"

"The Paris Police scoured the phones of everyone from the bar," Syn disclosed. "Before you even approached LaBarre, some American college girls recognized you. They sneaked in at least a dozen shots each. Moreover, a security camera from the street caught you and Max Brickham entering the pub together."

Her breath hitched. It was tangled so painfully, she could not even form a token cuss. At least thirty seconds of the struggle went by before she stuttered out, "So what does that mean?"

"For the time being? Nothing," Syn replied. "But *fembla* . . ."

"What?" she demanded, hating the trail-off that was so unlike Samsyn. "Damn it, *bonsun*. Just tell me."

"Some reporters are already speculating you as Brickham's accomplice. Not just LaBarre's assassination. In the last ten minutes, the assault on Carris has been added to the accusations."

Well, that took care of the breathing concerns altogether. Still she was able to retort, *"Assault?* So that's what the pig is telling everyone? Likely not including *his* contribution to the verb, right? The part of the evening where he pinned me down and was getting ready to—"

"Fuck."

"Not the verb I had in mind, but it lands in the neighborhood."

"I shall rip his goddamned balls out. And then break his filthy knees."

"Brickham already got that ball rolling for you."

Her brother roughened the line with a reluctant grunt. Something in his undertone took Jayd back to days when she had crushes on his friends, and how he always seemed to *know.* Did he discern the same thing now?

Except that Brickham was not the same as those boys. Not in everything she had shared with him. Done with him. Certainly *not* in what she still felt about it. Feelings they had both agreed not to have at all . . .

She only had to wrestle with that confusion for a few seconds longer, thanks to Syn's fresh snort. It sounded like he was back in Alpha Arcadian Security Chief mode, which she welcomed with relief—even as he uttered his next words.

"Well, now you know why I pulled a few favors and scrambled up the jet at Le Bourget."

Yes, those words.

The ones she had all but expected by now—but knew she would dread. Only there was her fatal mistake. Thinking *dread* could come close to describing the stinging sadness along her veins and the vast vacuum in her heart. Worst of all, the pragmatic princess that stomped back into her mind, bearing a scepter of shitty truth.

"Thank you, *rerda*," she told Syn with as much sincerity as possible. Regrettably, she still sounded—and felt—miserable. "You are right." *Creator on high, why did he have to be so right?* "It is time to go home."

She handed the device back over to Ozias as they sped out of the Paris city limits, and signs whizzed by declaring that Bourget was less than ten kilometers away. Too damn close— just like time was passing too damn fast, and Brickham's embrace was feeling too damn good...

And her heart was clenching too damn painfully.

Just like she was too damn sure that "home" was never going to feel like that again. Not the way it did before.

But what choice did she have about things now? The authorities were hunting her as equally as Brickham, but he would be able to leave the car at Bourget, take ten steps, and be just another face in a crowd. She had one of the world's most recognizable faces, with no time or materials for another impromptu makeover. Not that the first one had helped, in the end.

The end.

This was *not* that.

Maybe if she told that to herself a million more times, she would start to believe it.

Or maybe—likely—she would not.

And that would have to be okay too.

Who, under the Creator's vast sky, was she trying to kid?

The world would not be *okay* for a long time to come. She just wished she could think of a scenario in which it could be—without the vision involving Maximillian Brickham.

Saints help her. It was going to be hard.
No.
It was going to be impossible.

CHAPTER FOURTEEN

Samsyn Cimarron had a lot of friends in some damn high places.

Brick wished he could write off the conclusion as a trite quip of his brain, but this shit was on the level. The Cimarron prince had called in some big favors to get them cleared to drive onto the tarmac at Bourget. They'd barely gotten a sneeze from the guard at the security gate, let alone been stopped or searched.

Once they were rolling on the runway proper, their destination was glaringly obvious. Only one jet waited on any of the three airstrips, its nav lights glowing through the light mist. The sleek, white corporate jet wasn't an overly small thing, nor was it a C-130. Still, the sight was impressive. He kept waiting for some dramatic movie soundtrack to start, though it was best that it didn't. The quieter they handled this party, the better. Less importantly, his gut's churn of apprehension and desolation didn't need any more muses.

The former started edging out the latter as soon as Fox brought the SQ7 to a stop near the aircraft. Brick got out as soon as the Arcadian did, exiting from his spot behind the driver's seat. Jayd began sliding over, but he gave her a quick hand command to wait. Requiemme, stretched out on the third seat behind his Pixie, would also have to stay put.

For the moment, that was a good thing. The hairs on the back of his neck weren't reaching for their downtime beers yet.

Ozias made short work of jogging around to his boyfriend's side and shorter work of narrowing an impatient stare. "Pardon the mongrel on your moment, mate, but we've got a very specific time window for getting this bird off the ground."

"Acknowledged," Brick returned, lifting his hands in a pseudosurrender. "But also questioned."

"Because we are the only ones here?" Fox offered.

He slanted a grateful smirk. "It'd crossed my mind."

"Bourget has a pretty gnarly noise abatement rule thingy," Oz asserted. "Air quality for the locals and all that."

"Understandable." He swept a brief but thorough scrutiny of the terminals. Nothing but basic security lighting as far as the eye could see. "And in this case, advantageous."

Oz chuffed. "I love it when you invent fancy words for breaking the law."

"That makes one of us." Brick shifted his weight, still unable to shake his weird skittishness. The gray area between his instinct and paranoia was wider than the Puget at hide tide—not a surprise after enduring a DEFCON 1 panic attack in the middle of a Paris cemetery. "But I'm just here for the car keys, mate." He extended a hand, accepting the fob from Jag. "I'll make sure this beauty gets returned right." *Just get* my *beauty back to safety too.*

He held on to the thought far longer than he should. But it was the last time he'd be able to call Jayd his, so technically, hours wouldn't be enough.

"Ah. *Merderim mahaleur.*" Fox brought him back to reality fast enough. "My many thanks to you, Brickham, on behalf of the kingdom of Arcadia—for everything."

"Uh . . . sure." He ran his gaze back over at the terminals, certain the guy would detect the new trajectory of his thoughts. That *he* owed Arcadia for so much more than everything.

Fortunately, his cover worked. "Just call Gerard. His number is adhered to the inside of the spare tire well," Fox explained with his usual efficiency. "He will retrieve the car from wherever you finally park it."

"Well, damn." Brick was glad for the open opportunity at a deadpan. "You guys do take full service seriously."

"Actually . . ." Oz stepped forward again, jabbing a thumb at the waiting pilot and copilot. "They do too. And if I'm rightly calling the game on those scowls, they wanted to be wheels up five minutes ago."

"Yeah, yeah, Penelope Promptitude," Brick joked. "I got your *wheels up* in my jockstrap."

"Which has clearly been in places I don't want to know about tonight," the Aussie volleyed.

Shit.

The word jangled in his senses with every step he retraced to the Audi. All right, more than his senses. His mind borrowed a more stringent version of it too—especially as he swung a leg under the car's back end to swing open the tailgate. Once the door had risen and he'd helped Requiemme out, he circled around to where Jayd now waited, leaning against the hood with folded arms.

Despite the semistiff stance, she was going for a breezy beach vibe—or something like that. She had her ankles casually crossed and her chin held high. Her gaze was fixed toward a seemingly fascinating horizon. The mist was making it rough to see anything beyond a couple of hundred yards, so that part of her bluff was already up.

Her bluff.

Wasn't that a really rich case of the pot and the kettle?

Because damn it, he was just as pathetic. Who the hell was he kidding with fingers hooked in his belt loops and feet kicking stones like he was the perfect surfer boy for her beach bunny?

They were never going to be that matched set.

They both knew that. Had both accepted it as part of their decadent deal, so many hours ago.

Goddammit. A lifetime ago.

The lifetime that glittered, so bright and tortured, in the gaze she lifted as he approached.

In the memories held by each of her tears.

In the connection they refueled every time she blinked those lush lashes.

In the myriad ways she could touch him without laying a finger on him.

It all started with her eyes. And despite his vow to conclude it there, his self-control was dust as soon as he was near enough to haul her close. Within seconds, he embraced her as tightly as he dared. Her soft, spiky locks tickled his nose. Her honey-and-amber scent suffused his senses. Her lithe curves filled his grip.

She felt so damn good.

She felt so damn right.

And for the next wordless minute, she was.

The last minute he'd ever embrace her like this.

So selfishly, he took another. And, despite the way Oz pointedly cleared his throat, another.

From over Jayd's head, he speared a glare at Demos. While his friend was coming from a decent place, the guy would have to exercise a little Aussie-style chill. It wasn't like Brick planned on holding her forever.

Christ, how he wished they had forever.

He braced himself for the mental alarms that'd be clanging any second. Then the flinches in all his limbs, spurring the gentle step back that he needed. That they both needed.

Didn't happen.

Not even as Oz gave a hand signal to the pilot, and the officer moved inside to start his flight precheck.

Especially not as Jayd moved against him—but only to wriggle herself closer. Tighter. Warmer.

"Brickham." Her rasp on his neck was thick with emotion. "Sir . . ." Her lips were dotted with tears. She still dragged in a shaky breath, as if battling for more syllables but not finding them. Her exhalation was a slice of frustration, thickening the lump in Brick's throat.

"I know, Pixie," he grated. "I know."

Holy shit. That was it? That was *all* he could muster for her?

But summoning anything more to his mind . . . Again, not happening. But also not fucking acceptable. He'd talked children across war zones. Watched six on ordnance specialists as they'd worked on fields of live lego devices. Even delivered a few babies in hovels beneath skies lit up like Satan's birthday party. Never, through all those crazy fuck fests, had he been at a loss for the right words. Only one mission had rendered him that pathetically useless, and he'd completely bowed out of the game because of it.

He didn't want to bow out now.

God help him, he wanted to stay all-in on this one. But once more, not happening. Not now. Not ever. The classic eighties song was right. God did have a sick sense of humor.

And the next moment, he swore he heard the bastard laughing.

As the rest of the world decided it was Satan's birthday again.

One moment, he was stroking Jayd's back as her soft tears fell with the silver mist. The next, a flash charge turned the tarmac into blinding gold. Then another. Behind them, like Imperial stormtroopers with wasps up their asses, a dozen new visitors charged the soggy pavement.

"Maximillian Brickham! Stop where you are, by the authority of the Gendarmerie Nationale."

And there was D'artagnan Vader, right on cue.

"Brickham?" Jayd burrowed closer while throwing her arms all the way around his neck. Damn good thing, because she saved him from commanding her to do it. "Wh-What is happening?"

"It's all right, Pixie." It was good to know he could still pull off the I'm-terrified-but-you-don't-know-it trick. Because nothing about this was all right. A new glance to Oz proved as much. His friend, blinking to fight the effects of the flash bangs, was still reeling but fuming.

"Bugger me to Christmas. Our juice is spilled, mate!"

At least that was what the words sounded like. For all Brick knew, they could've been *bugs are shitless; our poop is swill, mate.* His ears were ringing like Quasimodo was riffing a solo between them. His balance was off. His vision was distorted. But it was inconsequential to the main object of his focus.

That plane.

And getting Jayd onto it.

Fast.

"Brickham!"

"I hear you!" He dialed back from the bellow at Oz once he tucked his mouth next to Jayd's ear. "And you need to hear me, sweetheart. This ride's about to get bumpy but don't you dare let go until I get you to the plane. You got that, Pixie? Do. Not. Let. Go!"

He waited for her brave *yes, Sir.* Instead, he got a couple of urgent nods. Good enough for now. It had to be. Neither of them had any choice about how this had to go down.

Or more accurately, what had to surge ahead.

His two legs.

Holy fuck, it was hard. His muscles, at the mercy of his brainwaves, fought to process the Mach 10 adrenaline spike. He force-fed the impulses to them, homing his attention on everything from his ass down. Everything north of that was on automatic do-or-die mode, desperately holding Jayd close. He added to the protection as much as he could, hunching over her while bolting forward.

Fuck. This had to go right the first time.

The only chance he'd have.

Mentally, he charted a course to the plane's waiting stairs. Yeah, it was a giant middle finger at fate, as well as his own mortality. But this wasn't a luxury buffet of opportunity. In the next few seconds, the Audi would be shot up like Butch Cassidy's poor mule.

Every choice mattered now. They needed to be the right ones.

But the last time he'd been in hot water this deep, he'd trusted all his eggs to the right choices. They'd ended in disaster.

Apparently, dysfunction loved company.

He even smiled about that one, as he got within two bounds of the stairway.

Then smiled even wider, looking up to see Requiemme ducking into the aircraft with Fox's help.

Oz was positioned halfway down the stairway, now brandishing—and using—a handgun. Brick almost tapped into some valuable lung power to swear at the guy. Was he really trying to give them cover fire with a pistol? There was no custom barrel or sighting system on his piece, so he couldn't be thinking of hitting anything at this long range.

Unless it wasn't such a long range anymore.

Fuuuckkk.

The word billowed in his brain as the air crackled and roared around him. And while the violence pushed him forward, it wasn't what compelled him to keep going, carrying Jayd up the daunting steel stairs.

The drive for that belonged to the whisper beneath it all.

The fervent words, in sweet strands of Arcadian, beseeching her creator with all the force of her soul. A force he could feel now too. A pull belonging to a bigger entity than him—or even her. A belief that overrode every screaming muscle in his body, wrapping him in powerful purpose, lifting his steps and filling him with determined fire . . .

Until the fire flared too hot.

And then too cold.

So. Fucking. Cold.

Every move he could still make. Every thought he could still form. Every awareness he could still acknowledge— though they were dwindling by the moment.

Until there was only one.

Jayd.

His perfect pixie.

Her ocean-and-earth scent. Her soft but strong arms. Her amazing aqua eyes.

Wait. Her eyes.

What was going on with them? Why were they so red and grieving and wet? And yeah, he knew that for a fact, because all those saltwater drops were now raining on him. But how?

How had she suddenly swung around to be leaning over him?

How had he gotten here, sprawled beneath her?

And how was his head now consumed by noise of a different kind? A revving hum, followed by the whine of high-powered engines.

Jet engines.

Shit. Wait. I'm not on this flight manifest, gang. This isn't the plan!

He struggled to transform the words from protests in his head to sounds on his lips. He had to. He had to get the hell off this flying VIP lounge, not on. It was the smart move. It was his only choice.

The right choice . . .

He opened his mouth to say just that. But again, it was as far as he got. The fuses between his brain and his mouth were severed. He could only lie here and silently panic while Jayd sobbed harder and the engines screeched louder.

But then, even the panic was gone.

As a black blanket got draped across his consciousness.

Before he fully succumbed to the night, Jayd's desperate rasp was once more a haven for his senses. And his soul. And his heart. But her entreaty wasn't for her Creator anymore.

She was pleading to him—with a message that pierced a thousand holes into his aching soul.

"Brickham! Brickham! It is your turn to hang on, okay? Are you listening to me, damn it? Do not even think of letting go, Brickham. Stay with me, Brickham. Please. Please stay with me!"

Can't... stay. Have to... keep you safe. You're... the most important thing now...

More things he had to say. So many things he had to tell her. All the important things in his heart and soul. All the ways she'd captured both of them, possibly forever. *Probably* forever. But again, none of it connected to his lips.

Tell her. You have to tell her, damn it!

"P-P-Pixie..."

It was all he could manage before the blanket rose up again, thicker and darker than before. Unconsciousness wasn't fucking around this time. It wanted him—and it was damn well going to claim him.

★ ★ ★

"Creator's blessed mercy!"

Emme's gasp barely dented Jayd's awareness. She could spare no extra energy on it, too consumed with threading coherent thoughts past the chaos consuming her every nerve ending.

"Mother of God."

Oz's low growl was no help either. His taut dismay was like a psychic butter knife, slathering thick dismay through her psyche. It weakened the fingers she still had twisted around Brickham's. Her other hand, attached to the arm that cradled his head against her lap, was clamped to the ledge of his shoulder—

Where a splotch of red had become a full bloom.

She pulled him closer, hating herself for causing his sharp groan. But letting go was not an option. When she had even thought about doing that, outside on the tarmac, fate had punished her by letting hell break loose.

No.

That was not hell. Not even close.

This was.

The rush of the tarmac outside the plane's windows. The abrupt climb of the sleek machine, threatening to separate her from where Brickham had fallen near the galley. His darker bellow, stabbed by profanities she did not even recognize.

But even worse, his sudden silence.

His formidable face was too damn still, illuminated in orange-and-amber shadows that chased them from the explosions below. Jayd pushed past the temptation to scream, funneling her attention in. Poring her focus over the most important thing in her existence right now. The downed warrior in her arms, so terrifyingly still. The leech of color from the rugged planes of his face. The shallow rises and falls across his mighty chest. The awkward sprawl of his timber log legs, stretching into the main cabin—where another dark-red pool gained traction across the light-cream carpeting.

"Creator's damnation." As the rasp spilled from her, unbearable heat gathered behind her eyes. But raw fear eclipsed her tears. She could only take that energy and push it all at the first person who would listen. That human should have been Brickham. She stifled a scream—barely—that it was not.

"Oz," she demanded of the man "lucky" enough to stand in for him. "Tell me," she stammered. "Ozias? Talk to me, damn it." Air clutched in her throat as she followed every move the Australian made, his cautious assessment interjected by barely audible grunts. "Is he all right? It—it is not that bad, is it?"

But the new pang of bile in her belly made her see those words for what they were. Stabs at the truth she was battling to mold. A reality in which a man was not limp, unconscious, and bleeding in her lap.

No. Not just a man. This was the hero who, in less than twenty-four hours, had broken past her defenses to uncover her, discover her, fulfill her. Who, in some ways, knew her better than most people who had known her for twenty-four years. Who had defeated predator *bonsuns* for her. Who had even confronted the demons of his own mind for her. Now she owed him the same bravery.

No. She owed him more.

Even as she watched Oz's scowl intensify as his assessment continued. Yes, even as the man scooted back up to look at the crimson deluge from the corner of Brickham's temple. The terrifying stuff flowed down through the rough chaff on that side of Brick's head, forming a gory topographical map she could barely look at.

Still, she forced herself to demand, "Oz? Please talk to me!"

Only when Emme dropped to her side, soothing her with sounds and touches, did she realize how deep she had fallen into the shrill shrew bucket. Jayd gulped hard and forced herself to breathe. That brought back a little clarity, though total victory there felt as distant as the ground below—

and yes, even the island homeland that was so far away. Too damn far.

At last, Ozias sat up. Her attention whipped back to him. After a decisive breath, he stated, "The nick in his forehead is long and elliptically shaped—and bleeding like a damn dingo with the runs."

"Which means what?" she pressed.

"That it's likely just a graze." He hauled in more air while settling his hands atop his thighs. "So that's the good news."

"The good news?" Jayd spat.

"*Rahmie Creacu*," Emme whispered, sweeping both hands in the air over Brickham's body. In other cultures, the motions were compared to witchcraft spells, but on Arcadia, they were a call for the Almighty to harness natural forces for physical and spiritual healing.

Jayd was grateful for the move due to other reasons. She needed a second to regather her strength.

"All right," she finally blurted, nodding at Oz. "The bad news?"

The Aussie nodded as Jagger dropped down next to him, bearing a half-meter stack of cloth hand towels. "As you can likely tell, he's also been hit in his shoulder and thigh. Best as I can tell, the bullets have hit solid meat instead of bone, but there's no way of assessing the damage until we can get the rounds out. And no way in hell can we do that here."

Jayd ground her teeth to avoid screaming. From the midst of that agony, she charged, "So where do we do it? Should we tell the pilot to land?"

"No." The denial was immediate, emphatic, and in stereo. After Jagger joined Oz to issue it, he determinedly went on. "The Gendarmerie has likely gotten some alerts out already.

If we put down anywhere in France, Italy, or Greece, they'll arrest Brickham first and ask questions later."

Oz backed it up with a somber nod. She copied the motion but not the attitude. With every authoritative tone she had ever been taught, she decreed, "So we push on to Arcadia."

Oz grimaced. "It's our best option."

Jagger shoulder-butted him. "My love, it is our only option." At the same time, he reached over and wrapped a hand around her wrist—but the reassurance only succeeded in stamping her skin with the blood on his fingers.

Brickham's blood.

Damn it, damn it, damn it.

She gave in to the inner rant again. Then again. It was her only thread of control in this surreal situation. They were helpless until the touchdown at Sancti, with naught but the droning engines and minor air turbulence to inform them progress was being made toward the airstrip on her island.

Where she would disembark this flying trap—before having to walk into another.

She harbored no illusions about machinations that were happening as they flew south. Most notably, the ones in Carris's control. Even with a shot-apart knee, the *bonsun* would be demanding a phone audience with Evrest so he could lay out every detail of the evening's insanity for her brother. Correction. All three of her brothers. She envisioned each of their unique reactions to Carris's caterwauling. None of them were pretty.

But none of them panged worse than continuing to watch as Brickham slept on.

Slept?

Her impression was presumptuous. She knew that

more clearly, and grotesquely, than the bright-red stains that seemed everywhere, especially as Oz and Jag labored without stopping to help their friend. Emme served as their runner, tireless in hauling as many supplies as she could from the galley. Her friends' efforts touched the deepest places in Jayd's heart but elucidated all her fears about her awful impotence. She felt like a wet tree monkey scrabbling on a massive oak. No purchase to be had. No advantage to be gained. The man in her arms was still so ominously quiet.

What if she was not doing enough for him?

What if she was not helping enough? Praying hard enough? Believing strongly enough? Holding him tightly enough?

What if, because of all that, Brickham died before they got to Arcadia?

"No."

She rasped it from dry lips and a parched throat, but refused to pause for water, air, or a respite from her exhaustion. If her suffering counted for the smallest credit in providence's bank, she could use it for Brickham's benefit.

He was worth it. So worth it.

Her incredible force of nature . . .

Forces of nature are not meant to die!

But this one remained horrifyingly dormant. So still. So quiet. So . . . vacant.

An anguished moan, swirling deep in her belly, finally tornadoed its way into her chest. She welcomed it. She needed the focus, dragging her away from the temptation of tears. She would not give them power right now. She would not give them her voice. There was still too much to say with her words.

"Brickham." Maybe the third time was the proverbial

charm. She enforced her hail with a twisted fist in his shirt and a desperate bite into one of his pecs. "Are you listening now? Because I can do this the whole flight, you know. Do you really want that? Do you really want me to hurt you for the next two hours? Because I guarantee, even then, you will not be in as much agony as me."

As she dropped her forehead back to the plane over his heart, she swore there was a skip of the beats in the organ just beneath.

"You want to debate the point?" she challenged. "Then do it. Wake up and do it with me, Max Brickham. Open your eyes. Give me your arguments. Fight with me! Damn it..." Her conflicted choke finally cracked the dyke of her composure. "Damn it, Brickham. Fight for me!"

Unless...

She was not worth it anymore.

Unless he had finally decided he had paid all the necessary tolls for her. For the mission of her. In the end, was that not the raw truth of all she was to him? An asset he had been contracted to find and protect, period? So there was probably an understood job definition to it, along with the acceptable extras list of job risks.

Things like rescuing her from a raping *soldask* like Gervais.

Then hiding her in a kink dungeon by disguising her as his submissive.

Then fulfilling her as his real submissive, giving her the most unforgettable pleasure of her life.

Then escorting her to meet her father—who became the drug addict he was framed for murdering.

Then rescuing her from another predatorial lunatic.

Then hiding in a crypt with her and enduring a full panic attack because of it.

Then continuing to protect her, even into a skirmish that had gotten him shot in the head.

Just the basic ticks on the list had her exhausted—and weeping harder.

Because maybe he really was done with paying all the prices for her. And maybe she could not fault him for that.

Maybe she really was not worth the ultimate fight.

As the surety sank deeper into her logic, sorrow clawed deeper into her heart.

Her hopelessness saved itself for her soul.

It seeped in, drenching her worse than the bloodstains on her skin and clothes. In equal measure, sadness welled from her gut and poured from her eyes. She was a mass of surrender, a wide wound past all hope of avoiding despairing infection.

This man was bleeding because of her.

And soon, he was going to die because of her.

And somehow, at some point, she had to be okay with that.

No.

She would never be okay with that.

Max Brickham had done more than just find her, rescue her, and protect her. He had opened her. Shown her parts of herself that she knew not were even missing. Perhaps the parts she had left Arcadia to search for in the first place. The woman she thought she could find by talking to her real father.

Wrong.

She had been so wrong about that.

But that was not why she sobbed now.

She cried because she could not stanch the pain. Because she could not avoid the truth. The pain was excruciating, but she made her soul take it. Forced herself to remain that way for the Creator to see, bared and broken...and willing to trade it all for the life of the man she had come to care for—to terrifying depths of her heart and soul.

Continue the Honor Bound Series with **Bound**

ALSO BY ANGEL PAYNE

Honor Bound:
Saved
Cuffed
Seduced
Wild
Wet
Hot
Masked
Mastered
Conquered
Ruled
Bared
Bound

The Blood of Zeus Series:
(with Meredith Wild)
Blood of Zeus
Heart of Fire
Fate of Storms
Bridge of Souls

Shark's Edge Series:
(with Victoria Blue)
Shark's Edge
Shark's Pride
Shark's Rise
Grant's Heat
Grant's Flame
Grant's Blaze

The Bolt Saga:
Bolt
Ignite
Pulse
Fuse
Surge
Light

Misadventures:
Misadventures with a Time Traveler
Misadventures with a Duke

Cimarron Series:
Into His Dark
Into His Command
Into Her Fantasies

Temptation Court:
Naughty Little Gift
Pretty Perfect Toy
Bold Beautiful Love

Suited for Sin:
Sing
Sigh
Submit

Lords of Sin:
Trade Winds
Promised Touch
Redemption
A Fire in Heaven
Surrender to the Dawn

**For a full list of Angel's other titles,
visit her at AngelPayne.com**

ACKNOWLEDGMENTS

Massive thanks to some incredible folks who helped get Max and Jayd to the page!

— The team at Waterhouse Press, for believing that there was more of the Honor Bound world to explore. I'm so grateful for all of you: Meredith, Jon, Robyn, Keli Jo, Haley, Amber, Jennifer, Jesse, Yvonne, Kurt, and Dana.

— Scott Saunders, Editor God on High: what would I do without you? Thank you for piloting this one to such great heights. You're incredible. I'm a better writer because of you!

— So many special thanks to the invaluable beta team who helped with this one in its messy "baby" phases: Tracy Roelle, Corinne Akers, and Kika Medina. You guys are so awesome!

— Beyond grateful for Martha Frantz, who keeps so many operational gears going. I'm so lucky to have you, lady!

— Worlds—WORLDS—of thankfulness to all the readers who believed in both Honor Bound and the Cimarrons all these years. Your love and encouragement has meant the world. I'll never be able to tell you how much.

— To Tom and Fortune, who have to hear me tapping late at night (even on vacation!). You are my rocks and my world. I love you.

ABOUT ANGEL PAYNE

USA Today bestselling romance author Angel Payne loves to focus on high-heat romance starring memorable alpha men and the women who love them. She has numerous book series to her credit, including the action-packed Bolt Saga and Honor Bound series, Secrets of Stone series (with Victoria Blue), the intertwined Cimarron and Temptation Court series, the Suited for Sin series, and the Lords of Sin historicals, as well as several standalone titles.

Angel is a native Southern Californian, leading to her love of being in the outdoors, where she often reads and writes. She still lives in Southern California with her soul-mate husband and beautiful daughter, to whom she is a proud cosplay/culture con mom. Her passions also include whisky tasting, shoe shopping, and travel.

Visit her at AngelPayne.com